Henry Aloysius Barry

Salvation through Mary

Henry Aloysius Barry

Salvation through Mary

ISBN/EAN: 9783744740562

Printed in Europe, USA, Canada, Australia, Japan

Cover: Foto ©Andreas Hilbeck / pixelio.de

More available books at **www.hansebooks.com**

SALVATION THROUGH MARY

"Lady, thy goodness, thy magnificence.
    Thy virtue, and thy great humility,
Surpass all science and all utterance;
        For sometimes, Lady! ere men pray to thee.
        Thou goest before in thy benignity.
    The light to us vouchsafing to our prayer.
To be our guide unto thy Son so dear."
                            — Chaucer-Wordsworth.

Salvation Through Mary

BY

Rev. HENRY ALOYSIUS BARRY

Author, "Am I of the Chosen"

BOSTON
ANGEL GUARDIAN PRESS
1898

O Virgin Mother, daughter of thy Son,
Created beings all in lowliness
Surpassing, as in height above them all;
Term by the eternal counsel pre-ordained;
Ennobler of thy nature, so advanced
In thee that its great Maker did not scorn
To make Himself His own creation;
For in thy womb rekindling shone the love
Revealed whose genial influence makes now
This flower to germin in eternal peace;
Here thou to us of charity and love
Art as the noonday torch; and art beneath
To mortal men of hope a living spring.

—Dante.

TO
THE MOTHER OF GOD,
WHO BORE US ALL IN THE SPIRIT,
WHO, AS

Our Lady of Mt. Carmel,

HAS BROUGHT SUCH BLESSINGS
INTO HIS OWN LIFE,
AND UNDER HER
TO THE
VIRTUOUS AND DEVOTED MOTHER
WHO GAVE HIMSELF BIRTH
IN THE FLESH —

Elizabeth Josephine White-Barry —

THE AUTHOR,
WITH DEEPEST LOVE AND GRATITUDE,
DEDICATES HIS
UNPRETENTIOUS VOLUME.

PREFACE.

THIS little volume with its mission of endeavoring to utter sweet things of the most gracious Mother of God owes its nativity to the earnest wishes of my family. What prompted them to suggest this particular and noble theme is, however, upon reflection, to my mind, very natural; and I venture to fancy that the relationship of cause and effect, from the nature of its particularity in the present instance, is invested with sufficient interest to warrant its being publicly set forth.

All the children of my virtuous and devout mother have been drilled in Mary-cult and no picture is so familiar to them as Our Lady's Shrine. From the beginning it was the custom with our family that all of us children had to tramp — if not always disposed to, bound — to daily Mass, by our mother's side, during Mary's month. The memories of those bright May days are with us never to part. I see the red lamp blinking, nodding, wriggling, to free itself, as it were, from the taper's clasp. I scent the young leaves and blossoms of the bower which Mary's lovers have weaved about her glorious image out of the freshest and most fragrant roses. I hear the melodic hymns of the innocents upon whose hearts the cold chill blast of the world has not yet blown its taint, its sorrows and its coldness. In the midst of all this comes forth the lesson of the day. In the beginning, we are told, it was Father Williams destined to be Boston's great Archbishop, to rule in troubl·us times wi·h the prudence of a son of Solomon, who read, I fancy, with sombre mein, but sincere, deep pathos and profoundest faith to the first-born of our family. Later, in my own boyhood days the devout Father Healy, now the Bishop of Portland, read to us bairns, with his impressive tone and accent, the story of God's Mother, so that things I heard him say in boyhood fastened themselves upon my memory to remain with me for life. Then comes Bishop Harkins, calm and earnest, to read to the youngest of our family, whose turn had come to carry out the May traditions. In delightful, old St. James, the nursery of bishops for our own dear New England, my family, with many others, became imbued with that interest in the Mother of God, which culminated in the present little volume. The dear Nuns of Mt. Carmel, having been apprized of my family's wish, urged me to take upon myself the pleasant little task, with the result before you.

In relation to the little volume itself, alas, so many times unworthy of heaven's mighty Empress, I beg the indulgence of an observation. It is designed, as my previous work, *Am I of the Chosen*, for such as are happy within the Fold, for such as have eyes and see, ears and hear. Its science is practical, its philosophy, its language, the grammar and syntax of its speech is the spirit of faith. This may be briefly made clear: If one were asked by anyone if, indeed, he could not be saved without Mary's aid, I take for granted that a theologian, would answer that he could, absolutely speaking, do so; and yet, whilst his lips would be in the act of framing such a reply, his Christian heart, his spirit of faith, his Catholic instinct, would compel him to entertain misgivings upon the 'fact' of that man's salvation.

'Can' a man accomplish this or that carries with it a certain speculative interest to be sure, but it is chiefly in the line of a real interest if I ask myself the question: "'Shall' I be saved without Mary?" Whilst in reply to the question, "'Can' I be saved without Mary?" the theologian would say, absolutely speaking, yes, he could not give the same affirmative answer to the question, "'Shall' I be saved without Mary?" and not be assailed with forcible doubts and fearful apprehensions. Whilst defending the position here stated, the author prays, and therefore hopes that he is at the same time fixedly enshrining the Virgin Mother of God in the hearts of such as patiently and sincerely consider his labor of love.

HENRY A. BARRY.

May 1, 1898.

INDEX.

SALVATION THROUGH MARY.

CHAPTER I.

MARY'S PART IN THE PLAN OF SALVATION.

WE must not undervalue the opinion of the wise and holy touching the true position or role which was played by the Mother of God in the unique, sublime and all-important work of the world's Redemption:—"All others should adjust their lives to that of the saints and make it their rule to do so." (St. Ambrose Brev. III. Sunday Lent). Saints concur in the belief so admirably sustained by them in word, pen and practice, that as God bestowed, in the first, the Redeemer of Mankind upon this world of ours by the intermediation of His wondrous Mother, He, no less, in our own day, goes on dispensing the favors and blessings of healing upon our miserable planet, as in former days—through Mary.

We cannot exaggerate, so to speak, the soothing helpfulness of Our Lady's intermediation under the One Necessary Mediator, Jesus Christ, Her Son.

This has been, is, and shall be, the economy of salvation:

Our prayers, our works and our hopes should be laid before the great white throne by the gentle hand that was chosen to wrap the Divine Mediator in His swaddles; that same dear hand that made, mended and washed for the Saviour. Let our motto, then, be: All the blessings of God descend upon the world and upon me individually through Mary, the Mother of God. All your prayers and mine—the world's supplication—the cries of the helpless, the sighs of the sinner, the groans of the captive, the sweet-flowered visions of the recluse, the lisping plea of the tender orphan—I repeat, the world's prayer, the Celt's, the Frank's, the Parthian's, the Hindoo's, shall go up, all, and be heard by the Lord when, and even 'because' we shall have requested Our Lady to present them in our behalf before the Face of God, Her Son.

'Tis true, the incense, whose sweet aromatic fumes wind themselves star-ward to *blind*, as it were, the Father's eye to mankind's follies, and to inebriate His Heart with the fragrance of love, pity and forgiveness, is the Master's prayer, and His alone. When Our Lord's lips moved in prayer, heaven moved; when His Heart beat fast with sorrow over man's misery, by the unity of the Godhead, the thrill of mercy swept o'er the bosom of the Eternal Father like the rippling of the blue waters of the Lake of Genesareth, or the Sea of Galilee, when the mountain wind blew across its liquid breast from the rugged slopes and wild gorges of Anti-Libonus, Carmel's blue chain and the broad plateaux of beautiful Galilee.

The cry of Ozias to Judith is the new Israel's confession before the Mother of God: " Blessed art thou, O daughter, by the Lord, the Most High God, above all women upon the earth. Blessed be the Lord, Who made heaven and earth, Who hath directed thee to the cutting off of the head of the prince of our enemies. Because He hath so magnified thy name this day, that thy praise shall not depart out of the mouth of men, who shall be mindful of the power of the Lord forever; for that thou hast not spared thy life by reason of the distress and tribulation of thy people, but hast prevented our ruin in the presence of God." (Judith xiii., 23).

When Joachim and the ancients sung it to the heroine of old Israel, truly may we sing it to the new Judith, the Mother of God: "Thou art the joy of Israel, thou art the honor of our people." (Judith, xx., 10).

In Mary we find the incense that rises in a holy cloud—She is a thurible.

In her the God of Israel found the beauty and power to captivate Himself, so to speak, and, with the sword, swung by God's Own hand to cut down the enemies of His people.

Our theme is forcibly sustained and beautifully developed by Bossuet: "I feel myself under the obligation," said this wise bishop, profound scholar

and godly man, " of calling your attention to a
consequence that flows out from the Motherhood
of Mary—a consequence which, I fancy, has not
found a place in your meditation to adequate
lengths.   The consequence to which I would call
your attention is to the effect that God, having
once found it agreeable to Himself to make us
the possessors of Jesus Christ by the Blessed
Virgin, this economy or order of things goes on
in the same way, at the present time ; and, Our
Lord does not take back His gifts. (His gifts are
without repentance).   It is true, and it shall not
cease to be true, that as we have once received, by
Mary, the Universal Principle of Grace, in the
same way we receive, up to the present, by her
mediation, the various applications of that Grace,
in all the different states that come together to
make the christian life.   Her mother's charity,
which gives birth to the children of the Church,
having contributed so largely to the work of
salvation in the mystery of the Incarnation,
which is the Universal Principle of Grace, this
very same charity, on the part of God's Mother,
will go on contributing to the work of salvation,
for all eternity, in all other operations which are
but the consequences of the Incarnation toward
which she has contributed. (Third Sermon,
Feast Imm. Conc.).

CONCLUSION :

IF we wish to find God and come into possession of His grace and favor it is clear that we should follow in the steps of the Magi and take to the road that leads to the arms of Mary. Here we shall find what we seek. Here Our Lord is always at home to us.

ILLUSTRATION:

THE Holy Bible sets forth in the case of Our Lady the strongest illustration of the elements of power, influence and authority that enter into the structure of intercession before God. The scene of the illustration is Cana in Galilee, and the occasion is a wedding-feast.

Joy and good cheer is the key to the hour. The presence of Jesus throws a benediction over the event and deepens the outward delight of the things terrene with the inner gladness, that only the nearness and overshadowing of God can yield. Our Lord is there to bless His children, to hallow their joys and protect them against harmful excesses. Our Lady is standing by with her eyes apart, and moving in a quiet, calm, keen but restless action, looking to catch sight of the needs of the guests and, with motherly proofs, to obviate the slightest embarrassments that might arise. Mary is present because her son is in attendance.

She is present as the mother of all there, with a mother's concern about the wants of her children. She has the mother's instinct, so sharp to discover a need. She does not think of herself. She thinks of her children only. She does not

blind herself to their needs because she loves
them truly; cheerfully and anxiously she em-
braces the discomfitures and sacrifices that are to
free them from their wants and blights.   The rest
are about their own entertainment.   They have
no other thought, no other concern.

It remains for Mary to detect, in the height of
the merry feasting, the failure of the wine.   This
is enough to set her sympathies into immediate
and rapid motion.   She takes upon herself the
distress and wants of her children.   Coldness and
indifference are sentiments the most foreign to
her heart.   Such deportment, under the circum-
stance, might become a princess, it being beneath
her dignity to be touched by so trivial a thing,
but Mary is the Mother.   The sympathy of an
acquaintance pours itself in upon us, during the
hours of trial, in fine phrases—voluminous but
empty; in graceful condolences, that are little
better than mocked friendship.   True love, embodied in the mother, scorns emptiness, repudiates
sham, contemns the vapid conventionalities of mere
acquaintanceship.   Mary is never, and never can
be a mere acquaintance, a mere friend.   She
must be our mother—the mother of all the world
though the world disown her.   So when now the
wine fails, love, real and active, shows itself; for,
love, like faith, and all other virtues, must be shown
to be true, in works.   True love scorns to seek
only what is merely of advantage to itself.   True
love does not stop at sacrifices, in the interests of

others.—"Charity seeketh not her own." (i. Cor. xiii, 5).

True love on earth reaches its topmost pitch when we are able to cry out Mother! We are not surprised to observe Our Lady in the present instance looking at Jesus. We find herein more than the mere, ordinary glance of admiration and love. There is a prayer in Mary's eyes. But the look will not do: A christian world must hear and recite from age to age the prayer in 'word.' At last, then, the word is spoken: "They have no wine." Here is Mary's prayer—of insinuation. She asks for wine. She prays her Son to perform the miracle in order to rescue her children from their difficulty. There was no other way for Our Lord to acquiesce in her behest but by miracle, inasmuch as, if wine could have been procured, and the emergency confronted by the natural and ordinary means, such as purchase or loan, Mary would not have tempted God, so to speak. Our Lord's reply implies Our Lady's prayer for a miracle: Woman, what is that to Me and to thee? My hour is not yet come. (Luke ii, 3). Here we find the interests of Jesus and Mary common—'to Me and to thee.' The Master couples His Mother's interests with His own, aye He makes, as it were, her interests His own. Does Our Lord not rebuke by His present atti- tude those who maintain that God's affairs and their own salvation are none of Mary's concern? The protestant world says: What is this to thee?

Our Lord in His answer to this question in behalf
of His Mother soundly teaches the world that
Mary is interested in us, prays for us and obtains
a sure compliance with the requests which she
puts up in our behalf. If this were not true and
Mary had indeed exceeded the bounds of her
power; if indeed she were, so to speak, over-zeal-
ous, Our Lord would not have sustained her nor
gratified her in her presumption. No, Mary knew,
indeed, better than any other, her own place and
her duty, and, therefore, Our Lord sustained His
Mother in Her action. She realized all this herself so well that she said to the waiters forthwith:
" Whatsoever He shall say to you do ye." (v. 5).
She knew that her prayer was proper and would
be granted. The issue confirms all this; for, Our
Lord commanded the water-pots to be filled and
then to be drawn off. So it was the Mother of
Jesus that pressed the button, as it were, which
was to summon into action those wonders with
which Jesus Christ will bewilder the world. At a
signal from her, began, I say, that long line of
miraculous cures and resurrections from the dead
that were to spread abroad over the world the
world's conviction of the Divinity of Jesus Christ:
" My hour is not yet come. " Yet this hour is
brought to hand at Mary's request. Strange !

His hour is not yet come for miracles; yet,
Jesus clearly advances His hour on her account.
His answer to His Mother: "Woman, what is that
to Me and to thee?" looks cruel in type; and, yet,

it seems as though we ought to fancy him twitting her. It was a serious affair, and yet the Child seems to be playful with the Mother.

His negation in word was, in tone of voice, in accent and expression of countenance, a lover's mystic affirmative. Mary could not by herself have furnished the wine that had been wanting to the wedding-guests, but she was able and willing to obtain all from her Child.

Our Lord carried out His Mother's wish in the highest fashion and turned the common element of the well into such exquisite and delicious wines as the guests had never before tasted. In the light of this example who will doubt, therefore, that, in the plan of God drawn up for the eternal destiny of man, Our Lady holds the power to intercede for us, and can, upon the strength of her intercession, transform us miserable wretches from turpid sinners into lily-white saints in quick order if we shall be wise enough to have recourse to her.

RESOLUTION:

IN our morning offering, or as often, in the course of the day, as we should renew it, let us be resolved to offer our thoughts, words, actions and all to God by the intercession of Mary, His august Mother.

PRAYER:

AUGUST Virgin, holy Mother of God, obtain for us all, and for myself in particular, the wisdom and precious grace to reach out for God ever and in all things by thy powerful intercession.

Through Our Lord Jesus Christ Who liveth and reigneth with the Father and the Spirit, One God forever and ever. Amen.

CHAPTER II.

MARY'S PART IN THE PLAN OF SALVATION.

(CONTINUED.)

LET us go ahead with the thought of yesterday so as to throw a greater distance between us and the danger of parting with it, and as we do so, let us endeavor to clasp the thought inextricably to our bosom.

The idea is of so great consequence in our life that its further strengthening is well worth our pains. The question before us is to ascertain precisely what place Eternal Truth has predestinated for Mary in the plan of the world's salvation and of ours in particular; and our next step shall be to award her that place, in our lives, that God has intended and selected for her. Devotion toward Mary, let us be assured, is not the creature of fiction.

What it has been our pleasure to have evolved in the previous chapter refutes such an impeachment. Let this be peremptorily understood in all its lights and shades, namely, that theology and philosophy, in a way, is agreed upon the pronouncement of the important place God has predestinated for Mary as a solid means toward spiritual good, beyond the mere straw of the drowning man, who reaches out in frenzy or false hope to what can be of no avail to him in preserving his life.

Let us repeat: Devotion to Mary is no figment of the zealot; no merely devout scheme, nor simply a pious, conventional emotion, but, on the contrary, a truth,—a substantial, solid, spiritually-scientific fact which faith and theological reason clearly maintain.

Auguste Nicolas, a writer of fine parts, whose word passes current among the thoughtful, presents the state of the question as follows: "It is an elementary maxim of philosophy, that effects, subsists by the same causes which entered into their production."

According to this principle the world does not subsist elsewise than by the same power that has created it. The conservation of the world is the world's creation made continuous. In the same way the christian world is nothing else than the Incarnation continued (the going on of the Incarnation). We are annexed to Jesus Christ, and form with Him 'One Body,' says the Apostle. Christ is the Head of that Body of which all christians throughout the world, all the chosen on earth and in heaven are the members. Now the members do not receive life in a manner different from that of the head; and as it is by Mary that Christ the Head received life, in the same way is it that we also receive life by Mary. As she contributed to the first generation of the christian world, she contributes even now to its conservation, which is, after all, nothing more nor less than the first generation continued or going on.

In bringing into the world the Eternal Light, it is she who has spread abroad its wings in the world—a fact which we find recognized by the Church in the song of the preface set apart for Our Lady's feasts—"O, thou who whilst thou didst preserve the glory of thy virginity, didst pour out upon the world the Eternal Light, Jesus Christ, Our Lord."

She is that garden of delights to which the spouse in the Canticles has been compared—which exhales afar, under the impulse of the South Wind, the sweet perfume of the Divine Flower that embalms it, the graces of Jesus Christ. "Arise, O North Wind, and come, O South Wind: blow through my garden, and let the Aromatical spices thereof flow." (Cant. iv., 16) (Nicolas).

So then we find that coupling the principles of philosophy with the dogmas of faith; knowing now on the one hand that the world's preservation is perpetual creation without interruption or sequence; or, as I might say, preservation is creation frozen in the act or action preserved and continually going on; and knowing, on the other hand, that Mary entered into the cause of the christian world by the Incarnation, inasmuch as she furnished life to Jesus Christ, and, consequently, life to us in the christian world, where we become one body with Him, it is clear that that christian piety which directs its attention to obtaining help from the Mother of God is sanctioned in its conduct by faith and reason, by philosophy and theology, and that these two principles dovetail nicely, making in the christian life a thing of harmony and beauty out of Mary-cult. When spheros or the world was set in motion we may say that our world was preserved. From that moment there has been no interruption of its gyration; for, motion is its life. This constant revolution of the world is like the continuous creation. What would be the effect if it were to stop in its motion? As order, life, being and everything depends on it, creation itself would cease. Worse than chaos, worse still than any one is aware of, would eventuate, if the world were to cease rotating. Neither will it pay to tamper with the perpetual causes of the christian world.

CONCLUSION:

I HAVE had and am still having my christian life of Jesus Christ by Mary. She is concerned about and prays for the Church. She is concerned for me individually and her prayers must obtain with God.

ILLUSTRATION:

WE find the following text in the Gospel: " And all these were persevering with one mind in prayer with the women and Mary, the Mother of

Jesus and His brethren " (Acts i, 14). We may well believe that joy filled the hearts of the Apostles, and the light was kindled in their eyes when they found the Mother of the Lord lodged in their midst, in that upper chamber at Jerusalem. Her presence breathed peace and comfort into them. The mourning look, expressive of trial, not regret, of grief not sadness, was on her face; and yet, though but a woman, she was able to suffer the Master's death better than those rugged men who had less grace than she and who found strength in the contemplation of her example of patience and hope to bear up under the awful shadow of Calvary's recent tragedy. The Apostles were, up to the present, weak, brittle vessels. They are assembled now to pray and fast together, and, in so doing, bring down upon themselves the Holy Ghost with His grace — that light and strength that was to show them all the roads to the ends of the earth and to warm their hearts with a brave wish to lay down their lives in the Master's cause. The Church of God is to be in their keeping. Surely it is an important hour when they await the means to carry out the ends of the Incarnation. Mary is by their side in this event helping the Apostles of her Son to obtain those sublime graces of which they stand in so great need. It is a scriptural fact that Our Lady's charity was the occasion of Our Lord's beginning to hallow the world before He was born. It was her sweet charity that brought her with her unborn Child

over the hills to visit her cousin Elizabeth when
Jesus presanctified John. It is the opinion of
many theologians that God's eager delight in the
immensities of the Blessed Virgin hastened on the
event of the Incarnation and advanced the birth
of Christ. This does not seem extravagant when
we study the economy of God's general conduct
toward His Mother as we know it: The pre-
sanctification of John taken with the anticipation,
so notably wrought at the instance of Mary, of the
time of His miracles, when He changed the water
into wine at Cana, and we may securely believe
that the prayers of Our Lady released the Spirit
from the embrace of the Father and the Son in
advance of the appointed time of Pentecost.
Forty days were spent by Moses in waiting for the
tables of the law. Now, ten days serve to open the
skies and bring the bright flashes of the law of grace
upon the minds and hearts of the Apostles. Ten
days! Why not forty—the favorite number and
length? Mary prayed. These facts are preg-
nant with meaning for us. They contain a
message for us. They inform us that Mary has
an interest in the Church, and, further, a positive
influence over her destinies. She influences the
Church as a body and as individuals. She was
present, prayed and fasted to bring down the
Holy Ghost upon the Church. She was present
in that same chamber and concerned when there
was a grace for the individual-Mathias. A bishop
was to be chosen out and praying they said:

" Thou O Lord, Who knowest the hearts of all men, show which of these Thou hast chosen." Mary was there, I say, and prayed.

RESOLUTION :

I SHALL never attempt anything in life without seeking the co-operation of Our Lady.

PRAYER :

VIRGIN MOTHER of God, as thou didst pray with the Apostles in that upper chamber of old, pray now for us that we may realize fully and always that all the hopes of our prayers should be based on our co-operation with thee, joined to thy intercession in our behalf.

Through Jesus Christ Thy Son, Who liveth and reigneth with God the Father and the Holy Ghost, One God forever and ever.   Amen.

CHAPTER III.

A CHILD IS BORN TO US TO-DAY THROUGH MARY.

"LET us proceed on with this beautiful mystery"—Nicolas is speaking—" and let one truth link itself to another. There is no such thing in God as succession. Only the present time may be applied to Him. 'I am Who am.' Only the present tense may be predicated of His operations, which, under force of necessity, share in the nature of God."

Accordingly, at this moment the Incarnation is going on through Mary. Saint Bernard carries out this truth: "There is born to you a Saviour this day." (Luke ii., 2). I hope no one is rash enough, by way of reply, to observe that this is an old affair, that this was said a long time ago. Aye, and I say, myself, it was repeated before, and even before that. Christ is born not only before our age, but before all ages. This birth has its dwelling in a light we cannot pierce. It loses itself in the profundity of the Father's bosom. With a view, however, to making it, in some way, manifest, He is born; but, this time it is of the flesh that He is born, and is made flesh. What is there in the fact to astonish us, that, because of this birth, Christ should go on continuing to be born to this very day in the Church, whereas, it was such a long time ago the words were uttered—"A Child is born to us."

Is it not true that the Son of God was yesterday, is to-day, and will be forever? It is no less true that Abraham, the father of all believers, leaped for very joy with the desire to witness that day, that he has witnessed it and drunk of its joys. And has not Jesus Christ said, "Before Abraham I am?" Exemplifying, in a way, eternity, Christ comprises within His vast bosom past, present and future things in such a way that nothing eludes Him, nothing goes before nor comes after Him. In the same way our devotion should eschew all that is merely fictitious and show to the letter its living faith in this high mystery of piety, revealed in the flesh, made just in the Spirit, made visible to the angels, preached to the nations, believed of the world, raised aloft in glory. Let us look upon that as ever new which ever renews souls: let us look upon that as never old which always bears fruit and never withers. In the same way as Christ is still, in a manner, immolated each day, as many times as we commemorate His death, so should He be looked upon as being born as many times as we commemorate His Nativity. (In Vigil, Nativ. Dom., Serm. 6).

We are incapable with our fathom-line to reach the bottom of this mystery with its perpetual nowness. We cannot understand it for the same reason that we cannot understand God Himself. Once, however, we come to believe in God and His Incarnation, we are driven to admit this mystery. The Eternal One making His entrance into time, must fill it with His presence and even overflow it, as if the ocean were to be poured into a vase. He must comprise in Him all its fulness. He should be a Temporal-Eternal just as He is a God-Man. For this reason, say the Fathers, all the mysteries of Jesus Christ, comprehending His Incarnation, birth, life, His passion and death go on and bear fruit in all ages; they are wrought out and fulfilled not only so as to confine themselves to the time when He was a dweller on earth, but for all time as well preceding and following His residence on earth. The result of this sublime truth is consequently that the gift of Jesus Christ to-day is nothing different to that primary and universal gift that had been accomplished by Mary; and, furthermore, that Mary to-day presents Jesus Christ to each one of us with the same gift that she once gave to the world. In the same way as all the wicked deeds done by mankind before the time of Jesus Christ and after Him were all present at His sacrifice and brought, all, their bitterness to the Chalice of His passion, in the same way, the graces, which were to be apportioned out to every one of mankind, were concentrated in Christ's Nativity from Mary. God, ' Who in His Providence makes preparations for effects in most far away causes,' as Bossuet alleges, has prepared likewise all those graces which were to be doled to mankind out of their chief source, Jesus Christ, and through their 'occasional' cause, which is Mary. The application of these graces is no more than the unrolling of this design, and, as it touches Mary, does not mean any more, consequently, than the extension and unfolding of her divine motherhood. The stream of graces poured out from the deep bosom of the Heavenly Father into the humble breast of Mary, like the public fountain, jets up to the very height of its source only to fall again and find a basin in her virginal soul, which it fills, first, and above all creatures, and overflows from Mary out upon those other creatures, passing, by a thousand outlets and channels, on its way to bear spirit and life to the whole body of the Church. (Aug. Nicolas la V. M. dans le plan divin. Livre iii, chapitre 5).

The devotion of the world toward the great Mother of the Redeemer should not be statuesque. The birth of Our Lord, of the wondrous Virgin should be more than an inanimate or historical impression as cold and heartless as the marble, bronzed or painted images of her which we see daily in our chapels and homes. This sublime truth that a child is born to us to-day of the Virgin Mary, must live, it must throb; and, we

must feel, as it were, the pulsations of the fact
with the same realization as the Magi, and
experience the warmth of its breath going out
over our lives like the warm summer air.

'A child is born to us this day' of the Virgin
Mary. It is a mystery and yet a majestic truth
that Mary gave Jesus to the world centuries ago
and that she, by the force of that gift and the
laws of divinity, bestows Him upon 'me' 'to-day'
and showers upon 'me' 'to-day' those first, original,
identical blessings of the Incarnation. The fruit
of Mary's fragrant womb is ever fresh. The
Divine Flower, Jesus, does not wither, neither does
the stock.

THOUGHT:

JESUS CHRIST is born to-day of the Virgin
Mary unto me.

ILLUSTRATION:

THE story of the Egyptian who, from a low,
wretched creature, rose to the very highest pitch
of holiness, is familiar to all, as it should be. The
sphinx and the mummies in Thebes should pass
from memory before this wonder of heaven's surpassing sweetness and benignity, flung across the
sinner's path like a golden bar of light in the
shadow of Our Lady's image.

History leaves no doubt about the woman's
character and lewd career. The victim of un-
governed passion, from the first breaking of youth,
Mary of Egypt chafed under parental surveil-

lance and fretted herself into open rebellion against her parents. She abandoned the old friends ; their good life rebuked her's, their counsels hurt her. She left her father and mother, breaking their hearts, sending them to their untimely graves with sorrow, shame, and tears for their ruined child ; and scuttled off to Alexandria to prosecute, without hindrance, a life of harlotage and dishonor. Right into the vortex of corruption she flung herself, with all the impetuosity of youth and the madness of untamed passions. She stopped at nothing. Now the inhabitants of Alexandria are going on a pious pilgrimage to Jerusalem to be present at the celebration of the exaltation of the Holy Cross. "Ah, this is a happy event for me," thought Mary, the outcast. "I shall join the pilgrims, and whilst they go to pray I shall have no end of good time with the husbands, brothers and sons of the devout female pilgrims." This was a desperate scheme of impiety :—to corrupt a crowd of pious men in the very act of their devotions. At all events Mary got as far as the church of the Holy Cross, and was on the point of following the band of pilgrims into the holy edifice when a hidden force thwarted her design. Some unseen hand kept her back. Strive as she would the corrupt woman could not step one pace forward— she was conquered. Mary of Egypt gives the account of the incident: "I recognized at once," said she, "that it was the wickedness of my life that barred the doors against me; so, I beat my breast, wept and sighed; and whilst doing so, was in the act of lifting my eyes heavenward, when an image of the Mother of God just above my head struck my eyes, whereupon, I cried out to the Mother of God for aid, conjuring her by her matchless power of creatures to look upon me with pity, and to offer to God my sincere repentance of my wickedness. When I had finished my prayer I felt the greatest comfort, and at the same time liberty to go into the church, which I immediately did. Inside the sacred temple I had the extreme happiness of adoring the precious Cross which gave forth salvation to the world. Upon my going from the church I again threw myself, at once, before the One who so mercifully had come to my aid; and, there before the image of the Mother of God, I renewed my repentance, and once more repeated the resolution to change my life. 'Holy Virgin,' said I, 'O thou by whom salvation is come upon the world, take me under thy care, keep me always and never desert me.'" Arrested in her course of evil, within the shadow of Mary's image, beneath the feet of her who was predestinated to crush the dragon's head and check the dark current of corruption, we may well anticipate the outcome of Mary's conversion. Called by the name of her glorious and heavenly Mother it was but natural the sinner should look with confidence to the bright Queen of Paradise; and that her cry would not fall upon a deaf ear.

Who has ever failed that placed his trust in Mary
with sincerity and docility?   St. Bernard says:
"O let not such a failure ever be said."   The Egyptian's repentance was not to be without struggle
and violence.   She withdrew instantly from the
occasion of sin which is always and necessarily
the first step toward a change of life.   She
buried herself in the deep solitude of a desert,
and remained there the rest of her life covering a
period of some forty-seven years.   The old lust
haunted her; and in that lonely desert heaven
alone witnessed between the poor lonely woman
of God and the powers of hell, the many a fierce
battle but uniform victory for the repentant sinner, who was aided in her struggles by the Queen
of Heaven, and who found in that help a sure
pledge of victory.   From the pavements of
Alexandria and the desert sands the memory of
the Egyptian penitent is wafted down to us all,
bringing with it a priceless two-fold blessing of
hope in God, in our worst guilt, and of confidence
that the Mother of God will aid us, if we turn to
her, to find Jesus, and after having found Him, to
keep Him till death.

RESOLVE :

I SHALL make the mysteries of God live and be
active in my life.   Especially shall I make the
Incarnation a blessing ever-present, ever-done and
ever-actually-doing, through Mary, for mankind
and for myself in particular.

PRAYER:

VIRGIN Mother of God obtain for us faith in the ever-presentness, ever-livingness and ever-actualness of the mysteries of thy Son, especially that of His Incarnation wrought through thee, the ever-estimable Queen-Mother.

Through Christ Our Lord.

CHAPTER IV.

CHANNEL OF DIVINE GRACE.

MARY is the medium or channel by which the grace of God and the mercies of heaven have been transmitted to the world. Upon this point St. Jerome expresses himself in the most highly lucid and poetic language: " Grace is vouchsafed," says this early Father of the Church, " to other virgins in restricted measure, or, in parts; whilst the fulness of grace, lacking nothing to its being entire, has been lavished upon Mary. She enjoyed that fulness, that unstintedness of grace which Christ owned for His humanity, viewed specifically as He was Divine in His 'Person' though, in the case of Mary, fulness of grace was to be found, as it were, in a 'temple' that has been made wondrously sacred.

To repeat this same, real truth in different language, the fulness of grace was found in Christ otherwise than in Mary; because, in Him, one perceives it as in its head, its source or spring which outflows; whilst, in her, the fulness of grace is to be seen as in a neck, a channel or an aqueduct transfusing, that is to say, conducting it through. "Therefore, Solomon," continues St. Jerome, " addresses Christ concerning the Blessed Virgin in Canticle of Canticles, Chap.

VII, as follows: "Thy neck is as a tower of ivory."
Because in the very same way as the life-giving
spirits are diffused through the neck and circu-
lated throughout the frame, in a way not unlike
this, the very vital graces that flow out from
Christ, Who is the Head, are being ever poured
out 'through' the Blessed Virgin and made
to circulate through His mystical body." (De
Assumptione). St. Bernard, who never misses an
opportunity to extol the Mother of God, and who
on this theme is a 'virtuoso,' furnishes the same
conviction with merely a change in metaphor.
He goes even farther in the development of the
thought for us. St. Jerome is rather the dogma-
tist on the point; he furnishes us with a sublime
and important truth, but leaves us to draw our
own conclusions.

St. Bernard is the moralist and places the
practical conclusion in our hands. St. Bernard
says: " O man, whatsoever that may be which is
in your mind to offer to God, bear in mind to en-
trust your presents into the care of Mary in order
that your favors may return to the Bountiful
Giver of grace by the same vessel that has brought
grace unto you. For, it was within the power of
God to diffuse His graces without any aqueduct
whatever, and to do so by whatever manner He
would, in His good pleasure; and, yet, as a
matter of fact, God, as we know, has been pleased,
He has willed to provide even the very means of
transportation for us." (De Nativ).

St. Bernard here lays down the truth in concert
with St. Jerome, that we receive grace through Our
Lady.   All agree that in God's dealing with men
He chose to transact His affairs with men through
the medium of His Mother.   Now, if God has
done so, St. Bernard concludes, we also ought
to conform to God's evidently established method
of conducting the affairs of salvation, and to send
back to God all we have to say to or do with Him,
through the same means of transport by which
He has clearly seen fit to communicate Himself
to us; that is to say, 'through' Mary His Mother.
We cannot in this matter set too much importance
upon St. Bernard's words: "God has 'willed' to
provide us with the vehicle or means of transportation back and forth between Himself and
mankind."   After such a precise declaration it
would seem as though no one should hesitate to
conform to God's plan, and that all our right to
dictate to God, or our liberty to offer God gifts
and prayers, gratitude and love in any manner we
see fit, should be done for, now that we come to
know the pleasure and will of God in the matter.
No sane man will doubt that God has a right to
make laws and rules for His Kingdom.   Why, let
us suppose Our Lady to be the mere servant in
the human sense; and, taking in its too literal
bearing the word 'behold the handmaid of the
Lord,' let us suppose her a servant, standing at
the door of the royal chamber to bring messages
back and forth.   Now let us further suppose a

subject of the realm coming along who says, — 'I
have something to offer or receive from the
king.' The appointed domestic replies in Mary's
words, ' Behold the servant of the Lord—I shall
take your message for you or I shall see the king
and know if he will entertain you.' 'Out upon
you,' replies the impudent subject. 'Who are you
that I should have to do business through you, or
that you should stand between my liege and his
subject?' Has any earthly subject, with even
the most barbaric etiquette, audacity enough to
claim independence of ' form ' and ' law ' in the
king's house? Yet this is what sectaries are
guilty of. They deny to God the right to make
His own rules for His own house. The common
idea of etiquette is absent from their dealings with
God. God is good enough to give us graces and
to accept our homage, even after our treachery
against His very crown. Shall God not have the
right to command 'discipline,' 'order' and 'respect'
in the manner of doing so? If God has provided
the ship which is to bear our gifts to heaven, it is
barbaric taste, if it were not grave disrespect, to
decline the appointed means, to waive the King's
carriage. What is 'apparently' a slight thing, a
mere conventionality, a point of etiquette, such
as the acceptance of a vehicle placed at one's
disposal, and, in the case of kings, commanded for one's 'disposal' may not be so harm-
less as sectaries fancy. It shows an incipient tendency, a spirit of impudence that reaches its logical

ending in the denial of the thing, itself, that is commanded to be done.   It implies, at the outset,
that God has not unlimited power and command
over His creatures, and that they enjoy rights in
contravention to His.   From small beginnings, mere
acorns, easily crushed, Cain and Saul developed
into huge criminals—oaks not so easily brought
low, giants in crime.   A spark is a trifle, but it
contains the living 'principle' of fire, the seed of
a conflagration that may destroy the largest city.
'Discipline,' 'form,' 'means' and right are mocked by
foreign churchmen.   Protestant demagogues make
these terms serve for many a gibe, and fling at
God's Church and saints.

These men forget that when God has commanded, in the least trifle, obedience is of obligation
because God has commanded.   They forget that
what is worthy enough to be the object of God's
will, is worthy of man's respect.   We are not to
delve into the possibilities of God, and to raise
curious enquiry into what is the extent or variety
of the omnipotent resources.   A creature's right
and privilege begins and ends in his obedience to
God.   All his rights of enquiry cease when he
has found the will of God.   Facts and not dreams
are what we want. Not what God might or could
have willed do we look for.   In all things we
seek the will of God, in all things, I say, great or
small.   Fidelity in small things, in the assurance
of God, is a sign of fidelity in the larger.   God
has instituted the sacrament of Baptism: He

mentioned the matter of it. He prescribed water.
"Why not oil or wine or milk?" say you. God
has 'willed' to prescribe water. It is a fact, also,
that God has provided a channel of grace in the
person of His august Mother, so that graces may
flow out to us through her. Why are we to
receive graces through Mary? Such a rude question falls on simple, humble, silent faith; but, if
the question must be answered for the sake of the
incredulous, or the sincere inquisitor, St. Bernard,
in a word, gives the following defence: "God has
willed it so." Our Lord is the Principle and the
Source of Grace, His Divinity constitutes Him its
author, essence, and complete origin. The
Lord's humanity is the chief instrument of grace,
whilst Mary is but a secondary principle thereof.
Our Lady has the grace communicated to her by
Our Lord.

She is, in relation to the Divine operations, a
treasure-vault, in which all the graces of the present life are deposited for man's use. St. Bernard
says again that "Mary was given the world as an
aqueduct through which God's graces are to
flow out upon us." "I, like an aqueduct, come
out of Paradise." (Eccl. iv, 41). On this account
no stream of grace was to be had for so long a
time, because, namely, there had been no aqueduct. Mary is the neck which joins the Head of
the Church, which is Christ, with its body.
Unless we cling fondly to the neck we cannot
cling to the Head, neither can the body be joined

to the Head without the neck. "Thy neck is as
the tower of ivory." As one who mediates, Our
Lady is the 'neck;' as one who protects and de-
fends us, she is a 'tower.' (Morales in Capit. i,
Matth. lib. 2, 9).

THOUGHT:

As a matter of fact, by the will of God, the
graces, predestinated for me, are enclosed in Mary
like the kernel in the nut,—"Blessed is the fruit
of thy womb, Jesus,"—and through her I am to
get at the helps and blessings of salvation.

ILLUSTRATION:

IT was a soft, balmy spring night in the Bene-
dictine Convent of Rodersdorf. The birds were
silent in the branches, without; and the toiler was
gone to repose within. There was restfulness and
peace diffused upon the air of the village. The
nuns in the cloister are chanting the Divine
Office, with more slow, solemn, measured sound,
for, to-morrow is the feast of the Annunciation.
There is a lingering on each syllable, as if each
were taking a long, deep inhalation from a rose
freshly plucked ; and gathered like bees around the
flower are they, the devout nuns, all sucking honey
from every leafy syllable, and by slow degrees
consuming the heart and meaning of every word
of the Divine Office. Fancy pictures the Angels
knocking at Mary's cottage in the long-ago. They
are seeking, in spirit, the face and form, the eyes,
the lips and the words of Mary. They are fancy-

c

ing the Virgin's rapture, they are yearning for a
wider knowledge of the great Virgin, begging a
fonder, purer love for her, and more faithful
devotion to her. Brought together in God's name,
God is in the midst of these christian vestals.
To honor the feast, the nuns are singing, at last,
the Ave Maria; and, Sister Gertrude falls to
ecstasy. Some strange rapture has seized upon
her soul and borne her mind, heart and fancy
away to the distance. To those around her
she is as one sweetly, exquisitely and peacefully
bewildered. What goes on within her soul is
reflected in her countenance in a bright, soft
radiance. St. Gertrude sees in that rapture
three copious streamlets, that flow out from the
Father, the Son and the Holy Ghost, and direct
their liquid steps toward the heart of the Virgin
Mary. They run out with anxious rapidity, but with
great smoothness, for all, into the heart of Mary,
and thence flow out again with the same characteristic of volume and motion back to their source
again. The saint is made to see that the effect
of all this action of the Blessed Trinity upon the
heart of God's Mother is that, after the Father's,
her power stands uppermost in all creation; that,
next to the Son's, her wisdom outshines that of
all angels and all men; and that, after the Holy
Spirit's, her mercy is the very first in heaven and
on earth. St. Gertrude was made to penetrate
the meaning of her vision. She was enlightened
so as to further understand that the Ave Maria

starts up these streams and opens their gates to
let them flow out from the bosom of the Blessed
Three; that under its spell they thence flow on
Maryward, singing merrily on their course, circle
her around, enter her Immaculate Heart and flow
back again to their source, dispensing tricklets
and distributing wavelets, in the bounty of their
joy, upon saints and angels, and, as well, upon
all such as upon earth repeat the Ave Maria;
whereas, in renewing the memory of Gabriel's
message, mankind renews the blessing of the
Incarnation and salvation of the world.

RESOLVE:

IN all my thoughts, words, actions and hopes
the Virgin-Mother shall be to me as that wonderful fountain whence the graces of heaven shall
stream forth into my soul and my life.

PRAYER:

HOLY Mother of God, obtain for us the grace
to approach thee for all that we need, or may ever
need, so that after having, in this, acted agreeably
toward God's plan for our salvation, we may feel
secure for our eternal end.

Through Jesus Christ, Thy Son, Who liveth
and reigneth with thee in unity of the Holy
Spirit, one God for ever and ever.

CHAPTER V.

WILLING INSTRUMENT OF SALVATION.

OUR Lady is more than a piece of mechanism in the work of the Incarnation: her share in the eminent project has the breath of life in it, energy, voluntary co-operation and, consequently, merit. Mary could have declined the august Motherhood on the ground of her free will, which no one will say God had taken from her; because, to do so, on the part of God, would be as if He were to diminish and disfigure Our Lady's human character, inasmuch as the beauty, charm and strength of human action lies in its freedom.

Bossuet contributes the following observation on this point: "I put it forward as a first principle that God, after He had made up His mind, back in eternity, to grant us Jesus Christ by means of the mediation of Mary, would not be content with making use of her as a simple instrument in this glorious mystery. It is not God's intention to have her rest a mere channel of such a grace, but a voluntary instrument which should contribute to this noble work not alone by her most surpassing disposition; but, more than this, by the action of her will. (Bossuet Serm. i, Nativ. B. V. M.). Our Lady is by no means a mere contrivance. Besides, there was nothing in the least automatic in her compliance with the will of God. Men listen with more or less pleasure to a tune discharged from a Swiss music-box or even a hurdy-gurdy. We admire the effect of the mechanic but we do not praise or honor the machine in or for itself; for, it can claim neither consciousness nor voluntariness, and hence cannot merit. Now if the same harmonies were brought about by a musical person we would applaud him, more or less, according to the degree of his proficiency in musicianship, technique, musical feeling, color and the rest. New achievements are inseparable from the honor or, say, merit of persons who perform them.

The godly understanding and appreciation of the talents bestowed on one, and the industry which one shows — industry being the practical development and voluntary right use or correspondence with one's gift — form the principle of praise and honor which are given directly only in the case of persons when they have behaved admirably in art, science or mechanics, but more than this, in ethics, and, above all, religion. There is no merit in an act or action that one could not help; in an act that is void of voluntariness. No one may withhold or stifle the proper praise of a good and truly 'human' action.

Perfection in work and the artist's praise are as two hands in the body. Science and the scientist are part of each other like the play and Hamlet. Mind and free will are the source of

praise or blame in all human action. Mary has
a full 'understanding' of God's design; she took
in its strictures, its struggles, its virtues, its
agonies — all the effects and consequences of the
divine Motherhood. Behold her in the presence
of the vast thought, the tremendous call. The
plan of redemption lies before her awaiting her
free acceptance and free and awful execution.
She enquires into the terms or conditions of the
plans — "How can this be?" Her mind was
made up to acquiesce; she wanted to know how
it is to be brought about. She freely accepts:
Very well, let it be so! — "Behold the Handmaid
of the Lord." Bossuet says: "Once God has
determined that the Blessed Virgin should co-
operate effectively, (that is really and actually),
in bestowing Jesus Christ upon mankind, the
first decree shall never change and we shall
keep on to the end receiving Jesus Christ by the
mediation of her charity." St. Germain, of Con-
stantinople, falls in neatly and practically with our
present thought in a fervid apostrophe to the
Virgin Mother. "No one finds salvation if it be
not brought about through thyself, O holy woman.
No one shall be rescued from the evils that surround him in life, if the deliverance be not effected
by thyself, O pure woman. There is no one
shall ever claim any gift whatsoever from heaven
if it come not by thyself, O most chaste Lady!
Only when they seek it through thyself shall any
ever find grace before God, O most glorious

Mary!" (Serm. sur la Ceinture de la Vierge Marie). If Our Lady were not a moral agent in the Incarnation, and had not acted with freedom, pure and noble, she could lay claim to no merit with God, or honor, in its true sense, in the matter, before mankind, or power to intercede for us. If she were no more than the unmoral agent, Scripture has needlessly brought her forward to blend her name and title with the Master's, and to commingle therewith His birth, His miracles, His life and His death.

The saints had been, besides, if Mary were not a moral agent in the Incarnation, extravagant and misleading in their practices, and in error under this head. As a matter of fact Our Lady has contributed effectively, rationally, freely, and, therefore, meritoriously so as to deserve the special favor of God and the honor, respect and thanks of mankind in the Incarnation. This has been the rule of judgment forming the root of action in the past. This has been the custom devoutly and lovingly cultivated by our fathers. Who now shall dare rob the Mother of God of one iota of her precious deserts? Christian ages have placed meadows of asphodel beneath her graceful tread; about her virginal memory they have wrapped garlands of honeysuckle, of pansies and hyacinths; in her hands they have placed branches of myrtle and of laurel; and about her waist they have fastened a cincture of white lilies. Encircling her brow they have made the victor's

crown of ivy. Heretics would destroy the garlands and crown. We do not support this vandalism; we resent it. We shall not forfeit a
solitary leaf; but, is there not some danger with
us that in the frosty air of protestantism, rational-
ism, and incredulity, the crown and garland of
God's Mother shall be bitten, or be suffered to fade
or lose sap? Yes, unless we have a warm place
for her in our hearts; unless we love, honor and ·
respect her with the saints, who have gone before
us, our devotion as Children of Mary must wither.

At our peril let this not be; for, when Mary
dies in us the Son will follow the Mother at once,
or, lingering, will follow her soon after.

THOUGHT:

THE burning charity of Our Lady gave, we
may say, the Redeemer to the world. That living, throbbing charity bestows Him on us to-day.

AN ILLUSTRATION:

ST. ANTONINUS who was, himself, an eye-witness
of the incident we now recall, and who furnishes
us with an account of the circumstances connected
with it, is, at the same time, a guarantee of the truth
being told us in the matter, and a pledge of the
absence of any illusion or exaggeration affecting
it. According to the saint, in his own time, during the year 1399, God saw fit to demonstrate
miraculously His Mother's potency and to verify,
in the means of its accomplishment, the saying of

David, that He would reveal Himself to the lowly
and to all such as in their own eyes would stand
of no account. God had a secret design in His
Heart which He wished to unveil: He had a
message of the highest possible import to deliver
to certain men affecting their salvation. He chose
a peasant, a simple, unlettered drudge to be the
instrument, under His hand, in the prosecution of
it. How characteristic of God in His selections!
for, as you know, David was but a ragged shepherd, and Peter a slimy-clad fisherman. The
story runs that this poor, guileless, humble peasant was loitering by a fountain, bearing in his
arms three loaves of bread, when it came to pass
that the Almighty deigned to appear to him, having in His company His own august and queenly
Mother.

The Lord gave, at once, command to the ingen-
uous rustic to hurl the three loaves, he carried in
his arms, into the waters that rippled in the basin
beneath his eyes, as a sign—for so God gave him
to understand—of his determination to extermin-
ate that portion of the world, comprehending the
neighborhood of the peasant's home. Though
fraught with cares that rose up in him that very
instant, and showing strong emotion at the time,
the peasant preserved his discernment, saw in a
glance the course of his duty, and flung himself
upon the point of complying with the order of
God when Our Lady put a check upon his movements, and at the same time threw herself at the

feet of Her Divine Son, appealing to Him with
arms outstretched, and with great emotion, to stay
His judgment, and to give the unhappy men,
doomed by His wrath, time to correct their ways
and repent of their wickedness. As usual, Our
Lady pleaded with success the cause of mankind
ever so dear to her, and the Lord amended His
recent command to the peasant, so far as that but
one loaf would be consigned to the fountain's liquid throat. God then laid the order upon the
trembling villager to go abroad as a peasant missionary, and warn the people thereabouts, on all
sides, to repent of their wicked ways, if they would
escape His stormy wrath. Processions were put
on foot, and the fear-struck inhabitants of those
parts were soon seen marching before the Lord
in white robes, with flames of compunction burning
in their hearts. St. Antoninus observes that he
himself was a witness of the admirable effects of
the peasant's warning; and further observes that
the number of conversions which followed, left
one no other recourse but to have faith in the
revelation. If the incident were to end here, the
full effect and harmony of the prophecy would
not be obtained; for, we find further on, how
timely the penances had been, and how providential the warning of the peasant, when a plague
broke out, shortly, which swept away about one-
third of the population—a proportion signified by
the number of loaves,—one, that had been cast into
the fountain, out of the three loaves, which the

peasant carried in his arms. The mercy of God and the power of Our Lady were shown even though the plague reduced the population by one-third, because such as were plague-struck had been warned in season to afford them the opportunity to settle up the affairs of their conscience, and to acquire by due compunction the solid assurances of the chosen, when their time had come, to stand face to face with God, and the eternalness of the life beyond the shadow of the tomb. We cannot draw the inference, from the recital, that the charity of Our Lady surpasses the Lord's, nor that her compassion could possibly exceed His, or equal it. The one thing we deduce from the event is the fact that *God wills* all blessings shall come down upon mankind through the Divinely appointed Channel, His Mother.

RESOLVE:

HENCEFORTH, I shall appeal to Mary's charity to find grace, and only by her aid shall I hope to preserve it, when found.

PRAYER:

O Holy Mother of God, secure for us grace to admire and venerate the charity by which thou gavest to the world a Redeemer, and also to put into practise, daily, the system of entrusting all our cares and interests to thy hands,—our mind, will, body, with all their various offices, so that passing through thy Heart, they may extract a fragrance that will render them agreeable to God.

Through Our Lord Jesus Christ Who liveth and reigneth with the Father in the Unity of the Spirit, one God, world without end.   Amen.

CHAPTER VI.

MEDIATRIX.

AT the mere mention of the word ' Mediation ' when predicated of Mary, a wave of terror, horror and,—if you please,—resentment, affected or sincere, sweeps over the bosom of those who are not of our faith. We tell foreigners in religion that Our Lady, with all her beautifulness, her moral symmetry and grace, is but a creature. We assure them, for they, too, are called by God to believe as we, that she holds all from God, her Son; yet the idea of illusion and the bug-bear of false divinity that rushes upon their mind takes such strange possession of them that, against all reason, it roots itself and clings to them in spite of all our affidavits. Granting that here or there some one has em-ployed an expression that could, under the glass, furnish a temptation to suspect exaggeration, the Catholic Faith, on this same point, is clear, and it could have only one meaning to be true, and the Church knows what she believes. The fact of the matter is, the devil tempts these people, just as he tempted Adam, Cain, Saul and all other men, not excluding the very Lord Himself; and they yield to his cunning. Coming down now to matters of fact, what is there in the word Media-

tor to excite or justify such wrath as is kindled
when it is applied to Our Lady?

All ages and peoples have stood for Our
Lady's ' mediation.' The Armenians, in the
hymn set for Christ's Nativity, addresses her
thus: "O Blessed Virgin! deliverer from the
curse, expiatrix of sin, through thee the decree
of condemnation was remitted and by thee,
our first mother, who fell by sin, has been lifted
to her feet." The Syrians, in the First Nocturn
of Saturday, say to her: "Blessed amongst
women art thou, through whom the curse of sin
has been uprooted and the sentence of damnation met its undoing."

The Greeks, in Menæ, for the fourth of February, and elsewise, most frequently used the apostrophe: "Hail, veritable treasury of virginity;
thou who hast annulled the first mother, thou who
hast released us from the curse which was visited
upon our first Father." The Latin Church employed these words, that are found in Peter
Chrysalog, in his sermon 140: "Heaven is filled
with dread, the angels tremble, creation can not
bear it, nature is powerless in the matter, and
one simple girl so takes God into her bosom,
receives and cherishes Him, as to exact as the
very rent of her house, and to levy as the price
of her very womb, peace unto earth, glory unto
heaven, salvation unto the lost, life unto the dead,
a parentage for earth and heaven, and the fellowship of God Himself with flesh."

St. Andrew of Crete says, in an ode to Our Lady: "O, thou, Deipara, the hope and defense of such as praise thee, release me from the grievous yoke of sin, and out of thy clemency favor me with tears of compunction." (Hurter. Theol. Dog. Vol. II. p. 412).

To be a mediator one has only to be able to bring his influence, by prayer or otherwise, to bear upon God, so as to draw down His favor upon some one. The saints are all mediators; and we, who still inhabit the earth, are mediators, inasmuch as we may pray one for the other. True, Our Lady's mediation outshines and even outranks that of the other saints, whoso they be or'whatso they may have done: Her snow-white holiness, from the first, her grace and intimate relationship with the Messiah, place in her hands powers of mediation in proportion to their own character, pre-eminence, degree and effectualness, and militate for her title to an altogether special mediation, such as, for influence upon the divinity, lifts her above the choirs of angels and sets her in a niche that overlooks the galleries of saints. Still the hypercritical need entertain no fear that we have in mind to obscure or to throw into the shadow the only absolutely necessary mediation of the Lord and Saviour, by speaking the truth of Our Lady's mediation. Nothing could be farther from our mind or the truth than to obtrude our most gracious Lady upon the sphere of God-head. We do not take

her, by anything we may truly say of her, out
of her domain of creatureship. To have any
creature stand in competition or comparison with
the Creator is above all things odious—this is
treason against the Most-High. God is beyond
us essentially. Our Lady is not beyond us, essentially ; though, as a matter of fact, she is. God is,
and must be so. Not Mary, yet, God has made
her as she is—great, sublime, wonderful, incomprehensible, though, compared to her Son,
nothing. How strange a zeal the Jews had for
the honor of Cæsar !   Was it, indeed, devotion and
love for Cæsar that made them charge against
Our Lord, that He sought the honor which should
have fallen, by right, to Cæsar?—"Give to Cæsar
the honor that belongs to Cæsar, and to God the
honor that belongs to God." Heretics reverse
the charge to-day. Now Our Lord repudiated
the charge of being the enemy of Cæsar: He
declared that His doctrine forbade any hostility
to the state. The Jews did not, or rather would
not, believe Our Lord; for, they charged Him
with this, later on, before Pontius Pilate. So are
we accused of giving to a creature honor that
belongs only to the Creator. We reply that our
faith teaches us Mary is but a creature, and can
have no part in any worship that should belong
distinctly to Divinity. Like the Jews, our accusers
do not choose to believe us. The Jews did not
love Cæsar so much, in their zeal for him, as
against Christ. Neither is it love and zeal for

God that inspires this querulous antipathy of
heretics against the children of Mary and the
Catholic Church. To all we answer: Give to
God the things that are God's, and to Mary
the honor that belongs to her; for surely she
is, at least, above Cæsar, though infinitely below
God.

Theologians assert that second causes subtract
naught from first. According to this, our fathers,
in the flesh, in the honor they receive at our
hands, nowise take from the honor that is due
to God; and, the respect we show the former is
in no sense prejudicial to the sovereign Father
that is in heaven. The Messiah and He alone
has made the salvation of the world a possibility:
no other could have done it. And if, indeed,
there are other mediators, Christ goes before all
as cause precedes effect. "For in Him dwelleth
all the fulness of the God-head, corporally, and you
are filled in Him Who is the head of all principalities and power." (Coll. i. 10, 11.) Without His
mediation there neither would nor could be hope
for mankind. So comprehensive was it in
character that Our Lady herself had very need of
it. The Messiah's mediation needed no props;
it needed no other besides. Of itself it is simply
without bounds in scope and value. Our Lady
could not, as a primary cause, I repeat, make
Salvation possible any more than she could be
the Victim, the Lamb, the Son of God—aye, any
more than you or I.

D

Our Lady's mediation assumes always that Christ and He alone has made Salvation possible; but, Mary's merits and intercession go far toward making that possibility a fact in our life. She applies it to us. The graces which Our Lord has laid up by His passion and death are, 'we may say, ready for distribution; but, as a matter of fact, we cannot come into their possession unless we can enlist Mary's influence in securing them for ourselves. A striking and terrible illustration of this fact lies before us in the sad catastrophe of protestantism. Why do so many presumably intelligent people come by such blindness to the light of grace and faith? St. Bernard has informed us of the reason under somewhat parallel conditions: "The currents of grace," said he, "have not flowed because the aqueduct was wanting." Protestants have not the real Mary in fact, as she is, in other words, as God made her; hence, they are far away from Christ, the Source of light and power. If those who have wandered from the Fold would but turn to Mary, the gentle shepherdess would soon lead the protesting nations back to Him Who said: "I am the Good Shepherd, other sheep I have who are not of this Fold." Let them accept Our Lady for all she is, and Christian unity will soon follow. To my mind, if one may dare express a personal impression, where Mary is absent from a religion there is not, for the most part, any real true and supernatural faith in the Divinity of Our Lord

Jesus Christ; and mounting from particulars to generalities, the faults, those beyond the pale find with us, have enough likeness to recall the fable of the wolf and the lamb. Men do not, in other words, like the Church of God, and, so, having in mind to pick a quarrel, and not being able to hit upon a just cause, behave like the Jews and the wolf, and trump up a pretext. Let all men beware of selfish illusions, and fear being tricked by the black fiend. Let all who see the light pray to God and Mary for all such as repine in darkness and flounder about in the illusions of sects, that the whole world may be made up of the faithful of Christ and the children of Mary.

THOUGHT:

THE graces we need, if we are to live virtuously and die with hope, find their source and origin in Our Lord; but, God has willed that we may not enjoy these graces without Mary's mediation.

ILLUSTRATION:

IT came to pass toward the middle of the eighth century, that the Moors got the upper hand in Spain. For a long time they kept up a violent antagonism toward christians in that part of the world. The deadliness of the Moors' hate showed itself in ruthless and bloody cruelties, which they exercised, without any pretence to mercy, upon all christians who had the misfortune ever to fall captive into their hands. Some they flayed alive; others, impaled, 'died upon the scimitar's sharp point'; whilst more found a sure death by flames, all the more torturous, wicked and fiendish, as they were purposely slow, so as to protract their victims' agony. Horrible indeed, yet a glory to record, are the deaths of the brave martyrs who perished under Moorish infamy; but deplorable, too, was the sight of those who succumbed to the tempter, and evinced their preference to life in apostacy, over death in grace and triumph if in blood.

Many showed, under torture, the white feather and the craven chest, and shifted their faith about to Mohammedanism. The Mother of Sorrows felt a sharp pang for this; the vision of so many captives, deserting the standard of her Son, refreshed the memory of the sword of grief that buried itself in her Immaculate Heart, in that olden time. Out of mercy and compassion, she inspired the raising up of a new order in the Church, whose mission was to be the deliverance of christian captives out of Moorish bondage. St. Peter Nolascus was the instrument chosen to do such work in Spain as St. John of Matha had done in France during the age that immediately preceded. Devotion to the Mother of God, and a glowing sympathy for the captives, were the chief marks of the saint's character and conduct. These he cultivated so well, that in the minds of all, the two things seemed to have been born in him. One day, as St. Peter was in prayer, that was attended with tears warm and copious, and with groans deep and sonorous, over the captivity of the christians and the arrogance of the infidels, the Mother of God appeared to him, and made it known, that if he, indeed, wished to afford her Divine Son and herself a pleasure, he could not do so in any way more suitable than to create a congregation under the title of Our Lady of Mercy, the purpose of which should be the redemption of christian slaves held amongst the Moors. The good man did not falter a moment, but fell to laying out his course immediately. Everything he had in the world, he sold, and with the help of St. Raymond and James, King of Aragon, both of whom had been honored with the very same revelation, he established, at Barcelona, in the year 1223, with the approval of the Holy See, the Order of Our Lady of Mercy, for the ransom of captives.

The Church of God, ever aflame with zeal for the honor of His Mother, to augment more and more the devotion, respect, love and gratitude she deserves at our hands as the Mother of Mercy, has made the twenty-fourth day of September a particular feast in thanksgiving for the raising up of an order which is itself a perpetual miracle of charity the most heroic. (Vie de St. Pierre de Nolasque). Moorish bondage, with its violence, fire and blade, deserved Our Lady's pity and intervention. Alas! we languish in a captivity worse than this. There the body was hewed and

hacked, burned and tortured, but all the while
their souls might be free. What, oh what, is that
captivity where the immortal soul is a captive and
the chains are those of human passions we ourselves have forged and placed in the hands of the
devil to fasten upon our wrists. Yes, if the
tortures of the innocent pierced the heavens and
reached the seat of mercy, what a pity must
touch the heart of Our Lady to see sinners, her
own children, the slaves of, aye, as St. Augustine
puts it, "the very food of the devil"? How it
must touch the heart of the Lord's Mother to
hear the orgies, the wild tumult, the brazen conduct, the mocking laughter, and shouts of the evil
spirits emanating from the souls of sinners when
the standard of God has been torn down and that
of Lucifer hoisted and unfurled! The Moor
could kill the body, but without their consent,
without their own voluntary sin, the souls
of their victims, through all the tortures the
dusky Moor rode them, had continued to be
free. The hand that lays this city of God,
my soul, in ruin, must be mine own. But Our
Lady will hear the captive's groan: the
sinner's cry is welcome to her ears: the call
of the weak and struggling comes to her like
the voice of a loved one absent, but returning
home. The plea of the outcast reaches her
within, like the starving orphan's sad, pitiful
wail comes upon the cold night wind to the
chamber of a kind and loving woman with an

appeal for food and shelter. Long live Our Lady, the ransom of captives!

RESOLVE:

GRACE is liberty and sin the only bondage. To obtain the former and be loosed from the latter I shall apply to Our Lady of Captives.

PRAYER:

HOLY Mother of God, obtain for us grace to realize the truth that all favors come to us from God, through thee ; and, furthermore, the grace to cultivate this economy of salvation set down by God.

Through Our Lord Jesus Christ, thy Son, Who liveth and reigneth with the Father and the Spirit, One God, forever and ever. Amen.

CHAPTER VII.

THE UNVEILED BOSOM.

MAN happily may stand, at the present time, in God's presence, with the comforting assurance of finding in the Son a Mediator before the Father, and in the Mother a mediatrix before the Son: "Jesus removes the covering from His side and wounds, and shows them to His Father; and the Mother uncovers her breast, and exposes to Jesus her hallowed paps." Such is the observation of Blessed Arnold of Chartres. Without question, this is a beautiful picture to adorn and enrich the christian fancy. What a power these red wounds must have! What sympathies they must rouse up in the Father's Bosom! What fresh hatred of evil and mercy for sinners! Grouped with the Divine Person stands 'humanity's solitary boast,' the Virgin Mother, tender, sublime, tragic in her strength, unveiling that stainless breast, those two fountains whence whitest milk flowed to nurse the Eternal Son of God. Without a word spoken, what could be more eloquent than this unveiling of the Mother's Immaculate Bosom? What a wealth of power and significance is implied in the silent act! Once and for all she stood between the wrath of God and doomed humanity, and received in that naked bosom the dagger's blade,—

not of steel, that frets only the flesh, but, of sorrow, that reaches down into the soul with a pain, sharp, terrible, sickening, and though silent, killing,—'a living death, more cruel than that which ends our woes at once.' What a picture for the soul to reflect a radiance of hope, from its warm colors, upon the weary, struggling, weak, human soul,—dark with its sin, sorrow-stricken over its miseries, and pained to the quick with the bitter feelings of its ingratitudes! Dumb as we shall be with over-pressure of guilt, before Our Great Judge, this picture will speak for us. O sinner, what a foil to your despair! O dying one, who can perish within the shadow of this Divine image of redemption? St. Bernard addresses to the Mother of God, words that furnish material for the same picture. "God the Father," says St. Bernard, "Who hath set up His Son for a Mediator betwixt Himself and mankind, hath, no less, set Thyself as mediatrix betwixt this same mankind and Christ, their Judge; and as thou art certain of ever finding grace with the Judge, the sinner is ever sure to find grace with Thyself. The treasure of Divine Mercies is all within Thy hands." (Ap. Dionysius Carth. lib. de laud., vitae solitariae. Art. 29).

Denis, the Carthusian, takes up this note and sustains it with the following expression: "Our Lord Jesus Christ, the Royal Messiah, having a mind to honor and glorify His Mother, hath 'established' her as an advocate before His own

Face and hath made of her a mediatrix between Himself, Who will judge us, and ourselves, who are to stand before Him in judgment. He hath entrusted the militant church to her keeping: He hath confided all the chosen to her care, in such a fashion, as that we shall be the recipients of no grace except such as shall come to us through her. It follows, therefore, that if our prayers are to be heard and we shall have received grace and mercy, we must bear in mind that all this good has come to us through Mary, and that it is she who has our salvation in her hands. (Lib. de laud Vit. Sal. Art. 7).

Here we do well to pause and consider the two elements that make for the solidity of Mary-cult. On the one hand we find that all graces and blessings come to us through Mary, and that we shall receive no other than such as shall have found passage through her intermediation. She is, if we employ a modern term, that 'main' (pipe) which runs through the city of God, connecting the souls of men to the reservoir that contains the blood of Jesus Christ and which has no other means of reaching us but through this main. We might call this the ' fact' of Mary-cult. Now the second element to be considered, the *raison d'être* though only a repetition with us, is well worthy indeed to be many times retold: It is as St. Bernard says that, "God hath set up His Mother," and as Denis, the Carthusian, has said: " God hath established her." Her power is God's doing.

The christian bends to God's will; and, as wave cries out to wave, the great confession of saints on earth goes up to God in that beautiful exclamation of the Lord's Prayer, "Thy will be done," and is echoed by celestial choirs bent in praise before the Lamb. In the language employed by saints to convey this economy of reaching God by Mary, which finds, in our own language, an apposite in the word 'established' or 'appointed,' we discern the elements of authority, stability and permanency. No one will doubt God's right to make this economy. Who will destroy what God has set up? No one has the right to change it. In order to be a supernatural act which any one performs there must be faith in that act; and, yet, every christian act is not specifically an act of faith. The virtue of faith, however, 'informs' it so to speak; its influence is upon it and in it. So too we know that the Church, in her prayers, appeals to God most frequently 'through Christ Our Lord' without specific reference to Our Lady. Here, whilst there is no 'specific' reference to her, the power of Mary's intercession is underlying, is presumed and understood. The characteristic of the Incarnation, as being operated through Our Lady, underlies the outward form of prayer but is never excluded from it; for, Christ is ever born of the Virgin Mary. It is just as in all christian acts which, though not, as stated, specific acts of faith, faith underlies with unbroken presence and influence. Those who absolutely

and on principle, so to speak, shut out Our Lady
from practical influence in religion shall — I
advisably say 'shall' in preference to 'can'—
only be saved, after having done so, on the score
or basis of ignorance or the like; though I am
constrained to observe that in this I speak practically and ascetically; for, I repeat, the great
question with us now is not: Can we be saved
without Mary, but 'shall' we be?

The spirit that animates the stand taken by
heretics toward the Mother of God, and their
defective view of her influence in religion is to
say the least in the sight of history, of fathers and
saints, suspicious and very self-opinioned. Those
who admit Our Lady in principle but do not in
practice make specific acts of belief in her power,
by prayer, for example, endanger their salvation.
Those do wisest and follow the rule of saints who
make a morning offering of all that is to pass,
throughout the day, to Almighty God, by the hand
that is always acceptable to Him,— His Mother's.
Such daily renewal keeps devotion to Mary alive
and preserves the assurance in us that we shall
gain over the Ear of God to our petitions and
that we shall obtain the graces and blessings that
are the burden of our prayers.

THOUGHT:

I SHALL not be of the chosen of God unless I
commend myself and my works to Our Lady
during my life.

ILLUSTRATION :

IT was the thirteenth day of May in the year
1856. The day broke clear, and the morning
was a cool, fresh morning of spring, so delightful,
under the beautiful skies of Oceanica, that I took
it into my head to take a trip; and, with joy in
my bosom started off with my Rosary in my hand
for a visit to the sanctuary of Our Lady of Grace
of Rocheford. When I had gotten over the holy
mountain, upon whose brow the monument consecrated to the queen of angels reared itself aloft,
I went into the church, which was presided over by
the Reverend Marist Fathers. I was edified, and,
in fact, very much touched with the sight of a venerable old man whom I saw kneeling on the steps
of the Blessed Virgin's altar, having by his side
a young soldier deeply recollected and bowed so
low in reverent attitude as to almost touch the
ground with a face that was bronzed by the sun.
When I came out from the chapel I was curious
enough to pick a conversation with the old gentleman and got him to divulge to me what it was that
occasioned so much devotion in himself and the
young man.

"That young man," said the old gentleman,
"is a soldier of the tenth regiment. He is
my son. He comes from the East where he
took part in the bloody encounter between the
Anglo-French and the Russians. Before his
departure for the wars we came, together, to pray
in this church. My son placed himself under the

protection of Our Lady of Grace; he was enrolled
in the scapular and thus put on the livery of the
Mother of God; and, at the same time, hung
about his neck a medal of the great Virgin, whilst
I, myself, in the meantime, conjured, with tears
in my eyes, the Sacred Mother that bore the
Redeemer to bring him back home to me again,
safe and sound to the family hearth. My son
kept up to his promise and has never failed to
address himself to the Mother of God each day
since; and, more especially, on those days when
battles were to be fought.

" In the thickest of the fight, when shot was
whizzing and shell was bursting about him, these
seemed, all, to respect him. His scapular served
him for a veritable breast-plate, that refused to
admit ball or shell, and seemed to avoid the
thrusts of the enemy. Finding himself finally, of
a day, in the trenches beneath the walls of Sebas-
topol, it seemed to him as though he heard a
voice which said to him, clearly: ' Change place.'
He moved forward two steps, and immediately
he did so, a shell fell and burst, which shattered
the body of the soldier by whom he was replaced,
and whose bloody head struck violently against
his kepi or military cap. He has come back
home to me and fancies that he is dead, but his
senses are coming back to him by degrees, and
he begins to show signs of realizing that the
blood which inundated him, was the blood of his
unfortunate comrade in arms. Preserved thus,

in a most special manner by the Mother of God, who has never failed to cast her protecting wings over him; snatched by her hand from the jaws of violent death, and a thousand perils upon seas and battle-fields, my boy has come back to return thanks to his great and clement liberatrix; and I, too, his father, have come with him on this pilgrimage of thanksgiving, to add my meed of gratitude to the most tender Virgin, who has heard our prayers and given back my son to me once again, the only support I have to look to in my old age."

So it is in all ages, Mary has had her knights whose swords have gleamed more with the brightness of her glory, than with the lustre of victory in war. Throughout history, and to-day, even here within our own midst at Mt. Carmel, in the Church of Our Lady of Perpetual Help, and in many holy places throughout the world, spiritual and temporal favors flow out in abundance, and miracles are performed, many of which, though kept hidden from the world, are none the less true, and a powerful incentive, in those who experience her wonders, to love the Mother of God, and to make her loved. Our Lady rewards devotion toward her in both temporal and spiritual blessings. In peace and in war, she aids us: In the one to victory, and in the other, goodness in prosperity and patience in suffering. "Devotion to the most Clement Mother of God," says Pope Pius IX, "heaps on all those who have recourse to her, gifts not only of a celestial and spiritual, but also of a temporal and terrestrial nature." (Letter to Henri Lassere).

RESOLVE :

IN spirituals and temporals, I shall always be and act as a Child of Mary: I shall confide all my eternal and temporal concerns unto her gracious keeping.

PRAYER :

O GOD, Who didst confide Thyself for all things, that a child should seek at its mother's hands, in Mary, grant us grace to always have recourse in all things, concern they time or eternity, to that same Mother.

Through Jesus Christ our Lord.

CHAPTER VIII.

WOODBINE AND POPLAR.

LET us not pass on before we shall have fixed Our Lady inextricably and deeply in our convictions, or in other words, anchored her down at the lowest foundation of our religious principles. She must become a part of our religious constitution, and be made to be cultivated as a primary religious habit with us. If we must be as those 'little ones,' those little children, whom the Master would have the world 'suffer to come unto Him and to withstand not,' then childship does not demean us, nor is it puerile in an odious and weak sense; but, rather a thing preëminently noble in us, to become positively children toward Mary, so far as to be, as it were, tied down to our Mother's apron strings. St. John calls us little children when he says "Little children, keep yourselves from idols." (II John v, 21). Do I err in pressing, or if I may say so, in sucking this conclusion out of these words of Our Lord: "Unless ye be as little ones, ye cannot enter the Kingdom of Heaven," and "Suffer little children to come unto me?" It is a glory and a beauty in our holy Church, that she offers the world a Mother, and enriches mankind with the luscious and abundant fruits of this entrancing prerogative. And what

E

is so natural and so apposite to childhood as
motherhood?   Yes, we must be always, in religion and piety, like these 'little ones' whom the
Lord pressed close to His knees: Innocence of
life, love, confidence, helplessness and depen-
dence!—Ah, what a noble thing is this christian
childship?   And, after all, what is that which we
term manhood?   What are the confines and
characteristics of that period in our life, so designated?   The Infant Son of Mary 'grew in wisdom
and age.'   This observation of Holy Writ, furnishes us with the key to the difference between
the estates of the child and the man, the seed-
time and the efflorescence.   The man is wise: in
youth one begins to expand,—concentrate, define and understand.   Fancy, impressions and
impulses have been supplanted in him by com-
prehension and motive, from which thought is
born.   Thought is the child of reason.   Do we
ever, in our christian life, pass beyond the point
where we have to surrender the mind to faith?
Should we ever be, can we ever be anything but
children, in a faith of such tremendous truths and
transcendent mysteries?   Can we ever define all
we believe?   Can we ever understand the adorable Trinity: though we grow in wisdom, in the
sight of such wonders, in the presence of such
mysterious sublimities, what are we above prat-
tling babes and mewling infants?

Who ever grows to that manhood in faith when
he does not have to hang about the neck of

Mother Church, depend upon her for life, and
take her word for many things that we see about
us in heaven and on earth? Do we ever out-
grow that chapter in our life when we believe our
Mother the Church fully and with a child's ingen-
uous trust? Faith is far beyond reason. Does
any one in life measure its altitudes? " Who
knoweth the mind of God?" queries St. Paul,—
" O heights of the riches of the wisdom and the
knowledge of God, how incomprehensible are His
judgments and how unsearchable are His ways."
From the mother the child takes its knowledge,
its hopes and fears. Like the willing, soft wax,
it takes in from its mother, its impressions of
right and wrong. It asks questions; the mother
gives the answer amid a shower of kisses and
caresses; this is enough for the child. It accepts
all, lays its infant head upon that bosom whence
has taken its faith, in calm trust and in unvexed
repose. Once again, then, in faith we are always
'little ones,' little children. The prophet thanked
God because He, the Father of Lights, unveiled
His secrets to the 'little ones' and hid them away
from the rest, from such as would be men where
they ought to be children, as would be wise where
they ought to be simple, as must understand all
things, as will have no loving trust, no depend-
ency, no child-like confidence, as would have
nothing that would exceed their understanding, in
spite of the kisses, so to speak, of God, His love
and His mercy, as find it incredible that there

should be a being superior to themselves to
whose judgment and will they ought to yield up
gracefully, lovingly and trustingly their own
judgment and will. Alas for those who will
believe themselves to be independent, and who
endeavor to effect locomotion in spirituals
upon the weak joints and limited resources
of a lame human mind, a shattered and frail will
and nature. Such wrest themselves from the idea
of motherhood as a weak, unbecoming, stupid and
undignified notion. The loftiness of childship
that made a shining characteristic of saints is
weakened in their eyes to imbecility. They abandon
the ship of Peter and sink out of sight in the
waters. From the fatal flood of heresy I hear the
moan, I hear the cry of the sincere heart calling—Mother! Mother! Mother Church, Mother
Mary! It is never weakness to depend upon God
—this is strength. There is peace, love and hope
in religious childhood, wherein we believe all our
Holy Mother Church asks us to believe. In any
other way there is unrest, vagary, desperation—
no hope, but a mad chance. So let us be toward
our Mother in heaven—little children clinging to
her virginal robes, dangling from her wrists, and
in that solemn moment when we have taken the
Precious Blood in the Holy Sacrifice, or in Holy
Communion, may we not in spirit hang about her
virginal neck. "O Virgin Mother," cries out
St. Bernard, "when thou hearest the verse 'Hail
Mary' it lies upon thee as an obligation to bestow

upon us a kiss. Advance then toward her image, my brethren," continues St. Bernard, "get upon your knees, plant kisses upon her whilst you say to her 'Ave Maria.'" (Hom. Missus Est.).

I confess that there is a kind of holy realism in such language. It is new to us because we have only known the sonship of Mary in theory, as it were, and have looked upon our Mother in heaven as one far off, and as a something almost as unreal as a myth. The idea of that familiarity which St. Bernard has expressed so humanly, so touchingly and ardently, is the fruit of a true, interior, pure life in Jesus Christ, and of constant meditation upon the adorable mystery of the Incarnation that was accomplished by the instrumentality of Our Lady. It is the result of daily communion, of a constant walking with Jesus and Mary which served to engender a deeper knowledge of the Mother and the Son, and to add fuel to the heart-fires which, under the abundant feeding of the soul, in spiritual reading, meditation, prayer, humiliations, sufferings and the like, waxed to a flame and broke out in tongues of fire and of noblest eloquence. Like causes produce like effects. In our life we walk remote from God and Mary. Like Peter, we follow the Lord from afar; hence, the failure or difficulty on our part to thoroughly fall in with the art of St. Bernard and to understand the truthfulness, the power, the beauty, and the exquisite language of his soul that to vulgar ears and groundlings might seem

affected or at least extravagant. What we need
in our own life is to make Our Lady a reality. To
do this, we must meditate on her, pray much to
her, and prove ourselves worthy of her in our life.
Only in an atmosphere of the most cultured
purity can the sacred art of Mary-cult bloom out
in anything like St. Bernardism.

THOUGHT.

I AM a child of Mary. She leads me to know,
love and serve her Divine Son. She promises
me, then, that, some day, I shall be up there in
yonder skies with Him: I believe her, I have
confidence in her, and rest my soul within her
keeping for the journey to my eternal home.
Why not? Mary is my Mother! .

ILLUSTRATION.

THE Rev. Father Guttierrez, of the Society of
Jesus, had been a good and faithful client to Our
Lady. The reality of his love for God's Mother
made so deep an impression upon his practical life
that all who came in contact with him were made
to feel it. The good priest who lived in bitter
times, during the days of Huguenotism, was placed
under arrest by the patrons of that mongrel religion in Gascony and consigned to prison walls.
With two companions he was thrust in a dark and
remote cell. Here the three holy priests were
made to endure countless rude trials, such as
insults, pangs of hunger, and killing, musty

dampness. Our Lady who never — to her great mother's-love be it said — deserts any of her children, could much less forget those in danger and affliction who had been the chosen weapons of her love. She could not but hear the prayer of her devoted and valiant son as he now raised his hunger-weakened voice from his dark, cold cell in the words of her own hymn, "Show thyself a mother." That word — mother — sharpens the arrow of prayer so that it enters the heart of God unfailingly; and, whilst God did not wish in the present instance to release the good priest from prison-bonds, the Mother of God made known to him the fact of his approaching death and prophesied the exact day on which he was to pass away, in order that he might dispose himself with fresh fervor for that solemn moment and accomplish it in the best possible dispositions. Our Lady deigned to visit him frequently and to comfort his soul with the most beautiful visions of her own august majesty. The day, at last, came upon which he had been foretold he was to die. Upon that very day his soul did actually pass away in that dark, gloomy, damp prison-cell. Eight hours after the passing of his soul, a lady entered the prison-cell. Her dress showed after the fashion of the French in vogue at that period in the south of France. She bore herself with serious and dignified mien. How indeed she had contrived to make her way into the cell no one could tell; for, in order to do this, she had, of necessity, to pass the guards, and these, as it was well known, were under strict orders to forbid any access to the prison or any communication whatever with the prisoners.

Upon entering the cell, she found the two priests keeping watch over their dead companion, weary, pale and starved. In a voice of unusual sweetness, the strange lady addressed them. "You have," said she, "here with you, a body for which you wish to find burial!" They answered in the affirmative, adding, that they did not have the advantage of so much as a shroud or winding sheet, in which they might wrap the body of their dead brother, nor again, any show of opportunity or freedom to go and procure one. With the same benignant smile, the lady heard out the statement of the two priests, and at its completion, drew forth with the greatest possible quiet, ease and grace, from under her arm, a linen sheet of snow-flake whiteness, and offered it to them, with the request that they take it and fold it about the remains of their dead companion. The esoteric air about the way things were going at this moment, robbed the two fathers of all speech; but under the influence of the wonderful kindness evinced to them, they made an effort to speak, and stammered rather than spoke out their warm thanks, with an ill-put apology, to the effect, that in reality it was too much ·to expect so much kindness, especially as the same was at the hands of a complete stranger, and that they hoped the

good lady might indeed suffer herself, at least, to
be made the recipient of some compensation for
all that she had done. With this, they started
into their pockets in quest of money, to carry out
their plan of compensation, when the good lady
intercepted their action with the most tender,
pleading, yet imperative no!—"I can have," said
she, "nothing at all by way of compensation from
you ; only be so good as to make use of the linen,
and dismiss from your mind any farther consideration. God wil make everything good." She
then took leave of the two prisoners, as a smile
of ravishing sweetness illumined and played
about her beautiful countenance. For a long
time, the two priests were at a loss to divine who
the mysterious lady was, how she affected an
entrance to their cell, and, above all things, how
she could have made out that one of them was
dead. All of a sudden, it came to the minds
of the two priests, by an inspiration, that the
lady was none other than the Mother of God,
who wished to bestow this testimony of charity
upon a devoted servant. It is recorded that Our
Lady pushed her charity so far, as even to put
her hand to the task of wrapping the remains
and sewing up the winding sheet; and further,
that she blessed the body. How, indeed, we are
rewarded for our agreeable pains to serve Our
Lady in life with devotion. What a reward it
is, to feel that we have found favor in her sight.
(Facts from Binet).

RESOLVE :

I SHALL cling to Mary as a child for support, protection and guidance in the dark shadows of life, and in the darker, denser gloom of death.

PRAYER :

O GOD, deign to grant us the sweet grace to love Mary as a Mother, in the simplicity, confidence, rest and innocence of the child, both in life and death.

Through Jesus Christ Our Lord, Who liveth and reigneth with the Father and the Spirit, one God, forever and ever.   Amen.

CHAPTER IX.

USE AND ABUSE OF MARY-CULT.

LET us retrace our steps and cultivate still further the thought we took up at the outset, and whilst we are but refreshing certain features of it, a maturer gleam of light shall come of our further acquaintance with Mary's part in the plan of redemption, and a new ray be added from the research. If we obtain a stronger light or a firmer grasp on the philosophy of Mary-cult, all the surer shall we be of salvation, and broader the foothold we shall have on our sovereign end. The ingenious and interesting Nicolas supplies us with a train of thought and keen observation :

The reasons which warrant the cult of Mary are woven, by virtue of sharp likeness, into those very reasons which militate for the worship of Jesus Christ Himself. So, as God has once made up His mind to let us have Himself through Jesus Christ, this order will go on ever after without variance. What has once taken place, and that for all, takes place always, and for each one of us. No one can come at the Father, but by the Son. In the same way, once Jesus has made up His mind to yield Himself to us, through Mary, why would one have this order repealed of coming at Jesus by Mary; and,

yet, not have the process changed of coming
at the Father through Jesus Christ? What
different reason could have urged God to send
us Jesus Christ, through Mary, once, if it was not
His intention to bestow Him upon us in the same
way always? Without doubt, Mary did not
furnish Jesus Christ in the sense that she was the
'first' and 'chief' cause of His advent: She has
been only the 'occasional' and 'instrumental'
cause of this gift on the part of God. It is God
Who has given Himself to us through Mary.
Mary, however, was ever attracting Him and
conceiving Him by her graces and virtues. But,
in accordance with this, we must not hold that
Mary is the dispensing cause of graces in any
other sense than that she has been the cause of
the gift of their author. (Nicolas Plan, Divin.
Liv. III., chap. v.).

Nicolas designates Mary the occasional cause.
Her graces and virtues were, beyond question,
an 'occasion,' though not a necessary cause.
Only as such did she draw down the spirit of the
Most High which culminated in the conception
and birth of Jesus Christ; and if this was not the
case, to the extent that she could not possibly
have been resisted, it survives, as a matter of fact,
that the spirit responded to the attractiveness of
her noble character and, we might say, was
drawn over by her grace and her virtue. Let us
here refresh our minds with the old reflection that
God is the chief cause of all things, even of

Mary's gifts and graces that now make up the instrumental cause of His coming. It is not for all to wander in the maze of curious speculation where elfish spirits adroitly conceal nets to catch the unequipped and unguarded mind. Theologians hunt here in safety even amidst the speculations that tend along the wastes of Divine possibilities. We ought to set aside, for ourselves, pure scholastic speculations and come down to facts. Wise men accept facts; humble men surrender in obedience to them: the stubborn resist them. It does not belong to us, rather would it be over-bold to inquire. Why this circuitous route? Why this lack of economy in God's reaching the souls of men by this winding path? Before replying directly to this curious interrogation, I might observe right here that the blood of Jesus loses none of its strength for passing through the immaculate channel; and, furthermore, if the path that stretches before the mansions of heaven winds, there is no lack of economy that is consistent with beauty. Salvation shows power and beauty. But it is not a question with us of what God might have done, or we would wish Him to do, or have done. As in the first, so now, Our Lady draws down God upon the world by her graces and beauties with the perpetualness of a divine fact — "Thy will be done on earth as it is in heaven." Could God have chosen another instrument of salvation is fruitless speculation. There can be no question

but He has chosen Mary as the instrument of
redemption. The eloquence of fact pleads with
us to have recourse to Mary if we would sincerely
wish to possess Jesus Christ. At this stage, it
will reward us to diverge one moment, in order
to attack a disorder and an abuse of Mary-cult.

Prayers in honor of Our Lady are an excellent
thing, and the traditional practice of the three
Aves uttered daily in her honor has left, un-
doubtedly, in its track, some very astonishing
marks of efficaciousness; but this pious custom
must not be pretended to supplant or purposed to
take the place of the sacraments instituted by
Jesus Christ for the sanctification of man or of the
Our Father; nor taken to repeal the law of
christian vigilance making it incumbent upon us
to shun the occasion that might lead us to sin.
To maintain that because one recites three Aves
daily one cannot be lost, is bad theology. Whilst,
on the one hand, in cold theory, Christ alone is
absolutely necessary to us, it is a mysterious fact
that huge sinners have been saved who had done
no other act of piety in many a day than to say
the triple Ave. How has this come about? It is
difficult to explain why, and yet it is a fact that
great sinners fancy salvation is not for them,
though no more potent fact emanates from revelation than the coming of the Son of Man for sinners.
' O what has the Immaculate Mother to do with us
foul creatures,' is an exact reproduction, in words,
of their sentiments. It was to inspire such men with

hope that Mary is proposed to them. Saints have told of the wonders of a few Aves. Now in the course of time, like all other things, this becomes the subject of abuse. "Ah, then," sinners began to argue to themselves, "we shall go on having a good time, we'll say the three Aves and Mary will save us ; she will make it all right with God." If such indeed is a translation of any one's thought and idea of Mary-cult it is an insult and a positive blasphemy farthest from the mind of saints and preachers, whose purpose in reciting the marvels of the Ave Maria is to check the course of evil and not encourage it. Devotion to Mary consists in using her power by prayer and otherwise to enable us to more successfully conquer our passions, acquire solid christian virtues, fulfil better the duties of our particular station in life, and to persevere in so doing unto the end. To go on in sin, laboring under the illusion that Mary's protection consists in her suffering us to err with impunity on account of our paltry contribution of a few daily Aves is, nothwithstanding the instrinic merit of a single Ave, for which Suarez would have made exchange of all his mighty learning, making Our Lady an abettor of evil; whereas, her mission in life being one with her Son's is to extirpate sin, subdue passion and bring along all holiness in mankind. Our Lady, like her Son, is for sinners, not sin. She loves the sinner but loathes the sin. Sin in the sinner is always a discomfort to the heavenly Mother.

Christ came to save the sheep that were lost to the house of Israel.

THOUGHT:

COULD God have chosen another instrument of salvation has nothing whatever to do with us. There can be no question that He has chosen Mary as the instrument of the redemption. The fact commands us to run to Mary without further ado if we humbly and seriously wish to possess Jesus Christ.

ILLUSTRATION:

IN the month of May, of the year 1850, a French officer was taking a ramble through the Vatican gardens, in company with his wife and children, two in number, one of them aged twelve and the other ten. The Holy Father was to be back in Rome in a few days. The officer's wife, Madame G., was a protestant at the time. There is no question but she had been a faithful wife and mother, and had always accomplished her duties up to the fullest measure of her lights. During the saunter in the Pope's garden she was just saying that she could not see how it would improve her in any way if she were to turn Catholic. Whether it was from presentiment, or out of pure curiosity, yet at all events, Madame G. urged upon her husband to indulge her with a glimpse of the interior of the Pope's apartments in the Vatican. The indulgent husband capitulated to her wish, and it took only a few moments before the doors were swinging apart,

and the officer's family were being ushered into
the Papal chambers.   Everything was examined
with interest.   One after the other bits of furni-
ture passed under scrutiny, till at last the family
found themselves before the door that opened
into the Pope's private chapel.   Here they made
no stop, but entered in.   There, before their eyes,
stood the Holy Father's prie-dieu draped in red
velvet.   This contrivance, with its high color,
caught the woman's fancy.   The conclusion sped
across her mind that that, of course, must be
where the Pope knelt to pray daily and to call
down God's blessing upon the vast world.   It
occurred to her that it might be a valuable idea
if she were to kneel upon that very prie-dieu and
pray down a blessing upon her husband, her
children and herself.   The next instant she was
upon it with bended knee.   Her elbows rested
upon the plane, and her head was supported by
her hands.   For some minutes she lingered on
in that posture, wrapt in prayer.   By force of a
habit, which, strange to say, she had for a long
time formed, and which she maintained and
practiced, in variance with other protestants,
Madame G. was now commending her family to
the care of God's Mother.   She then raised her
eyes and, casting a glance in the direction of the
altar, beheld a lady encircled by dazzling light
and holding two children by the hand, whilst,
before the altar, the Pope appeared, with glance
rivetted upon her.   The event agitated her pro-

foundly, and a paroxysm of terror and of solicitude for her children so stirred up her human
and motherly feelings that her emotion became
perceptible to her husband, before whom she
found an easy pretext of indisposition, and whom
she begged to lead her out into the garden air.
From that moment there was a strong impression
upon the woman's heart and mind. A few days
after the occurrence, on May the 12th, the Holy
Father made his arrival in Rome. Madame G.
was in a tribune reserved for the ladies of her
station in the Basilica of St. John Lateran. The
very instant the Pope made his appearance and
Madame G. set her eyes upon him she immediately recognized the features of Pius IX. just as
she had seen him in the vision in his private
chapel. This was not all ; for, very soon she was
stunned by perceiving just above the head of His
Holiness, in the very same apparition, and with
the same brilliancy as at the Vatican, the august
person of Our Blessed Lady. The woman's
emotion completely overpowered her, and she
fainted away. Friendly hands restored her to
consciousness, but even after this she concealed
within her breast the secret of the vision from
every one, even her husband. Providence had
another attempt in store for her in order to conquer her heart by a final assault in behalf of the
Truth.

On the day fixed by His Holiness for the reception of officers' wives, Madame G. was among

the very first to arrive. The ladies were arranged
in two rows, so as to allow the Pontiff to pass
down between them, and impart, as he went along
the two lines, his blessing to the right and left.
When the Vicar of Jesus Christ had arrived at a
point opposite where Madame G. was standing
with her children, as if providentially he paused,
as it were, to impress himself more deeply upon
her and took to caressing the children. With
great sweetness he enquired after the names of
the little ones, gave each of them a rosary and
appeared to have a wish to give them a very particular blessing, because he pressed his hand with
unusual earnestness upon their heads. The
mother of the lads was thrilled with joy; but what
was her feeling and experience when she observed
the old vision again, cast just above the Pontiff's
head and in precisely the same manner as on the
two previous occasions. There was no mistaking
the dazzling figure of Our Lady, the fair Mother
of God. Madame G. had begun to consider renouncing protestantism at the first apparition.
This consideration augmented with the second.
She capitulated wholly at the third. That night
she passed in tears, and the very next morning
made the announcement to her husband that she
had fully made up her mind to abjure protestantism. Her husband welcomed the announcement
and afforded her all the help he could in its accomplishment. She made her abjuration of false
faith with all the prescribed ceremonials in the

Nun's chapel of Holy-Trinity-on-the-Mount, and received the Sacrament of Baptism. On the following Thursday, Madame G. received, together with her husband and children, the Lord's Body and Blood in Holy Communion. The Cardinal Vicar of Rome himself administered to them the Communion, and after the Mass confirmed Madame G. Immediately his Eminence and suite left the church, the happy husband removed from his breast his decoration and penned a few lines as follows: "The graces I have this day received, together with my wife and children, are so great I cannot be too grateful for them. My decoration is what I cherish above all things, highest and most. I leave it at the altar of Our Blessed Lady as a token of my gratitude." That same officer, on the evening of that day, said to some of us, writes the chronicler: "Do you know I received Holy Communion this morning and I never was so proud or so happy. I tell you for making one happy there is nothing to stand in competition with the sacraments of the Lord." (Rome An. 1848-49-50).

RESOLVE:

WHEREAS, the rod of Moses had no natural virtues to call forth waters from the rock, but that God so willed it to be endowed with that power, so is Mary, by the will of God, empowered with a strange and wondrous power, and I resolve to employ the Mother of God as a wonderful rod to smite the bosom of God, when I need, that graces in sparkling radiance may fall in a cascade upon my soul.

PRAYER:

O GOD, grant us the grace to observe always, the order set up by Thee for the sanctification of the world, which prescribes that we shall seek Thee in Thy Mother's house, and through her find Thee: and may the whole world come to this sweet belief.

Through Jesus Christ Our Lord.

CHAPTER X.

INTERCESSION OF SAINTS AND MARY WITH INTERMEDIATION SET FORTH.

THE Abbot Godfrey, who is generally looked upon in the light of a man endowed with sober judgment found joined to consummate piety, says that 'we pay honor to the Son at the same time that we come to praise the Mother, and that upon our failure to give her praise, we can in no possible way be said to be pleasing to God; whereas, on the other hand, if we are found in the act of giving her praise, it is out of all question that we can by so doing, in any way, bring down upon our heads the displeasure of God.' (Mig. 157, 261.)

If, then, we have recourse to Our Lady, we are guilty of no such thing as piracy; neither can doing so be turned or twisted into any show of reflection upon Our Lord's mediation, in its scope or fulness. The central norm of Christian rectitude, the sun-burst of christian morality, is indisputably the will of God. In all reason, we cannot wish to think or do aught in contrariety to this, nor can we please Him if we contravene His will. Our end in honoring the Mother of God is, like in all things we think or do, His own ultimate glory, the narrow and only path to which, is to ascertain His will in any matter, and without farther debate put ourselves to its direct, speediest and best accomplishment; or, if it be true in temporals, it may be safely said to be doubly so in spirituals; namely, that we ought to take Time by the forelock. Had this norm been kept well in mind—the will of God even above kings—in the days when false prophets were disrupting unity, there would be no room for the fraudulent spirit, and protestantism would have been thwarted. But if Our Lady's intermediation is no prejudice to the adorable Master's, neither does it preclude, on the other hand, shut out, or minimize the value of the mediation of the other saints. Devotion to Mary is not designed to be so exclusive. Like her Son, her Model, and the embodiment, so to speak, of her will, Our Lady honors her children who have been faithful to her Son. True, she is the Moon, but she does not, for that, darken or shut out the stars that blink in the heavens, to warn and gleam for men's instruction, help and guidance. She is at the head of the saints, but her intercession does not run counter to the eminent practicability of prayers and vows to saints.

Here let us observe in passing, that it is a venerable custom, and one we ought to preserve and not let go into practical desuetude, to make, namely, promises to saints, conditional or in view of their prospective help. God wills His Mother's praise to flourish among men. He wills the

honor of all His saints. Mary wills only what
God wills. With her, as with us, 'Thy will be
done' is the one rule. St. Bernard of Sienna,
with all the charm of poesy and the authority of
a saint, sets forth the question of Our Lady and
the saints as follows: "Grace finds its source in
Christ," says the saint, "in Mary it finds a channel, whereas, in the saints, it comes across so
many little brooks. All graces are congregated
in Christ as in their spring or fountain-head, flow-
ing thence, off into their channel and brooklets.
But all these last come together and connect
themselves through the Virgin. It is so we find
it with the Church, which shows a fine proportion
and admirable blending, just as there exists between the Lord and the Virgin, a resemblance
and a union simply perfect." (Serm. Nativ.
Maria B. V.).

We come across our saint repeating this plan
again in his 'Glorious Name of Mary,' (Art. 2,
Chap. ii.), where he says: "No grace comes to
us from heaven, if this be not attained by the
intermediation of Mary." Such is the hierarchic
order that impresses its character upon the out-
flow of celestial graces. In the first place, they
flow out from God the Father, and roll on to the
blessed soul of Christ. 'Every excellent grace,
and all perfect gifts descend from on high, and
each perfect grace comes down from the Father
of Lights.' Thence they proceed downward into
the soul of the Virgin, thence into the Seraphim

and the Cherubim, with the other orders of angels, and still move on into the souls of the saints, until at last they flow into the Militant Church." What a sublime order! What beauty there is in heaven's first law! All creatures in heaven and on earth are bound together. The wails, the cries, the sorrows and the prayers of the christian soldier, writhing in agony on the battlefield, are all caught up by the lower order of angels, and, choir calls out to choir, till they reach Our Lady, and the message of earth is delivered with our Mother's hands into the very hands of God. When our prayers are heard and graces are decreed upon us, the first one to receive them from God's own hand, and to start them on their destiny, is the Virgin Mother of the Most High God. If, indeed, Our Lady intervenes by law between God and us, the graces that flow through her will contract no diminution of strength for this. At that moment, when such a possibility would harass our thoughts, we would have but to recall how the Saviour of the world came to us through her; how He took His flesh and blood from her, and how He dwelt in her virginal womb an unborn God by nature's law, so many months.

Round off this reflection with the impressive cadenza of the Doxology—"As it was in the beginning, is now, and ever shall be, one God." "Who was born of the Virgin Mary," adds the Credo, to which let the whole world echo forth Amen!

THOUGHT:

ALL the graces in life, the best and the least, concern they the body or the soul, are passed, all, out from the bosom of God to the world, by Mary's hand.

ILLUSTRATION:

IN the year 1830 the Mother of God honored, in one of her unusual ways, a novice of the Congregation of the Sisters of Charity of St: Vincent de Paul. The name which the humble maiden, so set apart, had borne in the world, was Catherine Labourè, and the way in which the Mother of God was pleased to honor the pious maiden was by an apparition. In honoring the devout novice, God's Mother was honoring, at the same time, the whole community of zealous Sisters of Charity, who do so much good for the Kingdom of God all over the world—here, on fields of battle, running red with blood; there, watching over the sick and caring for the poor and the orphans in hospitals and orphanages, toiling among the saddest features of human existence. The form of the apparition has since been made familiar to us all under the title of the Immaculate Conception. The vision shows us Our Lady mounted upon the globe, with hands outstretched, from whose palms, faced downward, two streams of light pour themselves down upon the globe that lies submerged in a very sea of dazzling brilliancy beneath her feet. At the same time, with the apparition, the scene was

accompanied by a voice which was distinctly
heard to utter the following words: "These rays
stand for the graces which Mary obtains for
men." A circle of supplicatory words ran round
the vision and revealed the following prayer in
clear, luminous letters: "O Mary, conceived
without sin, pray for us who have recourse to
thee." After some moments the vision withdrew,
and, in an instant, the reverse side of the apparition flashed upon the maiden's sight, plunging
her in deep wonder and showing her the device,
which, from that day, has been a part, aye, a
valuable part, of the spiritual stock-in-trade of
Mary's clients. This was the letter M, surmounted
by a cross, with the Sacred Hearts of Jesus and
Mary,—the former entwined with thorns, the
latter transpierced with a sword,—for a base.
Here again, the voice, that had spoken previously,
was heard, afresh, in an order, delivered with an
air of gentleness and command, to the effect that
a medal be struck off, which should be modelled
after the pattern of the vision. The voice
annexed to the command a promise that special
protection, on the part of the Mother of God,
should be guaranteed to all such as would carry
about their person this same image, duly indulg-
enced. The children of Mary should have about
them, at all times, some emblem of their queen,
some soft reminder of their Mother in heaven.
What more warrior-like than the chaplet we
see dangling by the side of the religious? It

hangs there from the waist, like a sword, with
the Lord for a hilt, and His Mother for a blade—
"and she shall crush thy head." What christian
man ventures forth in his daily life without a
rosary or some image, medallion, statuette or
other pious conceit of his Mother in heaven?
We are in danger, at any moment, of coming
upon the dragon in our darksome way. Our
path is strewn with snares. Let us not be without
this choice weapon to confront evil in our daily
life. Plunge your hand into your pocket, feel
the brazen medal, the bead, the crucifix attached
to it, at all times when the devil tempts you.
The very fact that you do so shows a will to
resist the tempter, and at the same time is a mute
prayer, a silent but eloquent plea for heavenly
help, and a noble confession that you do not and
will not surrender. In public places, where a
spoken prayer finds no opportunity to convince
us, we still cling to God in the interior darkness
and overwhelming sensibility of the temptation,
we see, by this sign, that we will not yield to him
and that we do not pretend to combat him, single
handed, but, rather, with the help of God and
His august Mother. Let no warrior of God seek
sleep at night without his scapular. This, too,
is both a sign of Our Lady's guardianship over
our rest and a help against the dangers which,
so general in life, do not spare mankind, even in
sleep. It is well for the faithful to know that all
priests who are members of the Eucharistic

League are empowered to indulgence medals and beads of Our Lady's Immaculate Conception. For the rest, the breviary, which the priests of God recite each day, yes, that great prayer of the universal church attests the wondrous growth of this devotion and the great things accomplished by it as by a great weapon designed by God for · the salvation of souls.

RESOLVE :

I SHALL never be found without my rosary, or at least a medal or statuette of Our Lady; and, I shall never forget to wear my scapular, night and day, and to renew it immediately it is worn out.

PRAYER :

O HOLY MOTHER of God, obtain for us grace to carry some emblem of thee about our person, always; and, grant, also, that we may have the courage to chisel out of our rough life, by humility, chastity, patience, and the constant practice of all christian virtues, an image of thyself. Through Jesus Christ, Our Lord.

CHAPTER XI.

INTERMEDIATION.

IN the motherhood of the Virgin Mary, the world finds its proof of the God-manhood of Jesus Christ.   If the wicked world could only succeed in obliterating Our Lady ; if they could do away with her, then would the vultures prey upon the Divinity of Our Lord, pick at it, and mangle it as they would.   Nestled in her arms what a beautiful picture it is to see the Mother protecting the child against the Herods of to-day.   To what tricks, resorts and machinations have not the vicious had recourse to riddle the idea of Divinity in Our Lord ?   They grant Him only what sheer reason drags from their lips, and their confession has no love in it whatever.   They strive to get one to match Him, and a doctrine to match His doctrine. They hunt up Buddha in India, Zoroaster in Persia, Confucius in China, Pythagoras in Greece, and the rest, and raise a comparison.   The idea of Virgin-Motherhood heads them off.   Here is not mere goodness such as is possible in the case of any other whosoever.   Here they counteract mystery.   What mere man would be born so ? Only the prophet could enlighten and put forward, on the part of God, this sign, that a ' Son of the most High,' an ' Emmanuel ' would be born of a

Virgin: " Behold a Virgin shall conceive and bring forth a Son and His name shall be Emmanuel," says Isaiah. So the Virgin-Motherhood outlives its adversaries, survives the bolts of its sneers and the shocks of the ' reformation.' It lives, it moves and influences millions of hearts, in spite of all fiendish efforts to the contrary to-day; for, the christian world looks upward to God's Mother, offers her flowers, sings hymns in her honor now as of yore. The world's best masters base their hope of immortality in art by making her outwardly fit the noblest christian idea of her within. When the Unitarian reads his novel and his biography, and his Scripture as a philosphy or code of ethics at home, the whole week long, the Virgin Mother has lights burning before her image in every quarter of the known world with myriads of votaries gathered about her; and their placid pooh-poohing does not serve to quench the myriad tapers; and, in their commingled rays and the prayerful whisperings of the myriad votaries, the world will read our confession in the Divinity of Jesus Christ. The Catholic world, unspoiled by protestantism, in spite of quibbling and theoretic distinctions, that haunt wilful sectaries, carries out its venerable and affectionate tradition of looking to the Mother of God with hope and confidence each day, each hour, and each moment. The child says its Ave in its mother's arms and at its mother's knee; with quivering, palsied lip the grandpa tells his beads with up-rolling eye and beaten chest; the youth recites his chaplet with his companions at the christian school or chapel; the monk lingers on it in his mountain solitude, the nun in her cell falls in ecstacy over it, the aged and learned professor and the Catholic statesman with the simplicity, hope and confidence of children say their daily Aves when and where they may.

This universal confidence of the christian world in the Mother of God is explained by St. Bernard in the following words : " Because she stands by us, when we tremble, to keep us up; stirs up our faith, confirms us in hope, drives away distrust and makes us brave.   Ye shook at the very thought," says the saint, "of having to approach the Father.   At the mere sound of His voice, in terror seized, ye made off for the woods. Thereupon the Father gave you a mediator.   Could such a Father withstand such a Son in any of His askings?   Indeed, the Lord will be heard ' for His reverence ;' because, the Father loves the Son.   But do ye not tremble at the thought of approaching the Son?   He is your brother and has taken upon Himself your own flesh : He has been, like yourselves, tempted in all things— though without sin : so that he would learn to be merciful.   In Him Mary has furnished you with a brother.   But it may be that ye still hesitate and are awed by the majesty of God which in spite of His humanity does not quit Him.   Ah, I see ye would have one to plead for you before

His face? Very well, be off to Mary. Ye will find her ministry the very thing because no taint attaches to it, of any kind whatever, and, besides, pure in the extraordinariness of its nature. I make bold to say, with certainty, that Mary also will be heard for her reverence. The Son will without doubt give ear to His Mother, and, of course, the Father will listen to His Son. This is the ladder, my children, placed beneath the feet of sinners. This is my own highest confidence; this is the ground of my hope. And why should this not be? Is it possible that the Son could dismiss His Mother's request ungranted, or that He Himself could meet with rebuff? Is it possible, I say, that the Son could fail to listen to His Mother, or He, Himself, to be heard by His Father? Neither most assuredly could happen—"Thou hast found grace before God," said the angel. Aye, happily, Mary shall always find grace and grace is all we stand in need of. (Serm. In Nat. B. V. M. n. 7.) St. Bernard gives the motive of Mary-cult: Man's humble, modest knowledge or consciousness of his own unworthiness coupled with a proper religious conception of Divine majesty makes it, as it were, a necessary plan of mercy and hope in mankind. St. Bernard does not denounce this humble disposition of christians. God has expressed His pleasure over this fact by respecting it and giving us Our Lady to be our advocate before His throne, Who, though man, is still God. Protestants fancy themselves self-sufficient and are bold enough to

G

burst into the presence of Divine Majesty without any ceremony whatever. With them and
us there is difference of cause and hence of effect.
They have no conception of humility as a religious virtue. The effect is, they see no need of
an advocate, of one who has unquestioned worthiness such as Mary. And, yet, nothing is more
general than to see the Madonna and Child hang-
ing from the wall in the homes of cultured
protestants. Is it not the 'idea' conveyed by the
portrait that prompts them to admire this mas-
ter-piece of Raphael and of the rest of the
masters? Would, then, that these people could
only rouse themselves, heed the wooing of the
spirit that secretly prompts them; would that they
could be courageous, break the chains of human
respect, be brave enough to do with less social
and pecuniary prospects, burst the bonds of
human respect, clasp Our Lady in their arms and
take her for what St. Bernard and the saints all
took her, and for all the merciful God has willed
her to be,—the hope of mankind. May the most
gracious Queen of Heaven bring back to us our
parted brethren to the sweet brotherhood that
goes along with childship and Mary.

THOUGHT:

FOR ourselves let confidence in the Mother of
God be our imperishable glory. For others who
are beyond the pale of Holy Church let us implore
the Mother of the Messiah to bring unto them the

blessings of Faith in Jesus her Son, and of confidence in herself—to Jew and Pagan, to heretic
and schismatic.   This is our duty: We owe it to
God, to Mary, to our parted brethren and to our own
souls: "Our Father Who art in Heaven hallowed
be Thy name, Thy Kingdom come, Thy will be
done on earth."

ILLUSTRATION:

GOD is not given to miracles by any sort of
levity.   Ends worthy of a God lift the wonders
of His hands infinitely above the circle of legerde-
main.   The deception of the juggler and the
sorcerer is, in itself, foreign to one, who is truth
itself.   There is, again, no reason why miracles
must necessarily have ceased in the Church.   The
very existence of the Church, meeting success
with a divine doctrine, and imposing such awful
sacrifices upon feeble human nature is itself a
perpetual miracle.   Miracles are, primarily, purposed to confirm the truth.   According to this
norm we ascertain the truth of its being the will of
God to have the world pay honor to His Mother's
Immaculate Conception.   The certitude of the
vision being duly witnessed of the Church, in the
case of the miraculous medal, struck off at the
instance of Catherine Labourè, taken in conjunction with the great, solid, spiritual advantages,
the real growth in holiness this devotion has
wrought out in souls, and we may, indeed, pro-
claim the miracle, not only credible, but worthy
of God.   This wonder has been confirmed, and

the will of God made doubly perceptible on the
point of Our Lady's Immaculate Conception in
its aspect of being a practical, active, living
instrument in the hands of such as wish to be
saved. The new wonder, also, has the sanction
of the Holy Church, and for this reason
commands our credence and respect. The phe-
nomenon is recited in the Roman Breviary thus:
Among the prodigies of the Virgin's power, we
find it specially deserving, and at the same time
a thing of the highest profit, to lay before all the
world the facts that occurred in the case of
Alphonse Ratisbonne, in the city of Rome, on
the thirteenth day of February, 1842; whereas, the
incident has found strength and confirmation in
the lawful witnessing of ecclesiastic authority.
Alphonse Ratisbonne, a broker, sprung from
Jewish parentage, was proceeding upon a tour
of the East, when it entered his mind to make a
halt at Rome. Whilst sojourning in the Eternal
City he struck up an acquaintance with a Catholic
gentleman, who had been some time before converted from the ranks of heresy, and baptized
in the Catholic faith. This gentleman felt a
sympathy for the young Jew, or rather took
compassion on him, and brought his best efforts
to work upon him to enlist, by argument and
persuasion, the Israelite in the faith of Jesus
Christ. Persuasion did not avail, and the argument failed of its end; but the apostle of charity
succeeded in one thing, namely, in getting the

Jew to accept, at his hands, a blessed medal of
the Mother of God, and to make the promise,
furthermore, that he would wear the medal about
his neck.   Whilst all this was going on without,
the good Catholic gentleman was storming the
Immaculate Virgin Mother's breast with prayers
in behalf of the Jew.   The answer from the Virgin
Mother came, speedily, for, soon after, whilst the
Jew was taking a stroll and wandered into the
Church of St. Andrea delle Fratte by the merest
accident, about the middle of the day, all of a
sudden, the whole sacred edifice became wrapt
in dense gloom, with the exception of the chapel
of St. Michael, from whence a bright light shone
forth, which was made all the more brilliant by
contrast with the prevailing gloom.   The Jew
was seized with awe, and had only just turned
his eyes upon the scene, when, lo! the Virgin
Mary revealed herself to him with a countenance
aglow with all sweetness and a bearing and dress
that matched exactly the image he wore about
his neck. Alphonse felt a sudden transformation
was being wrought within him, under the influence of the heavenly vision, and, all at once, his
heart gave way, and his lips broke forth amid a
flood of tears, in an abjuration of Judaism and
a confession of belief in the truth of the Catholic
religion, which he had but so recently held in
disrepute, and in a profession of his acceptance
of the Catholic faith with all his heart.   Alphonse
Ratisbonne was immediately instructed in the

Catholic religion, and in a few days received baptism, whilst all Rome let itself out in rejoicings and thanks to God. (Brev. Spec. Nov. 27. Noct. II., Lect. v.).

RESOLVE:

I SHALL beg the light of faith each day, for Jew and Gentile, for all unbelievers and heretics; and to advance this end I shall summons the services of the great Mother of God. For myself I shall always honor, in a special manner, Our Lady's Immaculate Conception.

PRAYER:

VIRGIN MOTHER of the Messiah, obtain for Jew and Gentile, for all such as are not of the true christian religion, the grace to believe in Thy Son; and, at the same time, we implore Thee, in our own behalf, that our faith may increase, and our confidence in Thine own power to intercede before the throne of redemption may wax fuller. Through Jesus Christ, Our Lord.

CHAPTER XII.

CO-REDEMPTRIX.

"Go teach all nations," spake the Messiah. Thus Our Lady is pronounced, by apposition, empress of all nations; for, her power extends over all the ends of her Son's dominions. She reigns, as queen, where her Son rules as king. The territory of her jurisdiction cannot be less in scope than the Master's. There is not one king for the rich and another for the poor; one for the Teuton and another for the Indian, one for the Saxon and one for the Celt. As the King Himself, Who is no acceptor of persons, the Queen-Mother has within her care and under the empire of her sweet, Motherly love, all the nations of the world; and she shuts out none from her. The brotherhood implied in a common motherhood shocks the æsthetic. The priceless jewel of an immortal soul lost in the mass of ill-formed joints, rags, squalid homes and the rest, is perceptible only to the eye of faith that has no cataract. Mary sees in every human being a likeness to her Son, and, for this reason, a claim upon her love. Matchless lady of such degree as none have nor ever shall have attained to, Mary is surrounded by spirits of light and love; housed admist luxuries, not of art and refinement, that are

merely human, but installed amid the sublimities
and brilliancies of Creation Itself, and the full
display of the glories of divinity, yet from her
lofty height, aye, from her throne in heaven, her
Mother's heart pierces through the light of peace,
happiness, and love to the gloomy earth, to its
filthy garrets, its haunts of shame and guilt, to the
home of refinement and the little log cabin with
its want and rags; and, woos, cares for, and watches
over the ragged outcast and—oh God!—loves
him, calls him to her, pleads for him before her
Son, whispers to his own heart and says to him
what Jesus says, " Come to Me all ye that labor
and are heavy burdened and I will refresh you."
She views the vacant chairs, left so by the angels,
and thinks of her absent children predestinated to
occupy them, but, now, wandering among the
valleys of earth with perils on every side.   How vast
and deep is our Mother's love !   The humanitarian
stops at a certain point, a friendly word, a pound
of tea, a letter to obtain employment more or less
sincere—yes ! but, what urchin would dare aspire
to the family-circle or the society to be met with
in the salons of the high-born dame, who has
gone to so much ado, has spoken so softly to the
outcast and made such great demonstrations of
love and sacrifice?   What, oh what a mystery of
love is that charity of heaven by which we wretches
of earth can hope to dwell with Our Lord and His
Mother in family unity, in peace, plenty and love
forever and ever !   " Praise the Lord all ye

nations," cries out the prophet-king. "Behold from henceforth all generations shall call me blessed," chimes in Mary. "Do not say that I claim for myself anything," is what we hear Our Lady saying, "why, He that is mighty hath done great things to me." So then, we hail Mary as the new Eve. "As," says St. Irenaeus, "by her disobedience Eve brought death upon the whole human race, so has Mary by her obedience become the cause of the whole world's salvation." Bound together from the first they are, now, Jesus and Mary, joined together as cause and instrument to mend that awful ruin that has befallen mankind, to despoil death of its booty and re-open the wells of eternal life. She is bound to the seed that would crush the serpent's head. (Gen. iii. 15).

She encircles the Emmanuel as the mother entwines herself about her son. (Is. vii., 14). She is bound to Him, as the root and flower— "and there shall come forth a rod out of the root of Jesse, and a flower shall rise up out of his root." (Is. xi., 1). "A woman shall compass a man," says Jeremiah (xxxl., 22). The angel that appeared to Jeremias, coupled Jesus and Mary —"And she shall bring forth a Son, and thou shalt call His name Jesus, for He shall save His people from many sins." (Mat. i., 21). Together they were found by the Magi, and the Evangelist makes mention of the fact—'And going into the house they found the Child with Mary, His Mother.' (Matthew ii., 2). Is there not tenderness, love and instruction in this scriptural relation, and a union of Mary with the Redeemer? The Evangelist tells us her name— "Mary"; and what she is—' His Mother.' What a name! what a character! what a dignity! what a power!—' His Mother!'—the Mother of Jesus, the Mother of God! The prophet Simeon did not shut Mary out from his terrible and tragic prophecy. He pronounced the Child as being set up for the glory of the people of Israel. And Simeon said to ' Mary,' the Child's Mother—the Evangelist, here, impresses upon us the title, dignity and power of Mary, and repeats her beautiful name: "To Mary, His Mother, behold this Child is set for the ruin and for the resurrection of many in Israel. And thy own soul a sword shall pierce." Why this sword to pierce that breast, ' white as hawthorn-buds that ope in the month of May?' It was not the blade of steel, I repeat, but of sorrow, that would bring a blessing upon the world, in the light of faith unto the nations. Simeon has revealed the mission of that sword—"That out of many hearts (yours and mine) thoughts may be revealed"—(Luke ii., 34-35) —"faith and love for God may burst into blossom, and the fruits of a pure christian life." All that we have been saying and just repeating we find suggested in St. Paul; for, the apostle mentions the cause and instrument of salvation: "When the fulness of the time was come, the Lord sent the Son, made of woman, that we might receive the adoption of sons." (Gal. iv., 5-6). Through His being born of the woman, we have come into the inheritance of salvation by the Lord. Here is the old truth, ever new, full of importance to you and to me. The prophets and apostles kept the fact well in mind. So must we—"And He was born of the Virgin Mary." —"For our salvation."

THOUGHT:

IF we should ever fall into any sin let us at once implore the Mother of the living, the new Eve, to intercede for us before Him Who said 'I am the Light.' If we desire faith in those who have it not, let us ask Mary to petition for it from the 'Light.'

ILLUSTRATION:

IT is a notable fact, that all those saints who have been predestinated, in the design of God, to found Orders in the Church, have been very exact and particular to cultivate Mary, and to commit their foundations, labors and hopes into her mother's-care. The saints have all been praised for this fealty to the Queen of Heaven; and, yet, after all, it is not by a new and special instinct of faith that this is so, but a matter of course or natural consequence, which follows upon the relationship of Our Lady with Jesus Christ her Son. The saints have but followed in this the footprints of the Master; only, they have cultivated, to its highest, that same instinct of Faith which we all

have, in the power and influence of the great
Virgin Mary. Mary watched over the cradle of
Jesus; she watched over the Infant Church when
the Master was dead; she prayed for the Apostles, she prayed with them, she sustained them
when they most needed to be sustained. All the
Fathers have patronized Mary, and phalanx after
phalanx of christian martyrs have been seen
marching into the arena, singing hymns of praise
and thanks to Jesus and His Mother. It is then
to be expected, that saintly founders would be
exact models of obedience to the precious example of the Master Himself, and of the venerable
principles that have permeated and guided all
traditions in the Church. Founders are not dis-
coverers, but cultivators and perfect imitators,
'other—Christs.' And, yet, these holy founders
have, upon their fidelity, their example, and the
strict injunctions they have laid upon their several
religious families touching Mary-cult, done Our
Lady's honor and glory no end of good, by creat-
ing a new obligation for such as are held in sweet
bondage of their rule, to pay respect and praise
to God's Mother. St. Bernard, first in the line of
holy founders, had a very tender devotion toward
God's Mother. From his Order, as from a root,
have sprung branches of religious institutions and
monasteries, that have world-wide fame for attachment to Mary. The Monks of Cluny, the
Cistercians, the Carthusians and the rest, have all
of them been hot-beds of Mary-cult. St. Dom-

inic, the father of the Rosary, has the distinction, in his one glorious inspiration, of placing Our Lady so near to us, that we may say we feel her presence or that we carry her under our garment. The christian world owes St. Dominic a debt it can never pay in time, and the christian world will never part with its heritage from St. Dominic —its Rosary. The religious of St. Dominic are, then, nothing, if not champions of the Rosary. St. Francis of Assissi, that incarnation of poverty, has specifically established the Mother of God as his own advocate, and that of all his spiritual family. To show how well his children have carried out their father's will, one needs but to pronounce the name of St. Bernadin of Sienna, who, one might say, lived on Mary. The Carmelites are a distinctly and directly organized Order of Mary. Surely no Order could wish for greater glory than that of having been the instrument of giving us, as this Order has, through Blessed Simon Stock, the scapular, that breast-plate of the christian soldier in the wars, that amulet to defend, as from harm, that pledge of being with our eternal love so very soon after our death. It was, as we know, because Carmel was so distinctly an Order of the Virgin, that St. John of the Cross embraced its rule and became so famous a Carmelite. St. Ignatius had, from the beginning, like his brother founders, the tenderest devotion to Deipera. Upon Mary's altar, the soldier laid his sword in renouncing the spirit of the world. In the church

of Our Lady, at Mont Serrat, he made his vow to
be forever chaste. In her church, on the summit
of Mont Mattre, the saint and his comrades pronounced their vow of poverty and that of a
journey to Jerusalem. The Jesuits have since been
true soldiers and gallant defenders of the great
Mother of God. To them belongs the great glory
of the institution of the sodalities of the Blessed
Virgin, which are, as it were, a Third Order of
Jesuits, and which have done such incalculable
good, in giving the christian world a chaste youth
and a womanhood that has purified society.
Their sacrifices and learning have ever been at
her disposal, and, it is our christian hope and devout prayer, that the Society of Jesus, continuing
in the spirit of abnegation and humility bequeathed to it by their holy founder, will go on
giving glory to God, to Jesus and Mary, and
augment the lustre of their beautiful history to
the end. If one would know the devotion of St.
Philip Neri to God's Mother, he has but to look
at the seal of the saint's Order which appears,
also, on the letter-heads of the Oratorians, the
spiritual children of St. Philip Neri. We find this
seal on St. Philip's own letters : It served Newman
and Faber, St. Philip's children, for the seals of
their letters. Whenever the Oratorians come to
write a letter, they come face to face with this
seal, showing the Virgin Mother of God pressing
the Child Jesus to her bosom. St. Alphonsus
Ligouri, the founder of the Redemptorists, yields

to none in his **great love** for the Mother of God. The consequence of this fact is, that the churches **of his** congregation are in the providence of God seats of famous shrines, centers of pilgrimages, whose wonders give glory to the name of Mary. But orders, like saints, must not be compared. All are beautiful, and each is perfect in its own circle. All work as helps to their mother the Church, and may they all grow and flourish, and be to the end bulwarks of Mary-cult.

RESOLVE:

I SHALL always carry my Rosary, if not like the religious, without, at least, within, where I may reach it like a dagger in danger moments.

PRAYER:

O GOD, Who didst inspire all those saints of predilection, who have been raised up by Thee for special service in Thy Church, with the marked and glowing love toward Mary, Thy most gracious Mother, grant us, through the intercession and good works of all these holy founders and their children, the grace to imitate them in this important point of salvation.

Through Jesus Christ Our Lord.

CHAPTER XIII.

THE AGE OF MARY.

THIS is the age of the Immaculate Conception. The signs of the times so read. A white star, soft and radiant, mild and brilliant, shines in the heavens. The Sun of God rises ruby in the morning, as, on the morning of Redemption, the red star gleamed above the grotto. Mary is fair as that Moon which shines in the evening — Ave Maris Stella ! The miracles and apparitions that have impressed the glory and truth of Mary-cult upon our age speak in behalf of God inasmuch as they are the distinct, critical evidence of His own hand and are designed to remind us that the time is come for Mary to have the place due to her and assigned her by her Son. This position is more or less denied her by all outside the Catholic faith ; hence, the mercy of God to check impiety and to glorify His Mother by the wonders that have come to pass in the nineteenth century. It is patent that where Our Lord is the object of tender and becoming piety, and is made a proper factor in the toil of santification, in the nations that rally round the image of the great Virgin, the faith in her Son and fidelity to the one true Church are so deeply rooted and go so hand in hand that the best efforts of political malice and diabolical instigation have

served ill to work it effective harm. All this is
most evident: As a nation, Italy is to a man for
Mother-Church, if we except some political differences created and sustained by the few. The
Madonna is the genius of that beautiful land of
warm sun, of art and blue skies. Spain is faithful
to the Church of her wonderful saints, of her
Dominic, of her Ignatius, of her Teresa. France
as a people still find no consistency in any religion
but the one, true, faith of Rome. In spite of
political demagogues, a dash of infidelity, social-
ism in some quarters, and the efforts of a handful
of foreign protestants and interlopers struggling
to make headway by force of money,—France, I
say, is still a nation of Notre Dame and from the
tall summit of Mt. Matre the national church of
the Sacrè Cœur announces the fact to her neighbors across the English channel who bartered their
God for a king made by the hand of man.
"Ireland," says our great Leo XIII, "is the most
Catholic country in the whole world." What else
could be said of a people who have always led the
world in true respect, love and devotion to the
Mother of Jesus Christ? Wealth and liberty could
have been theirs. Poverty and persecution might
not have been the lot of so many of her children
in strange lands were, indeed, the children of Erin
to surrender their God and His Immaculate
Mother. This they have not done, and this they
shall never do, by the mercy of God, come poverty,
come death. Protestant zeal emanating from the

H

tropical climate of another world has laid no re-
strictions on its purse-strings with the view to
purchase conversions in Ireland, Spain, Italy and
the other Catholic countries.   With the help of a
few apostates they make just show enough to fool
the dupes who support them.   These men are
humiliated at their failure to proselytize, but minis-
ters fancy they must live and support their wives
and children, and that the end justifies the means
when things come to such a pass ; though, indeed,
no man has a right to live who cannot live except
by evil.   When things do come to such a pass
starvation is the will of God.   In the lands of the
Madonna, heresy cannot effectually dominate.
Where she is, there is the Son : with her goes
her Son, as she took Him in the long-ago from
Judea off into Egypt.   Louis de Montfort is the
prophet, so to speak, of Mary's age, and the Church
honors his name though his augury may not suit
the ideas entertained by some moderns, within the
circle of the faith, who take their notion of the
Mother of God in its intellectual aspect from the
Church and in its heart-aspect from the unbeliev-
ing world.   But, of course, such is ever the
prophet's fate ; but, in spite of all this, a prophet, if I
may say so, is a prophet and his truth shall grow.

We have the apparition of Catherine Labourè,
the one vouchsafed to Alphonse Ratisbonne and
the one made to the maiden Bernadette, down
among the Pyrenees in the humble village of
Lourdes ; and all these lead up to and culminate

in the proclamation of the dogma of the Immaculate Conception by Pius IX.   All these have been forerunners of this last great pronouncement of the Church of God that speaks with a tongue that cannot deceive.   Is the will of God not clear? Are men not simply Pharaohs not to open their hearts in compliance with the will of heaven? Our own dear America has been placed under the special patronage of the Immaculate Conception. As Catholics in America, it is our duty to honor Our Lady with outward display and public pomp— processions, coronations of Our Lady at the hands of the children, hymns sung in her praise at Mass and society meetings, flowers, pæans and pageantry should characterize our Mother's feasts.   All this will impress us in childhood and live with us through hoariest old age.   To do this, I say, is a duty under which priests and faithful lie,—apart from general principles—of corresponding with the placing of our nation under the special patronage of the Immaculate Conception.   This is the call of the age.   God has not done these wonders in Paris, in Rome, and Lourdes in vain.   From the beginning, those who have the training of our souls must not leave us at the mercy of impulse, nor yet at the exclusive mercy of God, when this latter exacts co-operation from reason and industry; but, they must develop a character in us, carve traditions on our minds and hearts.   That is to say, from childhood, we ought, all, to be trained to interior and exterior devotion toward

the Mother of God.   The inward cult helps ourselves directly; the outward helps our brethren.
They owe it to us, we owe it to them that we
mutually confess our faith, and our great traditions.   We are individuals, but we are also
members of society and of the church.   In the
two characters we have distinct relations and
obligations.   This national devotion is of remark-
able import.   England, for example, as a people,
banished the Mother of God.   The true faith will
not return till Mary brings it with her.   I may
without irreverence, say, not 'where thou art
Caius, there am I, Caia,' but 'where Thou art
My Son there am I, Thy Mother.'   And why not?
for, on Calvary she was made the bride of the
Redeemer.   Our brethren of the faith, they of the
land of Newman and Faber, the one a brave
knight in armor clad to fight for Mary, the other
with twanging lyre and throat of a nightingale, to
publish her praise in exquisite song, our English
brethren, I say, know this.   They know the
desolation of their nation caused by the banishment of Mary, and they weep, groan, and call
her back.   Let us aid them in the task.   Let our
sympathy, love and prayer go across the sea that
Catholic England will be herself again, a nation
of the Madonna, like her green-robed sister, weep-
ing in chains of century-woven political servitude
and persecutions for her faith by the sad sea-
waves.   Let the Shamrock say to the Rose:
"Thou hast wronged me, sister, but I wish thee no

harm. God bless thee." "Father forgive them."
If in spite, however, of all we have said, some
Teuton, all head and no heart, there be, who is
still sceptical on the phenomena of spiritual hor-
oscopy and should be of mind that halucination
may be a considerable ingredient in all apparitions, he cannot but respect the living, present,
tangible edict of Leo XIII, instituting the month
of October as a month of the Rosary, and commanding public prayers in all the churches
throughout the christian world.   When we come
to consider the noble achievements of this great
Pontiff in behalf of christian unity, and consider,
at the same time, his supreme interest in encour-
aging Mary-cult, then we can have no doubt that
devotion to Mary and christian unity are closely
related ; and, we may well believe that the wonderful success that has attended the pontificate
of Leo XIII, a success that will make him live
forever in history, has been due to this noble
Pontiff's great love and devotion to the Mother of
Him Whose Church he rules.   The 'remnant'
saved, such as are of the 'chosen,' will be found
in the shadow of the eclipse when the 'Moon'
interposes between the eternal Sun and earth.
So much inferior to the great Sun in size, it
seems curious that the Moon can completely hide
the Sun from view; but, though it be so far
smaller than the Sun, it is millions of miles nearer
the earth, so that both appear to be of one size.
Mary is inferior to God infinitely.   She is nearer

to us. She is a woman, a creature like ourselves, and in the shadow of her mantle she shall conceal us from the wrath of God.

THOUGHT:

IT is the duty of the faithful to join with their worthy priests in fostering, by authority, co-operation and example, the outward cult of the Virgin Mother, in order to make it, as it were, a national feature of our Catholic-American life, so as to fall in so much the better with the design of God for the world's sanctification.

ILLUSTRATION:

THAT this is the age of Mary, has been, we feel, amply set forth, and yet, the evolution of this truth we fancy would be incomplete without recording specially the incident of Our Lady's apparition at Lourdes, in the south of France. There is no doubt of the fact, that the Blessed Mother of God has deigned to appear to the young shepherdess, for, in a letter to Henri Lasserre, the chronicler and critical examiner of the events that took place in Lourdes, a strict scrutinizer of all the episodes of the miraculous apparition, and student of the long line of prodigies that have silenced the lips of medical scoffers, Pius IX spoke as follows:— "You have just employed your best efforts in proving and establishing the truth of the recent apparition of the most clement Mother of God: and this you have done

in such a manner, that the very struggle of
human malice against the Divine Mercy, serves
but to bring out more forcibly the luminous evidence of the facts." (Given at Rome at St. Peters,
Sept. 4, 1869, in the year of our Pontificate 24,
Pius IX Pope.) Now there can be no question
but the devil comes as an angel of light to entrap
the proud of spirit, to augment in them their perilous delusions, and to bring down finally to ruin,
those whose faces are turned upward and whose
journey is set for the Lord. So, when apparitions
do happen, there is always doubt of their source
and truth, before authority examines and places
its seal of approbation upon the event, after which,
however, the faithful are at ease, and at liberty to
employ and enjoy the fact with security. Bertrand
Severe, Bishop of Tarve, in whose diocese Lourdes
is situated, makes the following declaration: "We
pronounce judgment that the Immaculate Mary,
Mother of God, really appeared to Bernadette
Soubirous, on the eleventh of February, 1858,
and following days, to the number of eighteen, in
the grotto of Massabielle, near the town of
Lourdes; that this apparition is invested with
every character of truth, and that the faithful
have good ground for believing it to be certain."
We learn from the approbation of the Holy
Father, confirming the declaration of Bishop
Severe, another fact; namely, the high end or
purpose of the apparition. The Pope says: "We
firmly believe that she, who from every quarter

attracts toward herself, by miracles of her power and goodness, multitudes of pilgrims, wills to excite toward herself the piety and confidence of mankind, to the end that all may participate in the plenitude of her graces." We learn, furthermore, that Our Lady wills to have pilgrims meet at her shrine in Lourdes. How wonderful! Here, as at all times, God glorifies the lowly and lifts them up. The Queen of Heaven makes a poor, starved, sickly maiden, her ambassadress to the court of the world, to announce her will and to spread her glory: "And, now, my child, go to the priests and tell them to raise a chapel to me here," said the Mother of God to Bernadette Soubirous. There stood the trembling child, then knelt she, bewildered. A worn out and patched, black dress encircled her body; a capulet was over her head, and coarse sabots kept out the cold from her feet. A kerchief covered her soft, black hair. Her brows were arched, and her eyes were brown but calm and profound, with a sweet innocence, all of which made her a most beautiful creature, interesting and attractive. Of course, she had a great protector in heaven, for, Bernadette means ' little Bernard,' and, no doubt, the great saint and doctor, for whom the child was named, taught her many things concerning Mary, to whom he had been so ardently devoted in his own life.

Bernadette was of the poorest of the poor in family, so much so, that, in order to obtain food she had to be hired out to tend the sheep. Bernadette knew no evil passion. Her soul was a limpid stream. She was as simple and innocent as the mountain snow that melted above her head; as fresh and fragrant in her purity as the wild rose, the eglantine, which grew out of the wild rock. It was to this innocent, hungry child of Nature, this ragged rustic, that Our Lady showed herself many times, and said: "I am the Immaculate Conception." The poor little child was so ignorant that she did not understand the meaning of the words "Immaculate Conception." "I repeated them to myself," said she, "all along the road, in order not to forget them.". The place where Our Lady appeared is at the base of a high mountain, in the huge rough rocks of Massabielle. Here, a miraculous stream sprung up at the touch of Bernadette's hand, under the inspiration of Our Lady; and here, wonders without end have since been accomplished, to the confusion of hell, the silencing of infidels, the lustre of the Catholic faith, and the glory of the Mother of God. The world, so stubborn, would not, at once, credit the apparition to Bernadette Soubirous, that tattered, unlettered rustic maid. They looked at her and laughed at the idea. Poor, innocent, humble girl! It was true, the Mother of God did appear to you, dear Bernadette, and if the world would take the pains to look aright they would have looked into your hands and seen your smirched fingers pressing the

Rosary, they would have followed you to the lonely mountains and heard your lips murmuring the Ave Maria night and day with the song of the mountain rill and the bleating of the sheep, as you picked, the while, wild flowers to make garlands for the Queen of Heaven. They would have looked beneath the black rags that wrapped your little, sickly body, and seen your sweet, innocent, pure and humble soul, and the mystery would have stood out revealed before them. Bernadette had many sufferings, the invariable lot of saints. Whilst the thousands gathered to praise the Mother of God in the grotto of Massabielle, the poor child was stretched upon a bed of pain and sickness in a public hospital, because her parents were too poor to care for her in her illness. There she listened to the groans of the sick and sorrowing about her, and heard not the chorus of praise and song at the fêtes being celebrated at the grotto in honor of Our Lady's apparition. God gave the dear child pain and poverty, in His mercy, to shield her soul from pride. She was the instrument of Our Lady to make Lourdes a magnet of piety, a source of unspeakable wonders and glory, and she must suffer, like all instruments, in the work of the Master, and remain under the test, like Jesus and Mary, humble and obedient unto death. It is the verdict of all pious christians, who have ever visited Lourdes, that the sights and impressions of that holy spot have been to their soul, like a visitation from the skies and the touch of heaven.

RESOLVE:

THOU art all beautiful, Mary, and there is no stain in thee. I shall cultivate, in a special manner, the honor and service of the Immaculate Conception of the Mother of God.

PRAYER:

O BLESSED LADY, who didst deign in thy great tenderness and love for mankind, to appear to the poor and humble Bernadette, and to announce to her the glory of thy Immaculate Conception, by thy love for souls and thy soft compassion for men, obtain for us that we may always honor thee in thy Immaculate Conception and learn from thy choice of the rustic child to celebrate thy praise and to realize the power of the Rosary, and the force of humility and purity. Through Jesus Christ, Our Lord.

CHAPTER XIV.

DIVINE MOTHERHOOD OF MARY.

PETAVIUS, the theologian, has expressed a noble, religious thought and a profound truth, when he said that 'the fountain-head or source of those wonders and stupendous things that God has heaped upon Mary, is to be sought after in her Divine Motherhood.' Yes, from this root, the differentiation, as botanists say, of all Mary's prerogatives is made as from a root. The great variety or play of brilliant color in her character and life, is but the opalescence of this sublime and noble quality; or, again, is like the corona that encircles the sun, and excites the wonder of astronomers. Yes, Mary is the Mother of God. What a world of meaning in that title! aye, what spheres of untold secrets in the philosophy of that name! True, she is a creature, and we must confess this as readily as we confess that she is the Mother of God, or that God is One. Besides, as creature, she could not possibly beget the Divine nature of Christ. But she had conceived and brought forth, in His humanity, a Person Who is God. We call those who brought us into this life the mothers of men; and yet, these have had no hand in the formation of the human soul within us. For this reason, we main-

tain, as dogma of the Church, that Our Lady is
not merely the Mother of the humanity of Our
Lord, but, that she is moreover the Mother of
God, inasmuch as Jesus Christ is truly God and
truly man.   The Son of God, in eternity, is the
Son of Mary, in time.   God has but One Son,
and He is, likewise, the Son of Mary.   We have
to believe and confess that Christ was always
One, and that the union of the word of God,
took place at the very beginning of Christ's Conception.   "Human nature," says St. Leo the
Martyr, "was not taken on by Him after such a
fashion, that it was in the first place created and
afterward taken on; but, rather, that it was
created by its very assumption." (Ep. 35).   We
cannot, therefore, withhold from Our Lady, the
prerogative of Mother of God.   On the other
hand, the denial of this prerogative would have
the same effect as crushing out the dogma of
unity that attaches to the Divine Person of Our
Lord.   In the past, everything went on smoothly,
as far as the Divine Motherhood was concerned,
from the very beginning well into the 5th century.
No one had challenged the doctrine.   At this
point in the christian era, Nestor rose up and
called the title into question.   The church of
God, that has had, in every age, Sampsons to defend her doctrine, found St. Cyril up at once, in
arms against the heresiarch; and, the Council of
Ephesus, thereupon, condemned the bold Nestor,
and crushed beneath the weight of its authority

his infamous negation. "If," says St. Cyril, "our adversaries deny that the Blessed Virgin should be called in any way the Mother of God, but, instead of this, the begetter of Christ, such are, evidently, guilty of blasphemy, denying, as they do, both the Divinity of Christ and His true Sonship. Because, if these people truly have the belief that He is truly God, why do they entertain any fear to call His Mother, the Mother of God— according to the flesh, I ask?" We have pointed out, in a previous chapter, the clear relationship of the Divine Motherhood with the Divinity of Christ, just as St. Cyril maintained. Under the prestige of such a glorious title, the natural consequence would be, that honor should be given to one of so exalted a degree of dignity, perfection, and even of family; for, let us know that, in the flesh, Mary alone belongs to the family of Christ, the rest of the world being of His family only in the spiritual sense.

When, then, a sect refuses to honor Mary as the Mother of God, the next stage in the dissolution of its faith is to deny that Mary's Son is God. Hence, the attitude of sectaries toward Our Lady brings their faith in the divinity of Our Lord justly under suspicion, as a matter of fact. The Third Ecumenical Council says: "If there should be anyone who will not confess that God is truly Emmanuel, and that the Blessed Virgin is, consequently, the Mother of God, inasmuch as she has begotten in the flesh the Word of God made

Flesh, let him be anathema."   The Church loves,
admires, and praises Our Lady, as the Mother of
God; but, she teaches us all distinctly that Mary
is not a Divinity.   St. Epiphany denounced the
Collyridians, who lifted Mary out of the circle of
creatureship up into the circle of Divinity, and
offered sacrifices to her as to a Divine Being.
These are the saint's words: " We cannot help
seeing," said he, "the hand and work of the devil
showing out of a practice so tainted with idolatry.
The body of Mary has been the temple of sanctity,
I confess; nevertheless, she has never been God.
Be she ever so select and superior, she is, in spite
of all this, a woman of the same nature as any one
else, howsoever great the honors may be which
have made her so holy in soul and body.   Now, in
the very light of this fact, however could the wily
serpent have been able to throw souls into this
error? By what manner of indirect and captious
insinuation could he have surprised them?   Let
Mary be 'honored'—by all means!   But let only
the Father, the Son and the Holy Ghost be
'adored.'   God commanded the first couple not
to eat of the fruit of the tree, but this did not place
the evil in the tree itself, but merely made it so that
through the tree, the crime of revolt was occasioned.   Let no one then taste the fruit of error
formed upon the occasion of Mary.   However
admirable the tree, it was not made to be eaten of.
Likewise, however admirable, however eminently
deserving of honor Mary might be, we must

not, for all that, bestow adoration upon her."
(Adversus Haeres, lib. iii.). It is difficult for human
nature to follow out an even, middle way, to hit off
a jog.   Too fast or too slow, too high or too low,
to the right or to the left, is its universal tendency.
This perverseness of our nature may operate in
the holiest of instances and in, I may say, the very
strongholds of piety; and scandalize on the one
hand by exaggerations and extravagances that are
little short of religious buffoonery; and, on the
other hand — so much are they bereft of dignity
and awe — by an exclusiveness that furnishes a
congenial air for the growth of any lurking self-
love.   All things, in due proportion and measure,
let there be.   The contrary in religion makes
one-sided, conceited, uncharitable, and altogether
deluded creatures out of people called to be saints.
Suum cuique — to God, to Mary, to all men be
given the honor each is due.   Our differences in
the christian life are functional, but co-operative,
and by no means mutually destructive, or contrac-
tive, or exclusive.   To the head, to the feet, to the
arms, to each its part be given, to each the right
and freedom of action with mutual respect and
forbearance; and whatever in us paralyzes another member, however great we may fancy
ourselves, and however small our neighbor's
function may be, is neither charity nor order,
but selfishness, ugly and scandalous, even only
made more so by its cleverest disguise.   Adored
be God, honored be Mary, helped be we one by

another to advance the kingdom of God and our own salvation!

THOUGHT:

MARY is the Mother of God. This she always shall be. I must praise and honor her. To my brethren in low or high stations, in all the great variety of vocations I am to give proper encouragement, due praise with christian co-operation. Another does a commoner function than I, one more ordinary in the christian body. I would not perhaps be so glad to accept so mean a vocation as he. After all is that other not humbler than I? Is there any jealousy in me?

ILLUSTRATION :

VEITH draws up a most soul-freezing comparison between the true believer in the Mother of God and the Pelagian, to wit: The Emperor of Greece, Constantine Copronymus, had no taste for religion, or if he ever had, had lost it. He despised religion and everything connected with it, and carried his impiety so very far as to refuse any respect whatever to the Mother of God. In his royal conceit and the ample recourses of a diabolical genius, this conceited monarch invented the following simile to portray his blasphemous unbelief in the august Motherhood. He carried a purse filled with gold pieces, and this he flaunted before the eyes of all such as were disposed to show any difference of opinion with him upon the point of the Divine Motherhood, asking, as he did so, what they should hold its value to be. When he had received their various replies, contrived to correspond with its value, he thereupon emptied the sack of its contents and then asked what they held to be the value of the empty bag itself. "Ah," said he, "as long as Mary carried the Saviour of the world within her breast she was blest amongst women, and deserving of the highest veneration; but upon her delivery of the Child her prerogative with its strict relations has ceased likewise." The unmorality of this comparison, so hideous indeed, and the total unlikeness of the two things—a law of nature on the one hand, and a mere matter of physiological convenience on the other—are so glaring as to be nothing short of wilful blasphemy and barefaced impiety. This is always the way with men. They will not have a thing to believe :—They cannot truthfully prove their own position; and, rather than give in, they suffer inconsistency of argument to pass current for logic, and finally wind up in resorting to chicanery and lying. To my mind, the most terrible thing in all the world to the human family is this primitive possibility or liability to self-delusion and self-deception, this benighting of one's own mind, as a consequence of our own wilfulness. When one wishes a thing, yearns for it, the next step is to remove obstacles and after this to set aside even that which lawfully stands in our way, even though that be the dictate or law of reason or faith. Sophistry, however, is not logic. A man who does a wrong and admits it to be a wrong, to himself at least, is merely weak ; but when a man justifies his conduct, even to himself, he is caught in the snare of delusion, and is on his way to the captivity of both his mind and his heart.   Now if such a one seeks farther to justify it before others, he is a perverse creature, a villain, and even a devil.   Abolish the Mother of God ! Dissolve this doctrine of the royal sophist in words that shall come from the Divine Son. What would this royal sophist have Our Divine Lord say?   Fancy the Master saying to His Mother : Thou wert My Mother once ; thou didst carry Me within Thy breast ; thou nursedest Me then ; but, now, thou art no longer My Mother, thou art to Me no more than the empty sack to the gold pieces that have been withdrawn from it — Unnatural, perverse doctrine—monstrous ! But the woman in the Gospel is sufficient to counterpoise the lamentable and cruel sophistry of the Grecian monarch : "Blessed is the womb that bore Thee," rose the confession of the Jewess in the perpetuation of Mary's prerogative of Mother of God. Blest indeed is Mary after the delivery of her Child and unto ages ; and, forever shall she be so.

The Byzantine despot, like other kings who have come after him in the world, ventured into foreign lands when he set up for a teacher in theology.   Christ and Cæsar are two.   As King, Henry VIII had undisputed rights and authori-

ty; but, as the Magister of theology, or the
head of the Church, he is a trespasser, a tyrant, a
deceiver—'to Cæsar the things that are Cæsar's,
to God the things that are God's.' The Jewess
looked upon Jesus as He was passing: she saw
the ravishing grace, in His manner and speech,
she caught the sweet charm of His doctrine as
He preached, felt the tender pathos of His
accents, was impressed by the massive grandeur
and mountain-like strength of His divinity, like
the power of suppression in art, that showed
forth in the Master's presence and was modulated
by the humaneness of a kind of motherly feeling,
all of which had the effect of driving the Jewish
maid into a rapture that had to find words, or
burn up her soul; into a fine frenzy that begs for
air.   Wonderful art Thou, O Son, and wonderful
must she be, that brought such a beautiful Son
into the world to give mankind hope, peace
and help.   Let the children of Mary echo that
cry of confession, of praise, of prayer.   In all
ages and tongues let the prophecy go on unfolding
itself: "For behold, from henceforth all generations shall call me blessed," and, when we look
upon Our Lord, the first-born of Mary, reposing
in the tabernacle, let the words of the Jewish
woman find echo in the hearts of the children of
Mary: "Blessed is the womb that bore thee, and
blessed are the paps that gave suck to Christ,
Our Lord."   "Thou art Christ, the Son of the
living God"—and of Mary.   ·

RESOLVE :

I SHALL honor Mary each day of my life, and show my honor in prayers for her intercession; secondly, I shall not fancy that I, who am but one member, am the whole christian body, or that the functions of others, of even the lowest christian, are not as valuable, in a way, as mine, in the work of God.

PRAYER :

WE thank Thee, O Lord, for having raised a fellow creature to the sublime state of the divine Motherhood, and hast in this so honored and ennobled our human creation; we beg to confess, at the same time, that she is, and always shall be, Thy Mother, and to ask the grace to enjoy throughout our whole life the great privileges of power and assistance embodied in this incomparable dignity. O Thou, Who livest and reignest with the Father and the Spirit, one God, forever and ever. Amen.

CHAPTER XV.

DIVINE MOTHERHOOD (CONTINUED).

In his epistle to Nestor, St. Cyril says that 'none of those who have taught the faith ever had any doubt touching the belief that the Blessed Virgin is the Mother of God,' and St. Gregory adds his testimony, along this line, as follows: "The Blessed Virgin is called at the same time both the servant and the Mother of God. She is, in truth, the servant of the Lord, because the Word, begotten from all eternity, is equal to His Father. She is the Mother of God, because the Word of God was made Man in her womb and of her own substance through the action of the Holy Ghost. Yes, the union of the divinity with the Saviour's flesh was brought about at the very instant that the body was conceived in the womb of Mary." (Lib. ix. Regist. Ep. 61.) St. Jerome is on record as follows: "Our belief is that God was born of the Virgin." (Lib. Contra Helvid.) The voice of Tertullian comes from the early days also in behalf of this doctrine: "It is a rule of faith that calls us to believe that the Word, the Son of God, brought down by the Spirit of God the Father, and by His workings upon the Virgin, was made flesh in her womb." (Lib. de Praescript xxc., c. 13.) St.

Ignatius, the martyr, wrote in his letter to the
Ephesians, that 'Mary bore in her womb Jesus
Christ, our God.' And St. Paul says the same
thing : " Concerning His Son, Who was made to
Him of the seed of David, according to the flesh."
(Rom. i., 3.) St. Ignatius informs us that
'the design of Holy Writ, with its proper and
formal announcement, is to the effect that we
should acknowledge in its language that there
are two ways of speaking of the Saviour, namely,
in the first place, that He was always, and is, God,
the Word, both the splendor and wisdom of the
Father; then, again, that for our sake, this same
God, taking on flesh of the Virgin Mother of
God, Mary, was made man." (St. Athan. Orat. 4,
Contra Arianos.): "Believe," says St. Cyril, "that
this only begotten Son of God was born of the
Blessed Virgin and the Holy Ghost." (St. Cyril
of Jerusalem. Catech. 4.) "A God is born man
of a Virgin," chimes in St. Hillary. (Lib. ix. de
Trinit.) There are not two Sons, one emanating
from the bosom of the Father before time, and
another conceived in time out of the bosom of
Mary. There is in Our Lord but one person,
one Son, one Jesus Christ, God and Man, and at
one and the same time, Son of the Eternal Father
and Son of the Virgin Mary. Those people who
have not the faith cannot see the power and
beauty in the Motherhood of God. In fact, they
cannot see it at all, in its divine aspect. If they
had that faith of the fathers and would stand in

the eclipse we referred to above, they would see all the halo and the dazzling beauty of the corona, that emanates from the Divine Son of Heaven. The glorious title of the Divine Motherhood cannot be denied and the christian religion be left intact.   When, then, the enemies of our faith run a tilt at the Mother of God, Catholics in society must not be deluded by the fact that those who quarrel with us on the score of Our Lady 'seem' to be sincere, and to be inclined to side with us in what they are pleased to term the fundamentals. The Mother of God is a fundamental, and I repeat that the body of Christ is ultimately meant to be the object of their sword-pass, which, in order to make a show of earnestness and sincerity, is delivered upon the body of Our Lady.   Under pressure from heretical quarters, and deceived by the false pretences which they so deftly put up, even some of our own brethren stop and ask themselves if, after all, we might not be carrying non-fundamentals too far. Let such of our brethren pray more, let them shun the occasions of sin, let them know that the devil works by deceit, treachery, fraud and sophistry, and furthermore, that in all things touching the faith there must be no inward debates. Let them beware that protestantism might not have affected them. Take the bold pertinacity of those who oppose our faith, and their clever disguise of zeal for Christ and honesty of purpose, in conjunction with their specious sophistry, and it is, indeed,

small wonder if some of our brethren, who court
dangerous environment, because it has a little
more social glamour, or purely intellectual flavor,
and especially where such are so poorly equipped
enough, and are sad representatives of staunch
Catholicity, in their knowledge or faith — small
wonder, I repeat, if such come home from teas
and club-gatherings with sentiments bordering on
doubt. Let those of our faith who venture into
heretical surroundings go armed with piety, and
clear, solid knowledge of their own ground in
religious faith, and, let them never quite forget
that they are not theologians, and, for the most
part, let them fight shy of all habit of debate on
subtle points of religious belief. It is a wise plan
and good policy never to engage with an adversary for whom we are no match. If our
protestant friends are sincere, and seriously wish
to ascertain a right knowledge of Catholic
theology and Catholic faith, and wish for more
than to merely gratify a wish to bring possible
confusion and a blush to their Catholic friends,
they know where they can ascertain the whole
truth; for, there are hosts of priests at hand
whose pleasant duty it is to do this work, and
enlighten them.

Let all such Catholics as patronize mixed society,
and more especially society with a pronounced
heretical character, examine their conscience on
the point of faith and see if they, by manner, word,
or silence, have or have not made concession to

the enemy, or by thought erred within themselves :
"Increase, O Lord, our faith." Say what you will,
living in the air of mixed paganism and heresy
can do us no good, whatever little harm it may be
alleged to be able to do us. The very most we
can hope for is that it will do us no harm.
Protestantism is a loathesome thing and whilst we
shall give our separated brothers kindness and
every civility, we must not have ourselves construed
into having any sympathy with protestantism
whilst we have charity toward those who unfortunately maintain it.

THOUGHT :

THE sweet and tender tie that binds the Mother
and the Divine Child, time can neither sever nor
weaken. Jesus and Mary love one another with
perfectly reciprocal affection.

ILLUSTRATION :

ALL Christians love the memory and applaud
the works of St. Gregory the Great, who has been
called a Thaumaturg, and another Moses. He
had been at one time a pagan and bore the name
of Theodore ; he sat in the school of Origen, became
convinced of christianity, embraced it in the full-
ness of his persuasion and made steady progress
in knowledge and piety, till at last he mounted the
Episcopal chair and ruled the See of Neo-Cæsarea.
St. Gregory of Nazianzen, and St. Basil, learned
from the lips of their grandmother the following

incident which the saintly lady had had herself from the mouth of St. Gregory of Cæsarea, himself.

The saint of Nazianzen relates it as follows: After he had been consecrated bishop, and before entering upon his See to take up its arduous duties and tremendous responsibilities, St. Gregory felt it his duty to go into solitude for a time, in order the better to fit himself for the just appreciation and understanding of the mysteries of Divine Faith, which the Episcopal office made it necessary for him to expound before the faithful of his bishopric. The mystery of the Holy Trinity was, it appears, a source of great perplexity to his mind from the fact that Origen, who had been his teacher, and for whom St. Gregory cherished a most affectionate and tender feeling, together with the profoundest veneration for his great knowledge, had imparted to him an opinion, touching this matter, that was not wholly in harmony with the prevailing Catholic mind on the point. Here he found himself at a point like that of a fork of the road, and in a very painful frame of mind to ascertain the right sentiments it was his duty to follow. All his efforts to come by a peaceful conclusion ended in failure, and after long and hard struggles and debates, and persistent endeavor to find the truth in the matter, he could, still, not turn the scale, till it happened at last of a night, that a person came to him in a vision. This person was clearly and distinctly visible, showed a most venerable appearance, all the symptoms of great age and a singularly chaste beauty, that, to his mind, looked all but divine. From the presence of this mystic visitor there exhaled and spread about through the air, on all sides, a peculiarly sweet aroma of grace and holiness. Gregory was affected by the vision, proceeded to draw himself up in his bed, and prayed the mysterious personage that he would be so kind as to inform him who he might be, and what might be the object of his visitation under such strange circumstances and at so strange an hour. The visitor made reply with all imaginable sweetness, and served with his manner to quiet all the Bishop's fears, as he observed that he was come upon the express command of God to extricate him from the meshes of his doubts touching the true doctrine that was weighing upon his mind. Gregory summoned all his senses and began to survey the venerable personage with commingled joy and astonishment, when the latter made a gesture that directed his attention to some object that claimed it on the opposite side of the room. Gregory obeyed the summons and turned his face to that quarter only to have his eyes fall upon the apparition of a woman. The woman showed above everything of a human character and condition by the dignity of her carriage and the distinction of her bearing, that was at once delightfully and awfully majestic.

Fresh terror laid hold upon Gregory at this sight and he made every effort to recall his eyes, not knowing as yet whether he could credit his mind and senses upon the affair that was going on about him, or upon how he was to esteem the vision of brightness that was too much for his eyes; for the whole proceeding took a new wonderfulness from the fact that the vision was appearing in the middle of the night, and in spite of the intense darkness created a brightness like in brilliancy to the blazing of a torch. Then he heard the two mysterious personages conferring between themselves upon the doctrine which constituted the object of his perplexities, and whilst they were doing so they made themselves at the same time known to him; for, he heard the female apparition, or that which bore the aspect of a woman, extend the invitation to John the Evangelist to expound to the young man, Gregory, the mystery involved in doubt in his mind, and heard John the Evangelist reply reverently that he stood ready to afford this pleasure to the Mother of God. The exposition of doctrine ensued thereupon, and this was carried on in the most precise and categorical order, at the close of which the personages vanished. All this goes to show once more that Our Lady has a mission and a power in the Church of God. Yes, her power of intercession has not closed with her earthly life: she lives, she moves, she influences the great mystical body of Jesus Christ her Son: she is gone from these vales of tears unto those eternal hills, but she favors us with the beautiful glimpses of her presence in the miraculous apparitions which she vouchsafes to saints from time to time, in behalf of the kingdom of her Son. She is not absent from us, she looks down upon us, she prays for us and has our eternal hopes warm in her heart. The whole body of the Church, I repeat, comes under the influence of the Mother of God, and my individual salvation is promoted by her.

RESOLVE:

FROM this moment, when I am groping in the dim fields of those little moral darknesses — personal, not of faith, I shall reach out for the hand of Our Lady to lead me unto the Light.

PRAYER:

O GOD, from this moment pour into our souls the mellifluous and rich grace to cling always, first and last, to Thy Mother, in all the Babel of confusion within our souls and the Egyptian darkness of our life, so that we may ever enjoy the sure benediction of her care, of her intercession and of her guidance unto the Light. Through Our Lord Jesus Christ.

CHAPTER XVI.

INCOMPARABLE DIGNITY OF DIVINE MOTHERHOOD.

ST. AUGUSTINE has observed that the 'Blessed Virgin could not set forth all that she herself had been led to know of her own dignity;' and St. Andrew of Crete is authority for the assertion 'that only God is able to praise the dignity of the Mother of God to the extent of its merits.' So high is the dignity of the Divine Motherhood that it passes the very confines of the finite, as it were. This is what St. Thomas maintains. "The humanity of Christ," says the Angel of the School, "because it is united to God; the happiness of heaven, since it is the enjoyment of God; the Blessed Virgin, because she is the Mother of God, have, as it were, an infinite dignity emanating from the Infinite Good, which is God. Therefore, as far as these things are considered, there could be nothing higher accomplished, inasmuch as there could be nothing higher than God." (Sum. Th. 1p. q. 25, A. 6.) St. Francis de Sales endorses this conception of Our Lady's dignity. "God could not create," says this saint, " a higher dignity for a creature. " No seraph has ever been able to say to the Saviour of the world: " Thou art my Son, and I love Thee as such;" and the Saviour of the world could never have said to any other creature except the

Blessed Virgin: "Thou art My true Mother and consequently thou art all to Me since I am thine only Son, and I am all thine since thou art the only creature to whom I owe My birth in time." (Traitè de l'amour de Dieu Liv. vii.) St. Bernardin of Sienna says: " It is the Blessed Virgin whom the faithful salute when they say Mother of God; for in very truth, when we breathe this name— Mother of God—we point out a title to glory of such eminence and dignity, one so far surpassing conception, that the like is not to be found among the divine persons save One, namely, the Father, nor amongst created beings except likewise one; namely, the person of the Mother of God. Besides, this quality or character of Mother of God is above that of sovereign of God's creatures, because the latter depends upon the former in the relationship of branch and root. So let us call her Mother of God rather than sovereign of the world." (Serm. 52. In Sulut. Ang.)

"What creature," says St. Thomas, "has been or ever could be so agreeable to God, or be found more pleasing to Him than Mary? There is no disputing she stands the most fair in His sight, is the most beloved of Him, and is the one toward whom He entertains the best wishes." (Sum. Theol. 1. p. q. 20, a, 8.)

St. Chrysostom asks: "Has there ever been found, in any epoch, or could there ever be, a more exalted or glorious creature than Mary? Taken by herself she surpasses the grandeurs of heaven

and earth.   What is there holier than she to be met
with?   Neither prophets, nor apostles, nor martyrs,
nor patriarchs, nor seraphs, nor cherubs, nor, in
one word, anything whatever in the shape of
creation, visible or invisible, could ever be found
greater or more excelling than Mary." (St. John
Chrysost. Serm. de Nat. B. V. M.)

"What greater creature could there be than the
Blessed Virgin, who held the sovereign greatness
of Divinity wrapped in the folds of her bosom?
Look at the seraph and remember this: All
that is greatest falls below the greatness of Mary.
Only the workman could be superior to such a
work." (St. Peter Domien en Serm. de Nat.
B. V. M.)

The immeasurableness, so to speak, of Our
Lady's dignity, is the conviction of the saints, who,
in the seclusion of their own thoughts, and in an atmosphere of pure, unselfish and upright purpose,
have made a mental computation, and followed out
a course of reasoning as far as human reason could
go, yet the boundary line of the Divine Motherhood has come within sight of none of them, even
the holiest.   The saints are our guides in piety,
because in their lives and practices is found the embodiment of the Catholic instinct with its true but
mysterious beliefs, with its knowledge that it is
difficult to impart to those who have not the
instinct; and, we must ever bear in mind that in
approving saints, Holy Church approves their
spirit and practices.   The Blessed Canisius is one

J

of those who, in the contemplation of the nearness
of the Son and the Mother to each other, concluded
the immeasurableness of Our Lady's dignity. "If
it is true," says he, "that the honor of a mother
advances with the glory acquired by her son, who
can entertain any doubt that the power and
dignity of Mary's Son, Who is infinitely perfect,
redounds upon His Mother, and is a source of
glory beyond measure, for her who, alone, can
say with the Father to His eternal Son: "Thou
art my Son, this day have I begotten Thee."
(Lib. 3 de Virg. C. 13.)

The world, materialistic, arrogant, aye, more,
impudent, and, farther still, blasphemous, will not
surrender to this instinct of Catholic piety; the
overtopping of reason by faith, and the superior-
ness of its atmosphere above that which lies upon
human judgments, though this must necessarily
be so, inasmuch as God and Divine things are
above man and human things, will not adjust
themselves to a standard of judgment that admits
only the unaided human mind and matter. For
example: There can be no doubt about how
materialists look upon the spirit of humility
which is the soul of piety, and the oxygen and
hydrogen, so to speak, of the instinct of faith.
They brand it as cowardice built upon ignorance
and superstition. The fear of God that emanates
directly and primarily from the wholesome spirit
of humility to the heretical eye is puerile and
unmanly.

What materialists say against us can, however, never mar our belief, nor ever shake our faith; but, the boldness of these men, aided by the unseen hand would like to destroy the 'atmosphere' of piety. A frosty air will kill the flowers. Humility and fear of God must charge the air of Catholic piety always. The 'spirit' of piety is a rampart. The very essence of faith means something that is beyond reason, yet a godly truth. This 'spirit,' I repeat, this 'atmosphere,' this 'bulwark' must be preserved in our lives. Applying all this to the case in hand, we do not understand the great dignity of the Mother of God. We salute it, we honor the truth, we believe it. To comprehend the kind of infiniteness, so to speak, which belongs to the dignity of the Mother of God, as a great writer has said: "If you represent its perfection by degrees more and more elevated, you will never attain to the last of those degrees, supposing that you would count up for a whole eternity, and that all the angels would count with you for ages without end." (De Rhodes.)

THOUGHT:

WE should conform our mind and heart to the glory of the Most High, exalting the daughter of David to the mysterious height of the Divine Motherhood.

ILLUSTRATION:

OUR Blessed Lady deigned to evince a decided predilection toward St. Brigitte in requital of the

saint's very extraordinary activity in the cult of
the Divine Motherhood. The saint lived in wed-
lock, but, upon the passing of her husband, which
left her free, she was not slow in bringing both
mind and heart to lay them in sacrifice to the
noblest service of God. So disposed was the
Mother of God toward this saint, that an angel
was delegated from His Throne to expound to
her the great glories of the Divine Motherhood,
and, the wonders, in the shape of privileges, that
emerged from her mountainous dignity. God sent
the saint stern trials from which no true saint can
wish to claim exemption, but the Mother of the
Lord came to her in a vision, and spoke with her
upon the necessity and the merit of sufferings,
and, in divers manners, besides, blessed her vo-
tary with signal marks of her motherly care and
very special protection and help. Our Lady com-
missioned the saint to confer with the Blessed
Hermingus, and to assure this devout priest that
she would bless him very particularly on his
death-bed owing to his devotion to her, so unfailingly evidenced by him in his never failing to
begin his discourses by making some allusion to
her, or some edifying observation on the virtues of
the Mother of God. The marks of Our Lady's
special tenderness, toward St. Brigitte, were well
defined in the saint's character, life and influence.
To honor this Divine Motherhood, St. Brigitte
stopped at no sacrifice, and bearded the most
suffering it would please heaven to send, if only,

by so doing, she could make the beauties of the
Divine Motherhood radiate any the more resplen-
dently, or have the great Virgin Mother come to be
more widely known or more ardently loved.

The world has recorded vows of saints that
have thrilled with their strength, and roused with
their ardor, but, none have struck a higher note
of love and chivalry than St. Brigitte. If those
without the faith do not catch the spirit or
instinct of christian piety, it is no less true, as
regards those within the faith, that there are
degrees of this virtue, and that those who have
risen to the highest mountain tops are not fully
understood by those who dwell lower down on
the slopes, and not at all by such as inhabit the
valleys. The culture, for example, of the refined
and intellectual, or the æsthetic, is lost upon
the ignorant masses. The classes all have
their language and vocabulary, framed to
suit their own thoughts, their progress, their
tastes, though all are said to speak, for example,
the English language. In heart-culture, in
development of love, in noble taste, in undoubted
self-sacrificing chivalry the saints speak a language
which all, even within the Church, do not understand. St. Teresa, speaking of intellectual visions,
says: "There is so much of heaven in this language
that it cannot well be understood on earth, though
we may desire ever so much to explain it, if Our
Lord will not teach it experimentally." (Coleridge, Life and Letters of St. Teresa, Vol. i,

p. 87.). They are like us, but higher up in perfection of faith and love. St. Brigitte offers us a specimen of this exalted saintship, an example of this spiritual culture and noble devotion in the cause of God's Mother: " O, my sweet and only Mistress," says the saint, " of all the loves of my heart, I experience such delight over the choice the Most High hath made of thee, to become the Mother of His Divine Son, that I would be ready to suffer forever in hell, rather than see thee deprived of a single degree of thy immense glory and heavenly dignity. So true is it, indeed, that I love thee more than myself, and care not to live except for God and thyself." (Binet, iv. p. 3.)

RESOLVE :

I SHALL always be mindful, especially in temptation, or when my devotion tends to wane, that Mary is my recourse, if I would enjoy the sure help of God.

PRAYER :

LORD Jesus Christ, Who didst honor the soul of St. Brigitte with the love of Thy Mother, so tender and sweet, quicken, through the intercession of this saint, the pulse of our sluggish devotion so that we, too, may be fervent in our attachment and constant in our devotion upon the sweet Queen-Mother. O Thou Who livest and reignest with the Father and the Holy Spirit, One God, forever and ever. Amen.

CHAPTER XVII.

DIVINE MOTHERHOOD IN THE FATHERS.

AN undoubted rebuke to the impudent, self-opinioned heretical moderns is conveyed in the unfolding of Mary's glories, as we witness it in the Fathers. Throughout their works, in all ages, her name is set forth by them in such sheen and praise that it shines like a jewel, next in glory to that of the adorable name of her Son. These glories the Fathers have upheld from the dawn, like the color-beauties of the pure clouds, which surround the red sunset and receive the blessing, in return, of its rich golden radiance. Under every kind of pretext, the most hypocritical of all being a view to maintain the honor of God, heretics have repudiated the Divine Motherhood and endeavored to belittle or bespatter Mary's dignity. What madness it is for men to adopt anything like a method of antagonism, as if, indeed, the christian world, impregnated with those patristic and saintly traditions, that have emanated from its own Catholic instinct, could for one instant hold it possible that God would be honored by a systematic, heartless banishment of her who brought Him into human life; of her who loved, nursed, watched, fed, and followed Him from the damps of the cave to the tragic hour

when, in the awful gloom of Death, she stood in
the darkness, a mother, loving, faithful through
all, to the end.   The scoffers of Mary-cult have
failed, as they must have done,—Mary is ours,
the world's queen, advocate, Mother!   She shall
be ours, and none shall take her from us: "The
quality of being the Mother of God," says St.
Augustine, "is so high a one that it fetches her
up beyond the angels, none the less than men,
inasmuch as being the mother of a prince
carries with it more honor and distinction than
being merely the prince's minister.   The reason
of all this is, that we rate a thing, in the scale of
perfection, according to its greater nearness to
God, Who is the Sovereign Perfection itself."
(Lib. iii. De Symb. Et. Catech.). Patriarchs,
prophets, apostles, martyrs and confessors show
themselves dim in the bright lustre of the august
Motherhood; all other trees display decrepitude
and weakness beside this stately palm-tree.   "If,"
says St. Gregory, "thou wouldst be made aware
of the nature and compass of her character, cast
thine eyes upon her Son, and from His greatness,
as well as by it, thou canst take bearings upon
the excellencies of the Mother.   Such a Mother
is worthy of such a Son, and, conversely, such a
Son is worthy of so great a Mother.   The Mother
gaveth human nature to the Child; the latter hath
filled His Mother with heavenly graces." (Super.
i. Reg.). Origen adds his word to the voices of
the great past, and it is by no means the least of

the Fathers; for, this Father's learning and culture took men's respect, as it were, by violence, and left them no alternative but to respect him. " Mary is the Immaculate Mother," said he, "the Mother unspeckled, the Mother of the only begotten God, Who is Lord and King of all. Mary is the Mother of Him Who had no mother in heaven nor Father on earth; Mother of Him, Who was in heaven, according to His divinity in the bosom of the Father, and, upon earth, in the bosom of Mary, by the assumption of human nature; for, it was not part only of the only-begotten that has come in the body; neither has He so divided Himself that half of Him should remain with the Father and half in the Virgin; but He is whole and entire with the Father, and whole and entire in the Virgin; whole in the bosom of the Father, and whole in the human body. Without abandoning heaven, He sought out the earth, preserving all in heaven and saving all on earth. If the human and corporeal word, when it is spoken into the ears of the many, is not divided amongst them individually, so that a part of it should go to one and part to another, but remains whole and entire, so that in each one it may be found whole, with what greater reason is the only begotten Word whole and complete, both in heaven and on earth; both with the Father and in the Virgin. Mary, then, is the Mother of the only begotten One. She is at once Mother and Virgin. She is a worthy

Mother of a worthy Child." (Origen Hom. 39. Ex. Diversis Sup., i. Mat.)

The light which the Fathers throw upon Mary makes her position, character and influence clear. That she occupies a higher position than it is possible for any other to enjoy, and is nearer to God than the very choirs of angels and circles of saints, is beyond dispute. The Fathers all found her greatness upon the Divine Motherhood. They bow reverently to its dignity and set God's Mother in a unique place. They make Our Lady, though, indeed, never divine, yet, all that creature can be, and more than any other creature can understand: " The terminating point of generation is the person, or the whole and integral suppositum" (hypostasis, or person). Now the person in Christ whom the Blessed Virgin brought forth is only One (alone in its kind, unique) and a Divine One at that, carrying a two-fold nature ; therefore, the Blessed Virgin, who brought forth the Divine Person, in other words, God, in the flesh He took, is truly and properly the Mother of God, and must be so called.   On the other hand, the Person of the Word underwent a true generation in the womb of the Virgin, and, therefore, contracted true Sonship toward her : therefore, the Virgin, likewise cultivated a true Motherhood toward the Person of the Word, Who is God ; therefore, the Blessed Virgin is truly the Mother of God.   On the other hand, again, the same Divine suppositum (hypostasis, or person) which, by means of

the Divine nature, is foreign to the Blessed
Virgin, becomes her belonging, and becomes
filial by reason of the human nature, through
generation; therefore, the Blessed Virgin is the
Mother of God. (Schouppe, Elementa Theol.
Dogm. Tr. 8, Ch. 2, Art. 4, N. 224.)

The reality and the power of the Divine Motherhood are best reflected by their practical effect
on the Fathers; namely, salvation through Mary.

St. Liguori says : "St. Bernard bids us run to
this Divine Mother, because her prayers are
surely heard by her Son. This saint calls her a
' ladder,' because, as one does not mount to the
third rung, except by supporting one's self on
the second, or mount to the second without
bringing the first into service, precisely in this
way, one comes to God only by means of Jesus
Christ, and to Jesus Christ only by means of
Mary. He calls her ' his greatest confidence and
the very foundation of his hope,' because he says
that God desires to have all the graces which He
is pleased to grant pass through Mary's hands;
and he adds, moreover, that all the graces we
desire we should ask for through Mary, whose
prayers can never be left unanswered." This is
the very teaching of St. Ephraim: "We have no
other confidence save that which comes to us
from Thee, O Most sincere Virgin!" St. Ilde-
fonse so teaches: "All the blessings which
yonder Sovereign Majesty hath decreed to impart
He hath wished to commend to thy hands, since

all His treasures are committed to thee — and the jewels of His graces confided to thy keeping." St. Germain does not differ from the rest: "If thou desertest us, what will become of us, O Life of Christians!" St. Peter Damien agrees with the other saints: "In thy hands are the treasures of the Lord's mercies." St. Antoninus keeps up the refrain: "Who seeks without the Lady herself would fly without wings." St. Bernardin of Sienna holds the same belief: "O Thou, dispensatrix of all graces, our salvation is in Thy hands. Through the Virgin the vital graces are transfused from the Head—Christ. From the time when the Virgin Mother conceived in her womb the Word of God, she obtained, so to speak, a jurisdiction in every temporal procession of the Holy Spirit. So that no creature has obtained any graces from God unless according to the dispensation of His own Blessed Mother. Therefore, all gifts, virtues and graces upon such as He wishes God dispenses by the hand of Mary." St. Liguori remarks of St. Bernardin of Sienna to the effect of that saint saying that not only are all graces handed down by means of Mary, but that the Blessed Virgin acquires, through Her being the Mother of God, a certain jurisdiction, covering all graces which are vouchsafed us. St. Liguori goes on: "St. Bonaventure is of the same mind. This is why theologians, framing their views upon the authority of holy persons, have piously and justly sustained the opinion that

God gives no grace without the intercession of Mary. Without question, since He desires us to have recourse to the saints, it will be still more pleasing to Him if we employ the intercession of Mary, so that by His merits she may make up for the lack of our unworthiness, as St. Anselm says. As for the dignity of Mary, St. Thomas assures us that it is, as it were, infinite. So is it evident that the prayers of Mary are more precious before God than are those of the whole Celestial Court. (De l'importance de la Priere, Ch. i.)

How delightful to hear a saint quoting saints. Like song-birds of nature, these saints have sung the truth, the power and reality of the Motherhood of Mary and Sonship of God, as their Catholic hearts inspired them. There is no false intonation, no artificiality, or affectation, but the clear, melodious notes of pure minstrelsy, free and unhampered. The mighty chorus of saints surges like an ocean of melody out of the past. We will not resist that mighty ocean, but add our voice to theirs, and swell the current of praise that will rush into the future generations, bearing on its bosom the honor, the praise and the power of the Mother of the Eternal Word and the reality of God's Sonship to Mary, His august Mother.

THOUGHT:

WHEN we shall have found Mary, the next step is to possess Christ. By means of her we shall

find Him. By the mud-pie Christ imparted the
vision to the sightless eye. By this beautiful
creature, Mary, God gave us the Light of salvation
and heaven. Why? "I will" (Matt. viii. 3).
"Is it not lawful for me to do what I will?"
(Matt. xx. Ch. 15.) "O Lord, Thy will be
done!"

ILLUSTRATION :

FRIENDLY hands had just laid a mother in the
grave by the side of a father. The few mourners,
who had come in their charity to assist at the
burial, had gone their way, and the orphan was
lonely beyond measure, and plunged in sadness as
she stood trembling in her poignant grief upon
the brink of her mother's grave, and bethought her
upon the cold, self-seeking world she now finds
herself forced to face alone, in direst poverty and
with no kinsmen to aid her in the struggle for
subsistence. Bitter tears the lonely child was
shedding. Sobs so loud and shrieks of grief so
piercing and heart-breaking came from the child
as moistened the eyes of the grave-diggers, who
had grown hardened by familiarity with the
emblems of death. These hardened men, so used
to mourning and tears, stood now in the midst of
their labors, sunken ankle deep in the up-turned
clay, to brush away the tears from their eyes as
the thought flashed across them that perchance
one of their own bairns would some day be so
bereft and helpless standing alone upon the threshold of the bitter struggle of life. "O my mother,

mother dear, sweet mother, " rose the wail, keen, despairing, penetrating.   The volume of emotion intercepted her breath, a short spasm ensued and again the cemetery rang with the echoes of the orphan's convulsions of grief.   " O mother, why did you leave your darling alone?—Come back, mamma, come back to angel—Oh mamma, who will give me anything to eat?   Who will care for me now?"   At last the orphan withdrew from the grave, exhausted, and, with slow steps wandered in a sort of dream to a wood hard by, led thitherward by no apparent motive; but, by the hidden providence of God ever leading us on, the child fetched up at the chapel dedicated to Our Lady set in a sylvan bower.   She paused, looked up, saw the church and entered in.   The next moment found her pouring out her heart in tears to her who is the Mother of the afflicted, of the lowly and abandoned.   The christian counsels of her good mother tell for her now.   The many nights she knelt at her mother's knee and prayed with her to the Great Mother in heaven sprang out of the past and laid their golden fruits at her feet. Snatches of the hymns she sang in childhood at the village chapel and at the christian school, the up-lifting strong counsels of a Sister Augustine or Sister Gertrude come back to her with a meaning, a message, a revelation; christian education demonstrates its precious effects.   Hope in the Mother of God lighted by memory grows in the orphan, inflames under reflection and culminates in an act

of sublime confidence, so humble and pathetic
that it pierced the clouds. "O Mary, kind and
Heavenly Mother," prayed the child, "my mother
is gone from me, there is no one left to care for
me now. Look upon the poor orphan because
I look up to thee for sympathy in my needs." The
child's lips fell to silence and upon the gloom of
that woodland chapel a light came, sudden, copious
and brilliant, and the sweetest, softest music she
had ever heard, or that human senses could fancy,
swept across the cords of the orphan's heart that
steeped her in a very lake of joy, whilst odors,
both exquisite and subtle, sweetly drowsed her
senses with the pleasures and sweetnesses of
spring-time.

In the height of the gorgeous scene Our Lady
appeared to the child wrapped in the folds of a
soft robe, immaculate in its whiteness, and bearing
on her glorious brow a diadem of brilliant gold,
whilst a troup of angelic troubadours ambled and
warbled by her side. With a beautiful countenance lighted by a soft winning smile, the lady
addressed the child. "My child," said she, "I am
Mary, the Mother of God. I have heard your
prayers and henceforth I shall be a Mother to
you." She pressed her hands upon the child's
temples and then withdrew with her band of
angel-songsters. The orphan suppliant lingered
after the scene in silence and rapture, even after
the echoes of the delightful strains of heaven-born
music had died away and the light had faded out

of her view. The sweetest memory of the vision clung to the child and her whole being felt thrilled from the touch of Our Lady's hand ; and, so it was with the strongest feeling of heavenly pleasure she walked back to her cottage with a new trust and with courage aglow in her breast. The dangers that beset a young and attractive but unprotected girl are many in life, but the Mother of God guided and guarded the footsteps of our orphan with a particular care from that memorable day in the forest, and the maiden grew, we are told, to womanhood, and charmed all who were graced to know her by the womanly dignity, the lily-white chastity and maidenly reserve she uniformly displayed in her life. After a long and devout life she went to join the Bride of Heaven, to meet with her, the Bridegroom, Jesus Christ, her Creator, Father, Lord and Master.

RESOLVE:

IN sickness, in poverty, and loneliness, natural or spiritual, I shall always have recourse to the Mother of God.

PRAYER :

GRANT us, O God, the grace to place our life, with all confidence, in the sweet care of Thine own incomparable Mother. O Thou Who livest and reignest forever and ever. Amen.

CHAPTER XVIII.

OUR LORD, THE IDEAL SON.

"HONOR thy father and thy mother," is a command that God has laid directly upon the human family. "Snatch the beam from the sun and it will shine no more," says St. Peter Chrysolog; "separate the water from the fountain and it will dry up; lop the branch from the tree and it will wither; detach a member from the human body and it will putrefy. In the same way a son who is no longer attached to his parents is no longer a son." What a dreadful imputation, what a treacherous suspicion to harbor in one's breast! — that Our Lord is no longer a Son, because He is no longer attached to His Mother. If certain men seek to make the Motherhood of Mary, or the Sonship of Christ a non-reality, a purely idealic notion, they defeat the purpose of God and the Incarnation, and accuse God of inconsistency, or lack of harmony between His law and His example. The reality of the mutual relationship, its perfection of character, and completeness of incident that belong to it, must go with the Mother of God and her Child. Here we may pause to observe that nothing is more common or more fashionable with our adversaries than to employ against us the force of such words as 'ignorance' and 'superstition.' The principle that obtains herein, obtains also, and is better perceived in the question of temperance in the case of those men who, becoming fully as bereft of their own senses with enthusiasm, and losing their own judgment in their own ardent spirits as fully as the victim of alcohol, get confused themselves and confuse others on their subject, by not distinguishing the difference between the use and the abuse of stimulants. So I say it is, that, though with less sincerity I believe for the most part, religious practices are dubbed by the charge of emanating from that very vague thing, 'ignorance,' or 'superstition.' The charge is most frequently designed to antagonize real faith used aright; but the charge is delivered in a cowardly way, like a blow delivered from behind one's back,—it is insinuated. We Catholics have a faith and we believe fully in it and carry this out in our life. We are able and willing to assign reasons for our faith and to defend the glorious heritage at all hazards and at all times. Our adversaries disown the consequences of faith in their lives, and because we are true and give up our judgment and will to God's law, and surrender them in obedience to His Church, the Visible Authority, it is insinuated that we are 'ignorant,' superstitious and servile. With us, faith is a reality, and this is a reproach to the shams about us. Ignorant! Indeed, is it a crime, is it an odium, is it a fault, to have a real faith, to confess that God really knows more than we creatures? Why,

the lowliness of spirit that makes Christ a motive
of sacrifice on the part of human will and judgment
is practically unknown to protestants as it is
absolutely to pagans.   Give in for common sense,
give in because you cannot help it, take an insult
to keep a man's trade—very well, but turn the
other cheek for the love of Jesus Christ, from a
motive of faith, and this is what protestants call
'servile.'   In theory they are Christians, but in
practise they are simply men. 'Superstition' is
another word much used but seldom defined.   It
is hurled at us by way of contempt.   Now what
is it that provokes this epithet?   It is but our
outward demonstration of the internal conviction
of our faith and of its reality.   This word, too,
whilst it could only be accurately applied where
there is 'abuse,' is, as a matter of fact, designedly
and with cowardice employed, promiscuously,
without distinction, to harm and to conceal the while
the process or purpose of attacking and harming
the true, real, divine, and just demonstration of
faith which is the objective point of the slander;
the whole fact of the matter is, outside of our
holy religion faith is a misnomer.   It is not a
reality.   Call it philosophy, call it a dream if you
like, but as a religion of Our Lord, it is not true;
it cannot be true.   Heretics throw over the
Mother of God as a practical reality; and because
we do not, because we love her within our hearts
and evince our internal love by outward signs, we
are designated as 'ignorant' and 'superstitious.'

I repeat, the provocation of the adjectives so generously bestowed upon us—ignorant, servile, superstitious—is the internal and external reality of our faith marching apace.   Let us examine the adjective 'superstitious' as it affects our subject.

Who fancies for one instant that Our Lord could be unsonly?   Who could fancy that He was not a real, but, on the contrary, a bogus, a spurious Son or a bare sketch of a Son?   Who can harbor such an irreverent thought as to fancy Our Lord denied, in the least, the Son's adequate tribute of love, respect, obedience and assistance to His Mother? And what a tribute! for, who knew better than Jesus the privations, the sacrifices, the devotion and, consequently, the merits of Mary, His sweet Mother?   Who could be swifter than He, the world's Exemplar, to repay all as a grateful and worthy Son?   Once a Mother, forever a Mother. So, too, is Jesus once and forever the Son of Mary.   Fancy, I repeat, Our Lord as being out-done in respect by a Joseph whom the ancients saw drive forward in haste from the palace gates of Pharaoh to embrace his aged and tottering father, and whom they saw leap from the chariot to drop at the feet of the feeble old man.   How admirable, noble and] sonly was King Solomon as he appeared once, and as we can fancy him, the brilliant and wise, rising from his seat upon the throne and stepping for-ward to lead his mother to a seat by his own side upon the throne!   It is no sign of greatness nor

mark of honor even in any man to fail in duty
toward his parents. "He is no longer a son," says
St. Chrysolog. When, then, a fraudulent religion would come to its senses and see its error,
what better symptom of its preposterousness would
it have than its effort or wish to de-naturalize the
Son of God? The Holy Scripture takes the
fulfilment of all the other duties of a Son for
granted in the case of Our Lord, and is silent
thereon, but it expressly makes allusion to Our
Lord's obedience to His parents, the epitome and
climax of a son's duty—"And He was subject to
them." A God subject to a creature! Yes, this
is true though the world, professing Christianity,
little knows its real interior essence. Subjection!
That very thing that heretics would call 'servile'
or 'cowardly,' the product of ignorance and
superstition, ah, such men know the name of
Christ but they do not know Him Who bore and
still bears that name. To bow before the Majesty
of heaven is not servile: to fear the Almighty is
not cowardice; "to serve God is to reign." We
would die for Him Who can kill both body and
soul. We wish to reach the power of the Mother
by the fidelity and dutifulness of Jesus Her Son.
The subjection or obedience of the Master to
His Mother does not imply any prejudice to His
dignity as King over all creation. "Nothing remained to be done but to fulfil his duties," says
St. Ambrose. "By no means is this subjection a
sign of weakness but rather a mark of piety."

(Contenson, Mariologia.)   Mark well the words
of the saint, ye naturalists brave: 'this subjection
is not a sign of weakness,' it was Christ's
duty.   Bossuet descants upon the text that recites
the Master's subjection, or what is the same,
obedience to His Mother—"He was subject to
them."   The illustrious Bishop says : "I am aston-
ished at these words.   Is this all that the Son of
God had to do?   Is this all His labor, His whole
function to obey two of His creatures?   And
wherein did He obey them?   In the meanest
pursuit, in the practise of the mechanical art.
We cannot discover that His parents ever had
domestics, but, that they were the same as those
poor people whose children act as their servants.
Jesus said Himself that He came to serve.   The
angels were compelled, so to speak, to serve Him
in the desert, but we can, no where, find that He
ever had servants about Him.   One thing is
certain, and that is, He worked, Himself, in His
father's shop — O God, I am startled again —
pride falls to pieces at the spectacle."   (Bossuet
Elevation sur les Mystere).   Now when a mere
friend frames a request to a friend it is the part of
friendship to feel itself under obligation, greater or
lesser, according to the degree of their mutual relationship, to acquiesce in the request; but,
when a mother requests anything at her son's
hands, something which she has especially at
heart and which carries with it no collision
with a son's prior duty toward God, toward

the universal economy and the common good, who shall say but the ideal son, such as Our Lord, will graciously, respectfully, obediently and lovingly comply with His Mother's request and accede to the gentle and filial pressure of maternal command? It is among the possibilities that a child would encounter collision between his Father in heaven and his parent on earth, in which event he is obliged to listen to and follow the voice of God; for example, in a religious vocation. And whilst the king's first duty is toward his kingdom, there can never be in Our Lady's requests, any element, clause or syllable that could be adverse to the universal welfare of the kingdom of God, or that her Son could consistently refuse. It is a wonder that God should take a Mother; but, it is not idolatrous but simply . natural that we should expect the Child to love, respect, obey and assist His Mother.

THOUGHT :

As a saint and friend of God, Our Lady has influence, but in the lights of the natural and divine laws, she, as a Mother, holds the power of command over her Son, and if this were not by strict right, it would be so at least in piety and the fitness of things.

ILLUSTRATION :

THE world needs no new proofs of Carmel's affection toward the Mother of God, nor to be

minded of the traditional and even constitutional
belief of all Carmelites in the commanding powers
of Our Lady, as they are found gushing forth
from the spring of her preëminent title of Mother
of God.   None are found in the world more often
knocking at Mary's door, more often following in
the footsteps of Gabriel, and crowding the aven-
ues that lead to the Immaculate heart of the great
Virgin, than Carmelites, the devout spiritual de-
scendants of Elias, in earlier times, and of Teresa
in a more recent day.   None know better than
they, and surely none reduce to practise better
than they, the christian instinct which teaches
that to enlist the Mother's favor is to set one's
mind at rest for the Son's.   The following incident illustrates one of their confidences, so
multiple, known and recorded in their pious history.   In February, of the year 1770, on the
eighth day of the month, the Carmelite nuns of
St. Denys, in Paris, awoke to the sad fact that they
should have to abandon their foundation out of
sheer poverty, coupled with the absence of any
visible hope of a more rosy prospect.   Yes, black
distress was at hand, and the outlook was blacker.
When the abbess announced this dark prediction
to her ewes, their bleatings were pathetic.   What
would Carmelites do, what could they do, Carmelites! in an hour of such gloom and disaster?
Tradition, hallowed by a long line of saints,
sanctioned and encouraged by everything connected with their institute and their education,

from the first moment they entered into a religious
life; tradition, that formed, at last, in all, an
instinct, told all, in that hour, that only one thing
was to be done: that they must look to the great
Mother of God. The natural course, and every
human prudence and precaution, had been
employed to obviate the disaster, so that there
could have been no temptation of God nor any
want of respect for His ways and laws in seeking
even an extraordinary intervention, since humility,
respect and fear of God and a high and noble
end were of one mind, so to speak, toward the
plan of prevailing upon God to grant succor.
Kneeling in their choir that day, hungry and
forlorn, these children of Mary, of Elias, and of
Teresa, sent up to God, in unison, their most
affectionate and earnest vows to heaven, if only
the gracious Queen of Heaven and earth would
save them from the misfortune of being constrained to abandon their nunnery. On the tenth
day of April, of that same year, Madame Louise
of France, daughter of Louis XV, forsook the
gay scenes of court life, the world, with its glitter,
its pomps and shams, to live apart for God alone,
a true life amongst true hearts; to dwell by the
side of the tabernacle, in the same house with
Jesus Christ, her God. The prayers and vows
of the good nuns of St. Denys were heard. The
Princess Louise chose the nunnery of St. Denys
for her religious profession, and upon her entrance
into convential life brought with her a dowry of

sufficient amplitude to guarantee the long life of
the foundation. The short interval between the
prayer of distress and the royal application for
admittance to religion made it evident that the
Mother of God had made a kind of extraordinary
intervention in behalf of the nuns of St. Denys.
When these facts became known abroad, besides
augmenting respect for and confidence in the
prayers of the devout nuns, they served to inspire
all christians with a freshly awakened trust in
the Mother of God. In the sublime confidence
of devout people, such as the nuns of Mt. Carmel,
there is no temptation of God when prayers
ascend for the afflicted and poor with such
unbounded trust. These prayers assume that
ordinary means will be respected and that God
shall act by ordinary, natural means. The good
nuns do not set aside God's laws to search after
exceptional and miraculous means. They will
not obtain bread for those who are too lazy to
work for it. They will not ask God to send a
raven or an angel to nourish indolent people, or
improvident, as Elias, Daniel and St. Paul were
fed. They will not tell you to refuse medicine
when you are sick, and to depend wholly upon
their prayers. We live in the natural order of
things, not the miraculous. Piety does not seek
a sign. Piety does not use God's extraordinary
power uselessly. To do so would be pride and
disrespect. Their prayers cause a blessing to
fall upon the natural means, such, for example,

as medicine, or even brings about the ordinary means, such as employment. When ordinary means fail, then the prayers of the nuns ascend to God, with profoundest respect and fear without any tinge of boldness, yet with confidence and resignation that if it please God to do so, He might be glorified by the extraordinary intervention of His Hand. After some years of daily ministrations to the nuns of Mt. Carmel, I cheerfully avow the great things they have wrought through prayer. Sickness has been sweetly borne with, because they prayed for the sufferer; instruments have successfully done their work in operations when danger threatened, because they prayed; the unemployed and depressed have found employment or patience to bear with their lot, because they knocked at Carmel's door, and the good nuns recommended them to God. As a matter of fact, it has pleased the Divine Majesty not so infrequently to do wonders, because these devout women have prayed. And all this is due to the confidence of Carmelites, a confidence which all christians may have, if they wish, in the Mother of Jesus. Long live Our Lady of Mt. Carmel!

RESOLVE:

I SHALL always have confidence in Mary in all things.

PRAYER:

GRANT, O God, in all things involving our own interests or those of others which should touch us, that we shall have speedy recourse to the commanding power of Thy Mother, with the loving but respectful confidence of children of Mary, O Thou Who livest and reignest, with the Father and the Spirit, One God, forever and ever. Amen.

CHAPTER XIX.

MOTHER IN NATURE AND RELIGION.

OUR Lord's humanity was real and complete. Therefore the Lord took with it as an effect all its relations. The very sublimity of the mystery lies in the reality of the Master's humanity. Viewed without the eyes of a faith, deep, solid, and given freely by God, the tendency will be to make the humanity of the Lord an unreality: "And we know that the Son of God is come, and He hath given us understanding, that we may know the true God and may be in His true Son." (1 John 20.). The Apostle points to Our Lord as the true Son, the true God, but when sectaries divest the Lord of the relations of Sonship, as is witnessed in the flesh, they no longer are in the true God. They have only the shadow of the Lord. There was in Christ only One Person and that was the Divine One. He took upon Him a human mind, a human heart, and a human body, and these became the mind, heart and body of God, so that the true God thought, loved and spoke: God took on human nature, therefore He took on Sonship from His Mother. God thought, loved and spoke. So is God the Son of Mary. The doctrine of the Eucharist, like the real Son of God, is also divested of its reality by heretics.

They make it a mere token, a symbol. The one is, the consequence, or rather the effect of the other. Practically, they view the Saviour as a sort of resemblance, a shepherd, like the sheep only in the outward appearance of the fleece. Our holy faith teaches the reality: "And He was made man." "Religion," says Nicolas the theologian, "is moulded upon nature." Now what relationship more logical, more necessary or higher than that of Motherhood? Remove the idea of the Divine Motherhood, or seek to diminish its consequences in the christian life, and you wound the reality of Our Lord's humanity in its most tender, human tie.

The Incarnation does not yield up its treasure spontaneously: "Ask and you shall find." The saints have toiled in meditation to work the mines, and have come back from their researches in the darkness of cloister and cave with nuggets and treasures of a golden knowledge of the Lord. We must toil in religion by the sweat of our brow, so to speak. This is the law—we must seek, knock, ask. The Incarnation was the first subject of saints. Its reality being so vast, so divine that only faith can make it true. The divinity of Our Lord is guaranteed historically, by prophecy and miracle, but the deep, practical reality which consists in its thousand and one relationships, its widest meaning, its extent, its consequences to God and ourselves, and its responsibilities, is the reward of saints who mediate and implore, who

seek and find, knock and have it opened unto
them.   Sectaries speak of the Lord at most as
they know Him, scientifically, so to speak.   The
saints know the Incarnation in prayer, fasting and
recollection.   It is one thing to know a person as
a friend, and another thing to know that same
person as a lover.   It is one thing to study to
know him, and another thing to know him in
order to love and serve him.   Now the Incarnation being true and real to the saints, they
naturally are found paying great reverence to the
Mother of God, and in so doing differ from those
who see the Incarnation on the surface or historically.   I fancy a Jerome, an Augustine, a Francis
and Ignatius in their prayerful solitude on bended
knee, with clasped hands, in meditation, with
this picture upon their fancy of the Mother and
the Child.   How sweet and intimate, how
deep, how lasting, how wondrous, how true,
thought they, as the Holy Spirit rewarded their
labors in contemplation with new discoveries of
the reality of the Incarnation.   How much better
we would all be if we would become familiar with
the knowledge of the saints, their lives and writings !   Soon, we, too, would grow to imitate them.
Of the mother's substance Christ was formed, and
O how pure ! for, no admixture was there to make
it otherwise.   Her blood alone flowed in the
Master's veins because He had no Father according to His human nature.   ''When the child
awakens to life," says Nicolas, " the first object

it meets in the obscurity of its first view is the sweet smile of its mother." The mother's milk preserves its life: for, how few infants survive the removal, by death or otherwise, of their mother? The best and most conscientious care cannot defeat the fearful mortality of infants deprived of their mother's love and nutriment and lodged in asylums. The mother cares for her child, trains him in the conduct most suitable to his mission upon earth, and to his future life when his present life is over. She directs and prunes his character as it were the young vine. When it wanders from the trellis of the law or good behavior her eye first notes the deflection and her hand is the first and swiftest to bring back the wandering young ivy. When sickness is upon us the mother's hand calms our temples, allays our fever; her touch and words give us courage. In time of trial and disgrace it seems as though she loves us all the more. At all events when all others have fled from us she is still by our side. The one link to bind a son naturally to hope is the remembrance of his mother: the one influence to check the despairs of his life is hers. The existence and reality of this relationship is fully verified in the prominence of Mary at Bethlehem and at Calvary, the beginning and the end. No! the Mother of Our Lord is not a chimera, but a great reality. The prophecy of Simeon confirms the relationship of the Mother: Good Lady, a sword of grief shall pierce thy heart. Thy Motherhood is a

L

reality, and as a true Mother thou must suffer with Thy Son; thou must be touched with the chill shadow of His life. Thou art not Mother merely in name — woman, thou art the real Mother of God! How beautiful is the ivy clinging to the tree! Who would tear it from its fond embrace? How like the Mother and the Child Jesus! What desecrating hand shall unclasp the divine shrub from that Virgin Tree? "Our Father Who art in heaven." So are christians a family, and the christian heart cries out for a mother to be at the very center of its life.

With trembling voice, with pathos in his heart the newsboy, with bare feet, lean and dirty face, carols his plain but honest ballad. Its author may not boast of his classic education on the legends of the woods, of harpies, sprites and gnomes, or on the enchantment of moon and star, or on the mystic beauty of the rose, like the great composers; but, he retains uncorrupted within his breast the healthy natural sentiments of a child's heart, and asks: "What indeed is home without a mother?" When the mother's chair is vacant children have, 'tis true, a place whereon to lay their head, something to eat they have and the like; but, the charm of home is gone. So much is she of the home that rarely does a father, if he be at all up in years, seared and yellow, linger long when this charm of the household has gone. Children marry and go to seek their fortunes in distant lands, but wherever they roam whilst the mother lives they all speak of that spot where she is as 'Home.' None can replace the mother. Children who are bereft of a mother's care, no matter how tenderly they are cared for, will suffer a void in their life. Combining the two things, namely, the idea of a christian family as evinced in the 'Our Father,' and the main structure of the christian religion formed on the mould of human nature, and we must have Mary. What! the christian family with the Mother's chair vacant! Ah, no! We want our Mother and we must have her; and by that same craving, by that loving child's longing and clinging of the human heart like the ivy, no one will tear us from her nor rob the christian fireside of the Mother of God. Whatever the rest of the world may choose to do, we shall keep Jesus and Mary side by side as they were at Bethlehem, at Nazareth, at Golgotha and are now in heaven. By the side of the altar her place shall be to guard the tabernacle as she rocked the Infant Jesus in His cradle and in her arms. There we shall find her. Our Father will be angry with us for our sins, our faults and imperfections, but that instinct of the human heart shall ever draw us home to Our Mother's side and she shall reconcile us to Our Father Who is in heaven. It is not that Our Lady loves us more than God—this is impossible. The mercy of God, taking Our Lady for a Mother unto Himself, extends to us; and, it is that same mercy of God that uses this instinct of our heart to more securely, naturally, and lovingly draw us unto Himself by the instrumentality of His august Mother.

THOUGHT:

As Mary is our Mother, we should turn toward her at all times with confidence. We should tell her all and hope for all at her kindly breast.

ILLUSTRATION:

WE have in a previous chapter indicated the neccessity, on the part of mothers and superiors who have at heart the real and lasting interests of their children and wards, to impress at the earliest hour, upon the minds of the little ones, the important duty of their coming close to the Mother of God. The beautiful month of May, so full of delightful recollections in the history of Catholic countries, should not be let pass among us without the morning Mass each day during that month of flowers, or at least without the Benediction of the Blessed Sacrament when the Mother and her children are found together before the throne of grace imploring light and strength from God, the grace of avoiding dangers, of eluding snares, of augmenting grace, and altogether building a sound, spiritual foundation upon which they may entertain a fair hope of raising the edifice of a truly christian life. "Know ye not that ye are the temples of God, and that the spirit of God dwelleth in you," says St. John.

Mothers should make their little ones children of Mary, and should, themselves, yield their own judgments and wills to the ways and wishes of her who rules from heaven's high arch over the destinies of her own children and theirs.   A child of Mary is the creature of another world. Whilst the child of the flesh and the offspring of the earthly womb may be but too often a being merely to live, or at most to work, to do this or that in the world, without the over-shadowing or the inspiration and abiding motive of eternal destiny, the child of Mary lives only to do the will of God, to save his or her soul, and makes everything else in life posterior and subservient to this higher purpose of existence, and, in all circumstances, secondary to it.   On these beautiful May mornings, whilst the children, with innocent hearts, are singing to Mary, and the sparrows chirp without, and the fresh blossoms of the earth sweeten the air that blows in through the open-windowed chapel upon the assembled mothers and their children, stirring the flames of a hundred tapers that burn before the image of their queen, O what blessings will come from heaven to the mother and her child! The mother offers her child to God at any cost. The child prays for eternal happiness, and that every obstacle threatening to stand in the way of that heritage shall be removed at any cost.   Ah, if we could only read the future or catch a present glimpse of those happy scenes behind the veil of

yon ebon cloud; if we could but see the design
of God as we stand beside the coffin of the youth
or maiden, what we say now we would not say
under the truer light. Alas, so early! fresh flower
or blossom or bud, nipped by the frost. Why
did God take one so young and tender, one so
beautiful, so rich, so full of hopes, one so good,
the only child? Why did God pass by the aged,
why did He pass over the wicked, why did He
not take one from the multitude in a large family?
The answer is to be found in that beautiful May
morning. Then the mother prayed for her child,
and the great Virgin in heaven obtained the grace
of death ere the child should be tainted with
evil, ere the lily should be smirched, ere
the young bud should be crushed. Weep
not, mothers of the early dead: weep not,
mothers of children of Mary; your pure and
innocent darlings are safe: they are at rest, far
from this troubled life; they are happy, they are
with Jesus and Mary in the embrace of Eternal
Life. But oh, weep, ye mothers who would not
have the Lord take unto Himself your young;
weep ye who rebelled against heaven's will in
the sickness of your bairns; weep ye who said,
"At any cost, O God, let my child live." Your
children were but your own, but they were not
children of Mary. They have lived as you
willed, but only to bring sorrow upon you and
destruction upon themselves. Would that God
had taken them in childhood and in untarnished

innocence, and they would be to-day angels to hover over your fireside, spirits of grace, of peace and love, to bless you and yours, your life and home, their lives and homes. The following history is recorded in a child's magazine, called the *Mentor des Enfants*, of a young Chinese girl named Mary, of the Imperial family, aged in the neighborhood of eleven or twelve years, who showed the strongest desire from a particular devotion to make her confession on the eve of the feast of Corpus Christi. Upon the termination of the child's confession, the missionary Father said to her: " I believe, by the mercy of God, that you are His, safe and secure, but you are young, my child, and this country is full of dangers for one's virtue. Who can tell whether you will persevere, or if some day you shall not offend the good God, mortally. I don't conceal it from you that I am uneasy at the thought, and the possibility of such a thing occurring to you makes me tremble." "O do not fear," replied the young girl, "I would, indeed, rather die than offend God." "If that is so," said the priest, " my advice to you, my child, is to implore the Blessed Virgin to obtain for you the grace to die rather than to offend Him by mortal sin." Upon the spur of the moment, the child wheeled about toward an image of Our Lady, which stood in the chapel where she had confessed, fell upon her knees, and brought her forehead to strike the earth in honor of the Mother of God. She dwelt for a moment in prayer, and rising up she said to the missionary: " Be easy about it, dear Father, I have hope that God's Mother will hear me." The young girl left the chapel happy in herself; and, with the good priest, she left an example that edified him. A few days after, the girl's cheek took on a swelling, but no one looked at the fact with any alarm, all about fancying that it was nothing more than a passing inconvenience. But the thing grew rapidly worse and ran into a cancer, that in less than twenty days had eaten away almost the whole of the child's face. The little one bore this painful affliction with the constancy of an angel, and died full of joy in the firm conviction that her death was the result of her prayer, which she addressed to the Mother of God, and also of the goodness and mercy of God, Who wished to draw her out of the dangers and perils of the world, and to make her sure of salvation.

RESOLVE:

I SHALL be first a Child of Mary and shall be resigned to all sickness, suffering and death, in my own case, and when it involves those near and dear, with the trust that all is for my eternal good, and for theirs.

PRAYER:

O GREAT Virgin, who hearest the prayers of the father, of the mother and her children, to bless the household, grant us all, sweet and, holy

Mother, grace of submission to thy love and of resignation to whatever form thy will may choose to shape our life, so that we shall be obedient to sickness, to suffering and to death. Through Jesus Christ, Our Lord.

CHAPTER XX.

MARY IS OUR MOTHER.

THE dogmatic truth of Mary's relationship with us, is based upon the economic law of christianity, the tendency of which is to share with us the relations of the Three Divine Persons. Under the action and influence of this economy, God's Son becomes also the Son of man and our first-born brother. The Heavenly Father becomes our Father; and it is by the Holy Spirit becoming in us the 'Spirit of Adoption,' that we become the children of the Father. It is always true and it could not be otherwise, that man has nothing in common by nature, with the Father, the Son or the Holy Ghost, as they 'are' from all eternity in the independence of their own Divine nature. The sovereign mystery of religion consists in the tremendous fact, that what the Three Divine Persons simply 'are' by nature, they have contrived to 'make' themselves toward us; that is to say, they have become our Father and our Brother. Mary is the bond of our union with them. Through Our Lady, Jesus was born, and through His birth of the Virgin, we are born into the life of brotherhood with Christ and of childship toward God: "Who, on our account, and for the sake of our salvation, hath come down from

heaven, and been made incarnate by the Holy
Ghost of the Virgin Mary," says the Creed. In
a certain sense, it is not improper to say that Our
Lady is co-redemptress, and, without adding
aught to our previous claims in her behalf, that
she is less the Mother of God than our own
Mother; because, after all, whilst she gave Jesus
Christ a mortal life, she has brought us forth into
an immortal life. Mary became the Mother of
God for the very same reason that urged Jesus to
become her Son; namely, that of having us become the children of God. Now the work of
Jesus, and consequently the work of Mary, was
not to come to an end with the very first, at the
outset of the Incarnation; or, when Our Lord became man. The end which Our Lord proposed
to Himself in coming into the world, and by a
parallel, Mary's purpose in her Motherhood, was
the redemption of mankind. Now we all know
that the Incarnation was only the beginning of the
redemption. The redemption is the whole, and
comprises the beginning with the end—Bethlehem
with Calvary. "It is finished," said Our Lord.
What? The Redemption; the end of the Incarnation is attained: "A great obstacle, lying in
the way of our understanding Mary's spiritual
Motherhood of mankind, consists in the fact, that
we separate the Redemption from the Incarnation.
We represent Mary to ourselves, once and for all,
as the Mother of Christ, just as any other natural
mother, and then we find it difficult afterward, to

conceive her to be the Mother of men; and, we come to consider that birth by which she became our Mother, at the foot of the cross, as a pious exaggeration." (Nicolas. Place cited above.)

This is a timely observation, because there is danger of our not seizing the reality, the breadth and meaning of Mary's Motherhood over men. Few mothers could witness the bloody execution of their son. St. Thomas is of opinion, and it is a matter of general belief, that God required the consent of the August Virgin in the taking of His Son, just as He asked it of her in bestowing Him upon her. Mary was to subscribe to the dreadful immolation at Calvary, as she gave her consent to His Incarnation in her virginal womb. What motive could sustain her purest love in such a terrible immolation? What interest could pretend to balance, as it were, such a horrible death, to which she, the Mother of the Victim, gives her fiat.—"Mary so loved the world as to give her only begotten Son," says St. Bonaventure. Wherefore? In the interest of the world's salvation. The gruesome features of a crucifixion, with its tricklets of blood, its bruises, its torturous, agonizing, and slow death under ordinary conditions, would dishearten a mother. But with the Son of God on the cross, and His Mother at its foot, we have a scene passing understanding. What motive, what strange power could have made her so firm in that place, at that hour, in the presence of that terrible scene? The body she nursed, the lips and face she had so often pressed and kissed! How could she look upon that adorable body, the Lamb of God, mutilated, bleeding, dying—dead! There she stood, however, calm, grief-drenched, torn with daggers throughout her feelings, tortured with a terrible sympathy. Jesus was God, therefore she loved Him more than herself. To have exchanged places with Him would have assuaged her bitterness. Ask first why Jesus was there, the gem of the skies, in that dark setting. Ask the Redeemer why He chose to be the center of that bloody scene, and to be mutilated and butchered to the death. I need not say it: we all know it was to give us life everlasting. So Mary's purpose in bringing Our Lord into the world was not yet completed. She stood at the foot of the cross till she presented Our Lord, before the whole world, not only a God-man, but a Redeemer. The end of the Incarnation, which was the Redemption, is here accomplished. Redemption had been impossible without a victim. "Behold, I come, O God, to do Thy will!" rang out the voice of the Son. Now a Mother is needed in the plan of God, to furnish a body for the Eternal Word. Our Lady answers: "Behold the handmaid of the Lord, be it done unto me according to Thy Word."

The two replies harmonize: They, Jesus and Mary, become co-workers in the great scheme of Divine Mercy, for the restoration of lost mankind,

joint-workers in the Incarnation. The loving,
heroic, parental union of Mary with Jesus, or the
spiritual Motherhood of redeemed mankind, began also at the moment Our Lord was conceived
in her womb, and was brought to completion at
that moment on the cross, when all was consummated, and she had brought us forth spiritually.
The festering sword of grief must be eliminated,
Mary must bring us forth. O how could she
have stood silent under the painfu' delivery, with
no groan, nor sigh, nor complaint? You ask
again, and we now answer. Jesus is near when
His Mother brings us forth. The parturition took
place beneath His dying glance. He sustained
her, and she helped sustain her Son, as the two,
Creator and creature, bore the pains and anguish
of labor in the world's birth, to life everlasting in
God. Mary is a Mother in the Incarnation and a
mother in our redemption. Be not amazed indeed that she is our Mother. The thing to
amaze is that she is the Mother of God, yet our
gratitude to that great Mother should be earnest,
deep and real, for she brought us forth like a
sword being withdrawn from her sore and sensi-
tive heart, where it hath so long been lodged—
from the conception of Christ. This gratitude
should not have to be wrung from us, like coin
from the miser. We shall not question either the
gift or its magnitude, but seize upon it with ardor
and thankfulness, whilst we say : God be praised
for our noble lineage ! God be praised that Mary

stood Mother to Jesus in the Incarnation, and
Mother to us in the Redemption, when she became the world's Mother.   St. Augustine teaches
that Mary is justly called our Mother, because
she has co-operated by her charity to give us
birth to the life of grace, as members of Jesus
Christ our chief. So as Mary has co-operated
by her charity, in the spiritual birth of the faithful, God desires still further, that she shall co-
operate by her intercession, in making them
acquire the life of grace in this world, and the
life of glory in the other.   It is for this the
Church desires that we call her our life, our
sweetness and our hope.   (De Symb. et Catech.
lib. iii, cap 4.)

The Motherhood of Mary toward the Redeemer, and her spiritual Motherhood toward the
human family, achieved at Calvary, form the basis
of that tradition in the Church, framed in language clear and powerful, to the effect, that her
maternal power with her Son is beyond measure,
and that she has but to ask in order to obtain
what she wishes.   St. Anselm resumes all when
he says: "As it is impossible that they shall be
saved, from whom the Virgin Mary turns away her
eyes of mercy, so is it necessary that they, toward whom she turns her eyes by praying for
them, shall be justified and glorified." (St. Anton.)

THOUGHT:

MARY is by 'right' my spiritual Mother, and
hence I should look up to her for nutriment, ad-

vice, and the direction of my spiritual formation
and education.

ILLUSTRATION:

THE following example is commendable for
quotation, as embodying the beautiful effect that
is obtained when the clergy, the parents and the
teachers of children, shall have done their duty
toward making Our Lady a real, practical element
in the life of children. It goes without saying,
that, in this, as in all other things, moderation
must be observed, proportion kept. Her place
must be set forth with becoming dignity, if it
would be impressively done; and, then again,
with an eye to prudence and opportunity. I
do not say that children must be stuffed with
piety, as if the Word of God was to be their
exclusive food in life. Mary-cult must not
be made to purport the transplanting of God,
but be set forth solidly and practically as a
powerful help toward salvation, by augmenting
grace, and enabling us to elude perils, and
conserve all virtues in the tempests of lust
and unholy passion. As the story runs, a vast
estate spread out its broad acres near Marseilles,
a sea-board city in the south of France. The
estate was thickly wooded, and in its center a
huge castle stood to house the lord and family
of the domain. The good priest who records
the incident, confesses to having had it from the
lips of the Lady Emma herself, the mother of
the child.

It was vacation, and Jules, a child of some eight years, had been given the freedom of the estate, a respite from his books, and liberty to romp as he would in order to recoup his strength after the season of more or less confinement and exhaustion incidental to study. The child used his permission to its fullest extent, according to his own interpretation of his privileges, and, as we may well believe, soon found the boundary line of the estate. Here a high fence mentioned the fact to all intruders and contiguous owners of land. The iron bars of the fence terminated at their tops in a row of glided iron lances. A child's innate hardihood and natural love of danger goes without saying; and, Jules was no exception to the rule. Judging, with a boy's judgment and conscience, that the boundary line of the estate must be the tops of the fence, nothing would serve but Jules should climb the fence and indulge in a promenade along its lofty and perilous ridge as though it were a level and green sward. The ascent was accomplished in safety, and this emboldened the young acrobat to venture on a new plan his mind of fiery mould conceived. Surmounting the iron posts that upheld the fence, rose far above it, and divided the fence into sections, bronze vases stood as ornaments to the boundary line and estate. "Now what in the world can be in those things away up there?" thought Jules. "I'll see," said he. So up he went and made the side of a vase in safety. But, now

M

he finds after all his pains that he is not tall enough
to peer into it and discover the nature of its contents; and any one conversant with human nature
in the least, must know that to be baffled thus will
never do at all.   Accordingly he grasped the edge
of the vase and strove to draw himself upward to
satisfy his curiosity.   The next moment the huge
vase toppled over and followed him down, trans-
fixing his little body under its great weight and
momentum upon the lances of the fence.   Their
sharp points penetrated his body to a considerable
depth and his shrill cries of distress soon brought
help, when he was delivered, after great trouble
and much pain, from his dangerous embarrass-
ment.   The mother of the child took him fondly
into her arms and the little lad, weak and bloody
as he was, evinced a grit and patience worthy of a
brave man and even tried to smile and be merry.
The agonized mother started for the castle, but
the boy would not have that just yet.   He
struggled and wriggled out of her arms, knelt
upon the ground, joined his little bloody hands,
and in tears of pain and love recited St. Bernard's
prayer to the Mother of God, "Remember, O most
pious Virgin Mary."   When his prayer was concluded, he said, "Now, mamma, take me home."
In eight days, the mischievous but brave and
devout little lad was wholly cured and said, with
great enthusiasm and faith: "I told you, mamma,
that Mary would cure me."   The reconteur
makes the observation that the child had learned

and retained what his good priest, his devout parents and religious teachers had inculcated in him; namely, to have recourse in all dangers to the glorious Mother of God.

RESOLVE:

IN every danger I shall have speedy recourse to Our Lady.

PRAYER:

O MOTHER of God, who didst protect the Child Jesus through tempests of blood, and bear Him away in safety, obtain for us the grace to have recourse to thee in all the dangers that may beset us in soul and body.   Through Jesus Christ Our Lord Who livest and reignest with the Father and the Spirit, One God forever and ever. Amen.

CHAPTER XXI.

THE WORLD'S BIRTH-CHAMBER.

"MARY stands Mother to our Head in the flesh, and occupies the same relation in spirit to us, His members," says St. Augustine. St. Ambrose makes allusion to this spiritual Motherhood of Mary over the world. "Whom," says the saint, addressing Our Lady, "thou hast begotten in One"—that is, in Christ. Calvary was the scene where the climax or the finale took place. Here on this blessed spot, the most sacred on earth, culminated the delivery of Our Lady, and the spiritual birth of the world was wrought out to her Motherhood. And it is important that we ground this fact well in the mind; for, the place and time being identical with the place and time of Our Lord's death, there are volumes to be learned from the fact in meditation, when in quiet moments we come to search out in the light of God's face the real union existing between Jesus and Mary, their co-workings, and the great Virgin's relations toward the children of men. Mary's work was not ended at Bethlehem as far as the world was to be concerned; like her Son's, her mission was to be consummated on that renowned hill-top, the birth chamber of redemption. The words that Our Lord addressed to St. John, on that terrible day, 'Son, behold thy Mother,' are the 'consummatum est' of the spiritual Motherhood. These bequeath to John a title of justice, and as the beloved disciple, in the mind of all the fathers, represents mankind, all the children of men own the right to call Mary, Mother. There is more in the words than a bestowal of a gift. "It is certain," says St. Bernardin of Sienna, "that Mary, by her loving co-operation in the mystery of the Redemption, has truly given birth to us on Calvary, a birth to the life of grace; and in the order of salvation the sorrows of Mary, like the sufferings of her Son, have given birth unto all; and in those precious moments Mary has become in all strictness our Mother by the immensity of her love and the generosity of her martyrdom."

Let memory escort us back through the ages unto that day in the garden when God raised the war cloud and informed the evil spirit that his malignant work would be resented. We may well fancy the wrath of God and flashes of fire when He issued the pronunciamento: "I shall put enmity between thee and the woman—She shall crush thy head." (Gen. iii. 15). That promise is fulfilled. The woman has come at last. 'Woman, behold thy Son.' Mary is that 'woman' whom God was to ordain for the crushing of the serpent. "We all know," says St. Augustine, "that the serpent signified the devil, and the 'woman' signified the Virgin Mary." (Ad Catech.) "Woman, behold thy son." Let us examine why

the Lord did not say, "I give him to you for a son
—I give her over to you for a Mother;" but on
the contrary simply said: "Behold thy Mother,
—Behold thy son." If in this solemn declaration it was a question of merely giving a
recompense to St. John, or a support to Mary,
the expression, 'I give her over to your care—I
give him to you for a son,' would have been
better selected and more opportunely; because,
Mary, not having engendered St. John, either
corporally or spirtually, as a particular individual,
he could only become her son by the gift of
Jesus Christ. But supposing that there is question
of all christians, even of all mankind, the expression: 'I confide thee'—'I give thee over to,'
would in some sort have hidden away the part
Mary had had in their spiritual birth and dimin-
ished the glory thereof. This would have
conveyed the impression that Mary had become
our mother 'by favor,' so to speak, and nowise by
title of 'justice'—'Behold thy son—Woman, thou
hast this moment been delivered; and behold
before thine eyes the son to whom thou hast
given the light of day; it is the Christian people
of whom John is at the same time the first fruit
and the figure.' (Ventura.). "John is a particular name. Disciple is a common name in
order to denote that Mary is given to all as
Mother," says Silveira.

Justice operates in that Motherhood which is
consummated in natural delivery. A right

emanates from Our Lady's spiritual delivery of
the world — a right for her and a right for us.
Mother is her title in justice, and child of Mary
is your title and mine, by the title of justice set
forth in the 'Behold thy son.' By the Incarnation, as the Mother of Our Lord, Mary is
indirectly our Mother: 'Whom thou hast begotten
in One.' (St. Ambrose.) But the direct and strict
Motherhood over the world, emanates from the
title culminating in and set forth in the words,
'Behold thy son.' As we have intimated, Mary's
delivery of the vast world was not painless, as was
the case with her delivery at Bethlehem, where
an Innocent Child was born to her. To-day, at
Calvary, she begets sinners to light and life, and
the curse of sin, 'Thou shalt bring forth in sorrow,'
is felt by the Immaculate Mother 'whose belly is
like a heap of wheat set about with lilies.' (Cant.
vii., 2.) "The sorrows which," says St. John Dama-
scene, apostrophizing Our Lady, " thou wert
spared in bringing forth Jesus, thou hast borne in
the hour of the passion." We may say that what
Our Lady had been spared at Bethlehem was
demanded of her with multiplied interest when
we contemplate the number of sinners to be born
unto her. Great were the mysterious pains of
labor that crowded upon the Virgin Mother at
the foot of the cross. " Now thou payest with
usury," says St. Bernard, " what thou hadst not
to pay to nature. Thou feltedst no sorrow in ·
bringing forth a Son, but thou hast suffered a

thousand times over during the Death of thy
Son." The reason is that Mary was joined in
Motherhood to the spiritual fatherhood of Christ.
We cannot imagine the agonies of a birth nor
conceive the bitterness of a delivery. In bringing
us into the world our mothers suffer more than
they can tell. To know all and appreciate the
sharpness of their sufferings is only for mothers,
although the joy over the child that is born
obliterates the remembrance of the pain. No
creature suffers as the human mother in this
event of life, and yet St. Bernadin of Sienna tells
us that "Mary has suffered in the death of her
Son and borne the bitter pains that would
establish her the mother of all the faithful, because
her sorrows equalled those of all mothers collec-
tively, and the sorrows of all who give birth have
conspired against her." (Ventura, p. 12, ch. 14.)

THOUGHT:

REMEMBER the sighs of thy heavenly Mother.

ILLUSTRATION:

IN the days when St. Francis Borgia was per-
fuming the city of Rome with the aroma of his
eminent virtue, he was approached by a great
sinner with the most earnest request that the
saint would condescend to look into his soul,
which was in a very bad way. He invoked the
aid of his wise counsel and the assistance of his
prayers to set matters aright in his conscience.

St. Francis, with a saint's intuition and a skilled physician's judgment of symptoms, saw at a glance that the suppliant spoke truly, and that his conscience did suffer need of speedy and judicious healing. St. Francis Borgia was a man of knowledge, prudence and piety; and these elements must concur, as we know, in a sound spiritual director, that is, in one who does good work and builds surely. Yet, the saint evinced a great modesty in the present case; and, instead of taking the sinner in hand himself, even though he was requested by the penitent to do so, he turned the case over to a Father Acosta, whose ripe experience and judgment in the direction of souls the saint held in high esteem.

St. Francis declined this case, and yet we know that it was he who first of all assured St. Teresa that her spirit of prayer was the work of God, and not a delusion, as other directors suspected. We all know how much St. Teresa endured for lack of skilful dealing in the affairs of her soul, and it is well for us to realize that we all have a right, and it is prudent besides that we enjoy that right, to be directed by skilful guides of the soul who, by knowledge, prudence, and holiness, obtain the fulness of the wisdom and discernment of the Holy Spirit. The young man obeyed and knelt in confession to Father Acosta. It is to be observed that the following unveiling of a sinner's heart to the whole world was brought about by the urgent

solicitation of the penitent himself who would not
have the world in ignorance of the mercy of God,
if, indeed, after Our Lord dying for it, the world
could be ignorant of how He willed the sinner to
live. The penitent insisted that the universe
should hear of the pity of the Mother of Jesus
toward the sinner, and of her tremendous power
before God. "My father," said the penitent to.
his confessor, " from my tenderest years I have
been endowed with the gift of religion; I invoked
the Mother of God, and praised her always; I
approached the Holy Table frequently. In my
inner self, however, in those hidden recesses
that are closed to the world, and where only the
eye of God may look in and see what lies there,
corruption held the mastery over me. There, in
that inner, hidden secret heart of mine, I was perverse, wicked, corrupt; and to crown my wickedness, I concealed my secret enormities to myself
and withheld them even from my confessor. In
that way, my dear father, did I go on, rolling sin
upon sin, piling guilt upon guilt, till my soul fairly
reeks with the blood of guilt, and my conscience
is haunted by its awful redness and dread. There
were moments through all this when the light
came to me and then I promised to correct myself, but, in all cases my resolution melted away
like ice in the first warm breath of temptation, or
disappeared like tow at the smell of fire. Ever
onward, crime succeeded crime and shame was
multiplied by shame. Many a time Jesus Christ

revealed to me the awful picture of myself, and said to me : 'Why, O unfortunate man, dost thou go on treating Me thus — Me, Who hath evinced so much goodness toward thee ; was it not enough that the Jews crucified Me? Shall thy heart be another Calvary?' But I had grown accustomed to sin and remained insensible to the warnings. My dear father, I have been reduced to my last mercy—only one drop remains. This morning I seemed to have seen my guardian angel. He held up before me the vision of the Sacred Host. 'Seest thou,' said he, 'thy Saviour Who hath loaded thee down with favors and Whom thou hast profaned and insulted all these years? See now the retribution of thy ingratitude,' and with these words he laid hold upon a sword to strike me dead. I was losing my senses in awful dread, with the fate of damnation staring me in the face, when the Ave Maria rose from my lips — Ave Maria ! thou canst save me. This saved the day for me, for thereupon the angel made reply: 'This is your last mercy. God, upon account of the protection of the Queen, accords you a longer time to live and expiate your sins.'" When the trembling penitent had told his story he remained silent. Father Acosta was tossed by many emotions. On the one hand the guilt red and ghastly, on the other, the mercies of God and of His august Mother. So he endeavored to confirm in the penitent the realization of his great guilt, but balanced this by pointing out the vastness of the

mercy shown to him by Our Lord and His
Mother. Furthermore, he assured the penitent
of how essential it was that he should make atone-
ment for the bad life he had led. Then the
poor sinner received absolution. With a heart
lightened of its dreadful weight, that old familiar
weight, that sickening weight, the penitent rose
from his knees light, happy and free, prepared
for and resolved upon a new life. His days afterward, were attended with struggles patiently and
nobly borne and characterized by a spirit of
penance deemed adequate to expunge the past, to
purify and strengthen his soul and to fit him for
the happy eternal life beyond the grave with God
and his great benefactress, the magnificent
Mother of us all.

RESOLUTION:

FROM this day I shall recite the Memorare or
equivalent prayer as a pledge of my last trust in
the Mother of God. Jesus is the Mediator of
Justice and Mary is the Mediatrix of Grace, says
St. Bernard.

PRAYER:

O GOD, when we contemplate our sins and
miseries, bound as we are in the prison of the
flesh, chained by passion and pride, grant us the
grace to employ the Mother's power over Thy
Heart and our hearts so that we may never despair
of forgiveness. Through Jesus Christ, Thy Son.

CHAPTER XXII.

MARY, MOTHER OF CHRISTIANS.

VIEWED as co-operatrix or co-sacrificatrix, Mary is Mother to all mankind. All races, all peoples, all classes, all colors, are embraced in the circle of her maternal interests and loves. Surely the title is superb, grand, unique. She blazes upon the horizon, — the vast world's Mother! But Our Lady is in a very peculiar and distinct way the Mother of christians; the Mother of the disciples and followers of her Divine Son; and this comes about by that mysterious unity which characterizes the Mystical body of Jesus Christ. Within this mystic sphere of magic one-ness, we are all found, who, by the sovereign mercies of heaven, are made able to confess the glorious name of Jesus Christ: "And the glory which Thou hast given Me, I have given to them; that they may be one as we are also One." (John xvii, 22.) St. Paul teaches this unity: "For, as in one body we have many members, but all the members have not the same office, so we, being many, are one body in Christ." (Rom. xii. 4, 5.) St. Paul alludes in another place to this spiritual unity: "For as the body is one and hath many members, and all the members of the body, whereas they are many, yet are one body, so also is Christ. For in one spirit were we all baptized into one body. Now you are the Body of Christ and member of member." (i Cor. xii. 12, 13, 27.) In baptism we become thus united to Christ— "As many of you as have been baptized in Christ have put on Christ." Now the effect of this baptism, or this putting on of Christ, is that 'we are grafted on the tree of Life, and become partakers of the Divine nature.' (ii Peter i. 4.) Our Lord is the Redeemer of the world, and yet, all do not choose to profit by the redemption, or at least, do not actively and practically profit by it; nevertheless, He is the Redeemer of all men, inasmuch as He has paid the ransom, though to complete the work in each, the individual must come under the touch of baptism, and by it be put in the actual enjoyment of all the graces and privileges, treasures and glories of the Lord's passion and death. Christ is the Saviour of the whole world: He is the Redeemer of all those savages who dwell in dark, impenetrable forests, in the tangled woods and jungles of remote and dark continents,— though, these have never yet profited, that is to say, practically profited by the redemption through baptism, howsoever they may profit by it speculatively. I repeat: Jesus is the Redeemer of the world, but Christ is distinctly, practically and perfectly, that is actually, the Redeemer of such as are christians. These not only 'may' be redeemed, but 'are' so. Now what we say of the Redeemer and of His distinct relations with christians, as the name christian implies, namely, to be of Christ, we may say correspondingly of Our Lady. She is the world's Mother, but in practice, and as a matter of fact, she is perfectly and distinctly the Mother of christians. Let us keep in mind that we, as christians, form, with our Divine Head, 'one body,' as this is the key to our theme. What happens to a member, happens to the body. What the body comes by all the members share in, and *vice versa*, what befalls a member the whole body feels, by the very fact. If this spiritual unity in the mystical body of Christ was only better understood, there would be more charity, sympathy and harmony, and less independence and selfishness in the christian world, less sectionalism and stoppage of circulation. This unity is far-reaching in its effects if piously observed, and it is a very vital element in the christianity that aims to be true, sincere and not fraudulent. This mysterious absorption of our spiritual entity, without losing identity, this being grafted on Christ, makes us all form with our Head, one Son of God, and likewise one Son of Mary. "I no longer live," says St. Paul, "but Jesus Christ liveth in me." How this mystical unity of the christian body makes Mary distinctly the Mother of christians, is most powerfully presented by Origen — The thought is deep, but admirable and exact. This unity was the object of Our Lord's prayer just before His death, and St.

Paul, as we have seen, insisted on it with his accustomed ardor.

"No one," says Origen, "can grasp the meaning of the Gospel delivered by John, only he who shall have reclined upon the bosom of Jesus, and received, from the hands of Jesus Christ, Mary for his own Mother." "If Mary has no son," say they who have thought well upon the matter, "except Jesus, and Jesus said to His Mother: 'Behold thy son,' and did not say, 'Behold this also is thy son,' it is just as if He had said: 'Behold, this is Jesus, Whom thou hast begotten; for, whoso is perfect doth himself no more live, but Jesus Christ liveth in him.'" (Origen, In. Joan.) Our Lord, then, said as much as that John was Himself, Jesus; and as John represents all men, but in a distinct, practical and perfect way, all christians in whom 'Christ liveth,' all christians are but one Jesus, and Mary is the Mother of that one Jesus. Beautifully as truly has Origen said that only loving faith, one close and familiar to Jesus, comprehends this unity: "that one must recline on the bosom of Jesus Christ" in order to receive the knowledge and inspiration of the great law of christian unity and charity. " As God strengthens our faith, love grows," says St. Teresa. This mystic unity, this absorption of St. Paul in Christ dwells in an atmosphere of love commensurate with one's faith. In the aspect of our being christians, that is to say, true disciples of Jesus Christ, united with Him, incor-

porated with Him, and becoming with Him one
and the same thing, we are the children of Mary,
just as Jesus Christ Himself is, and we are no
longer distinct from Him. Forming, as we do,
but one body, we do not become more than one
son. As a consequence, though, under this title,
Mary has as many children as are reckoned
among the true faithful, it is none the less true
that she has but one Son, Who is Jesus Christ,
because it is Jesus Christ Who liveth in us as
long as we are truly united to Him ; and all the
faithful make up with Him, only one and the
same Jesus Christ, of Whom Mary is the true
Mother, and therefore our true Mother. (Ventura La Madre di Dio, Madre degli uomini,
p. 1, ch. ix.) This intimacy and unity of the
faithful with Our Lord is sublime. It is in line
with that peerless mystery of the Incarnation. It
surpasses, like it, our human understanding, and
nevertheless, is not a mere fancy-picture or
Utopian's dream, but a reachable idea, one consistent with our present life, or, indeed, a wise
God had not called us thereto. Upon this mystic
unity we are nestled snugly together in the arms
of our Heavenly Mother—One Son, one Mother.
" Woman, behold thy son." Thou hast, then, O
woman, in the person of John, who stands at the
foot of the cross, the same Son thou seest upon
the cross, thy Jesus, Whom thou hast begotten,
and Who is found in His disciple, just as the
head is in the member to whom he is united.

N

See in him the fruit of My redemption, the traces
of My blood, the inexpressible communication of
My graces, even to the very participation of My
divine nature. There is nothing wanting to his
being My other self, one thing with Myself; and
since I am thy Son, so also is he, and so are
all such as shall demonstrate the same title and
condition as John, from that same moment be in
Me and with Me, thy Only Son." (Ventura loco
citato.) The Gospel of the widow of Naim, after
what we have been saying, may serve to throw
out a new light on this unity and its consequences.
Grievous sin not only robs the soul, that is dead
to God, of a Father, but it deprives it, likewise, in
a sense, of a Heavenly Mother. With the flight of
God's grace disappears that sublime, mystic unity
of Christ; and, we may observe in the widow of
Naim the Mother of God, lamenting over a dead
son, and, in a new and awful sense, a dead Alter-
Christus. Yes, when the soul of a christian dies
by sin, Christ is dead in him. Mary is still the
spiritual Mother of the man. Alas, practically,
the christian is dead to her. Let it be a new deter-
rent against sin to reflect that it excludes us from
the special and distinct maternity of Mary, and let
it be our first and highest purpose to conserve
the mystic unity of Christ, which springs from
sanctifying grace, by determined adhesion to
God's commandments and a more pronounced
aversion for the one thing on earth that can ever
disrupt this mystic unity, and that is — sin !

THOUGHT:

WHILST I conserve the grace of God within my heart I am an other-Christ, and as such Mary is distinctly My Mother—O mystery of kindness! O truth surpassing men's wits, O love supreme! O privilege above recounting! Mystic unity— Ave, abide always.   Grace of God be ever with me!

ILLUSTRATION:

ETERNITY alone will tell of the many who shall have found the intercession of Our Lady a last opportunity of scaling the eternal heights. God alone can say fully, how guilty they are who, upon principle, so to speak, discredit her power and banish Our Lady from their religious life.   No moralist can hit upon any useful purpose served by disentwining her name from her Son's in the religious standard.   It is nothing short of vandalism to disrobe the spiritual tower of that great shield or even of the graceful ivy that has clasped its walls and grown about it from the days of Bethlehem.   What has the protestant church to replace the Mother of God?—Nothing.   What figure could replace her? None.   Those who strive to dethrone her from the hearts of christian men and women, and to assail her place in the economy of christianity, in contradiction to Jesus Christ, the Father, and the spirit of true faith embodied in the lives of saints, will have much to answer for.   Sectaries speak of hope and yet they dull, by only feeble references to her, or

conceal altogether from the sight of men, by
ignoring Mary, the sharp weapon of the poor
sinner in the last struggle for life and death. Say
what you will, at least there is no priest familiar
with death-beds and the sacrament of penance
who has not been the witness of the tremendous
force of Our Lady in asserting the authority and
influence of her Motherhood upon her dead
children, the poor sinners of the world. Many a
youth and young man have been wayward and
brought around by her. There are always young
men, and some others, too, who, though not proud
in their judgments, are still not in their conduct
all they would like to have been when they come
to die. They have been foolish, but, for the most
part, weak: "The spirit is willing, but the flesh is
weak." They have not acted and thought of the
great Mother of God suitably; but for all that,
they never failed to reverence her when she did
appear in their thoughts, nor to shield her dignity
against the calumnies and innuendos of defiling
lips in their daily walks. If the world is amazed
at Our Lady's tender action toward such frail
members in the evening of careless lives, may we
not impute something of power to the spirit of
these same black sheep who would lay down their
lives to defend her name? We know that a
martyrdom washes out all, and does there not
loom up in such sinners, after an incongruous
fashion, a sort of spirit of martyrdom? In any
case, they have not been unnatural children:

They would not deny their Master nor their Mother in heaven. They have clung to the faith. In the end when death comes to call them up before God in judgment, they look back from their death-bed through all the years. The grizzled old man to-day, lying on his death-bed, recalls his childhood, his boyhood, his manhood days, and sees how good a mother Mary has been through all. And oh, how much it serves him now, calms the death-scene and smooths his pillow to have never denied her! How it softens and helps the weary heart to realize that even after so many faults she is still his Mother and he is still so much to her. At the bed-side of the dying sinner the devil has no better enemy than she, no adversary so worthy of his steel as Mary, for she is the only creature the devil has never in any way overcome. Let the dying sinner turn toward her his dying eyes and lift to her a child's wish of his sinking heart, and all is well. At once her maternal arms shall enfold him. The warm breath of the Mother shall enliven the chill of his brow; the sunny face of Mary shall chase away the great shadow from his heart. Shall the Mother's-love not out-do the hate of demons? Do we measure her love?

An instance of all this : The Rev. Charles Soler, of the Society of Jesus, is authority for the ensuing incident: A young man fell dangerously ill. Four priests approached him in succession, but he drove them all out of the room. I went to see

him, myself, and met the same fate as those who
had gone before me. As you will easily understand I came off with a feeling of great grief over
the obstinacy of the young man. On the following day the young man's mother came to me
again in great distress. I told her finally that I
felt a strong repugnance to returning again and
that I could see no greater prospect promised
from a fresh visit. However I did go again to
see the young man. I drew near to his bed-side,
I spoke to him with all the kindness I could
command; but, all my reasons and reflections
made no impression whatever on his hardened
heart. He persistently replied: "I don't want to,
I don't want to," and turned his back upon me.
Finally in despair of conquering him I said, "My
child, I shall not speak any further of confession,
but before I go I want to say how much pain I
feel over your lot; and I want besides to ask a
little favor of you. I do hope you will not refuse
me because I know after all that you have not
parted wholly with your christian sentiments.
Remember that the Blessed Virgin is our Mother
and the Refuge of Sinners: Come, join with me
in reciting five Ave Marias." The young man
grew silent and thoughtful. After a while he
said in the coldest manner, "Very well, I shall
follow you." We proceeded at once to say the
five Ave Marias, and who would believe, as we
were finishing the fifth Ave he begged aloud to
have his confession heard. There and then he

confessed his sins with the greatest sincerity and fervor. It is impossible to express the feelings of gratitude which he felt and expressed afterward toward Our Lord Jesus Christ and the Blessed Virgin. (Messager du Cœur du Jesu No. de Mai, 1878 p. 573.)

RESOLVE :

I SHALL have a never-dying trust in the Heavenly Mother, now and at the hour of my death, as the spouse of Christ, Holy Church, teaches me.

PRAYER :

O GOD, Who didst give unto mankind a Mother to love them, and especially to the christian world, with a new title to endear her to such as confess the Holy Name, grant us grace to be sensible of the meaning of Mary's Motherhood, and in life and death, in sorrow and sin, to cherish undying trust in her power and her willingness to aid us on to forgiveness, perseverance, and life ever-lasting. Through Jesus Christ Our Lord.

CHAPTER XXIII.

OUR DUTY AS CHILDREN OF MARY.

Is our duty to our Heavenly Mother, indeed, fully done, if left to consist in mere speculative attachment, or restricted to barren sentiment? To profess her and to think kindly of her, is, indeed, commendable; and yet, unless this sentiment should proceed farther onward, and shoot forth, develop and grow into action, and a conduct in keeping with our profession of the lips, ours is far from true, honorable, and complete devotion to our Mother in heaven. And if such a barren scheme of piety be not in truth entirely at fault, it falls within the nearest possibility and juxtaposition to an unsatisfactory thing which one may imagine. Let us demonstrate : Children, if they are judged by what they say of themselves, or should be accounted according to the weight of their own tongue-evidence, are seldom anything but good children. But are they such in the light of fact, in truth or conduct?—"You honor Me with your tongues, but your hearts are far from Me." Is their life an honorable reflection on their parentage? Are they indeed, before faith or reason, faultless children? Do they utter the truth when they say they are children, if, by their wicked life, they torture a mother's heart, grizzle her locks, and hasten her to an untimely grave? Are they children more than in name, who lie and deceive, or steal, or make use of scurrilous and unclean words, or cultivate undignified company, or even if they do not fail in all or the most of these things, fail in one of these points when they know they disobey their parents, and when they know that their malicious defiance or careless disregard of a mother's counsels, framed upon and delivered with that one deep love that is peculiar to her, will make her days full of bitterness and her nights full of misery, teeming with anguish, void of rest and slumber? Is it true that there can be love where there is no sacrifice? It is not true. Children who will not retrench their wicked pleasures, children who do not choose to forego their lawless satisfactions, where they know their conduct brings bitter pangs and weary nights to loving mothers, who bore them in pain and mother's pride, are selfish. In name they are children; in action they are matricides. Sorrow, repentance and tears, will obliterate the blot upon their childship, long after the flowers have withered on the graves of the mothers whose hearts they had broken, but it is still true that actions tell for true sonship, and not empty words. Which is to be admired? Which the true son? The son who toils day after day, lives up to his faith, accomplishes all his duties, makes every sacrifice, supports and comforts his poor, aged mother, or the conceited and selfish dolt of a fellow that loafs and debauches, and is the crucifixion of his devoted parent? The answer goes without saying. The one is a son, the other is a brute. The one creature on earth that loves us for our own sake is she: and, yet, the mother is most often the victim of the child's forgetfulness and ingratitude. Is this so in the case of our Heavenly Mother and us, her children? Mary has brought us forth to the life of grace. She watches over us and guards us from peril; she, as we know from the saints, softens the Father's heart toward us; she shows herself ever to be tenderness toward us. Yes, indeed, Mary is our Mother. The world views, aye, stands aghast, at the courageous, lasting attachment of a mother to an ingrate, a vicious, malignant offspring. The world does not understand the mother's untiring devotion to brutish, selfish children, nor comprehend her undying forbearance; because the world at large does not, neither is it given to all to understand love: The charm of the mother, her secret is love: "And He was subject to them." He never disobeyed. Here is the child's duty to his mother accomplished by the Son of man. Holy Scripture makes the point of insisting upon the fact that Our Lord was a real Son, and conformed to all His duties as such. Moreover, we cannot but believe that in this duty, as in all the other functions in life, He was Jesus, the Model. Now a child's duty is, as all agree, to respect,

love, obey and assist a parent.   "Unless you be
as one of these little ones, ye cannot enter the
kingdom of heaven."   We, too, must be children
of Mary, imitating Jesus, her first-born, in His
grand obedience to Mary, His Mother and ours.
We must respect her ; and, this all happens as long
as we are found respecting God, to the extent
that our fear of Him will prevent us from offending Him.   It is true, we cannot offer our Mother
assistance like our Divine Brother, but we can
comfort her by a good life.   When by sin we dis-
please God, we, at the same time, so to speak,
afflict her Mother's heart: "Behold what manner
of charity the Father hath bestowed upon us,
that we should be the sons of God." (I John iii.
1.   If our life be so ruled, that we are in our
conduct worthy sons of God, it must follow as a
consequence, that we shall walk as children of
Mary, denoting with our bearing before men, our
noble family and exalted lineage.   The providence of God has effected, in the nature of the
child's disposition, an admirable balance, lest any
one particular sentiment should deform the whole
by too great preponderance.   Children respect
and fear the father.   His strength and stern ways
are like the frontiers of his love.   The one pre-
dominant but not too preclusive idea of a mother,
the all-absorbing sentiment of the child toward
the mother, is love.   First, last and always, the
child loves its mother.   Our Lord took human
nature in its healthy characteristics. He loved His

Mother, like a real boy loves his mother; and we
must imitate Our Lord in all things, His virtues,
His loves and all. So, as children of Mary we
must love her. And what a beautiful Mother we
are called upon to love! She brings us into life
and rejoices in her large family; she never finds
us an encumbrance or a barrier to ambitions, especially to such as unsuit woman for domesticity.
Mary is a Mother—that thing which we all not
only respect and admire, but love wherever we
see it. Alas, some modern women, losing their
nature and misconstruing their mission, deviate
from their own sphere, and become neither man
nor woman, but a pitiable and often times hideous incongruity. Would that such would turn to
Our Lady for a pattern! Mary, I repeat, rejoices
in the number of her children; she has room in
her great, Immaculate Heart for the whole world;
she sets no obstacles in the way of our existence,
but accepts the great Motherhood of us all with
its cares and consequences, and is in the fullest
sympathy with her mission, that comprehends
the Motherhood of all mankind. "Be it done unto me according to Thy Word."

There before the first altar, erected to Jesus
Christ,—the Cross; within the great deep and
dense shadow of the Master's death; there, amid
that bloody scene of murder and ribaldry, the mystic
marriage to the Saviour and the mystic birth are
accomplished—"Behold thy Son!" For a wedding
ring our Mother received a band of sorrows set

with a sparkling gem of hope, and for her neck a chain of dolors brought around and fastened over the heart with a sword that sank into her bosom. She plighted her troth for ever; when the tomb should claim the spiritual Father of the christian family she would care for His children. When, at last, she, too, was to pass away, from the stars above she would love, nourish, guide, and protect God's children and her own. Is there a heart on earth that cannot or shall not admire, honor love and obey the Bride of God, and the Mother at Calvary? Since now we love Mary we must look upon her as a model. We must imitate her. Many earthly mothers make sad models for imitation. They tell their young to be good, patient, pure, humble, mortified and the rest, and then their pernicious example gives the lie to their tongues. But actions speak more forcibly than any word-advice. A parent's words will die; his or her example, good or bad, will live after to help his or her children to good or to encourage them to evil. Mary is a perfect model of a mother. Our imitation of her, in which after all consists the final result of Mary-cult is to bring forth Jesus Christ in our hearts; to find Our Lord through Mary His great Mother; to follow and cling to him in the dark hours of temptation and to die for Him,—yes, die for Him, not indeed to this material world which men call death, but to our passions, our vices, and faults, which christians call death. "If any man will come after Me, let him take up his Cross and follow Me." "All they who strive," says Venerable Bède, "to conceive and bring forth the Divine Lord in their own heart through faith, and endeavor to keep it there, must do so in suffering." "In sorrow shalt thou bring forth," said the wrathful God. Suffering offers the only passage into life. It was so with Our Lord, it was Mary's lot and it shall be ours if we are really children of Mary and are really saving our soul. It will bear repetition; that when a life is smooth, without obstacles, void of sufferings and humiliations, such a life is not a life that one may say with confidence is destined to be crowned with salvation.

THOUGHT:

I MUST love, obey and imitate my mother in heaven, and this I am doing as long, but only as long, as I am disposed to suffer all things in order to preserve the grace of God in my soul, therefore I shall love the sufferings and humiliations God sends me.

ILLUSTRATION:

ST. BRIGITTE'S son had departed for the wars, and during his absence abroad died. The news of his death threw the soul of his saintly mother into a state of great anxiety. The excitement of war, the great variety of characters one must meet in the line, the characteristic chivalry of military persons, so often found adapted to romance rather than religion, the spirit of comraderie,

most particularly in seasons of victory, are not
calculated, when viewed in the ensemble, to afford
a young soldier's mother peace of mind concerning the state of a son's soul, when he dies away
from her side. It is, indeed, true, that a man
can be a saint in any station of life to which it
has pleased God to call him; that he has graces
adequate and judiciously adapted to his position.
Ignatius had been a soldier, and before him Sebastian, the noble Sebastian who died so splendidly
for the faith. It is folly to believe that God does
not wish a soldier's, or a sailor's, or any other
man's soul to be saved, as well as he wishes
yours, or my own, or any other man's; or that he
puts us in a sphere, without giving us all that is
necessary to get on well in it, and be saints. We
hear so much from one-sided people, who are
continually talking about this or that being a
more secure state of life, that the rest of the world
are led to believe that their prospect of salvation
is gloomy. This cannot be said in so general and
absolute a way. The state of life to which a man
may be called, is the one secure way for him.
If there are perils God is with one. This view of
things must be entertained by all such as would
feel happy in knowing that they are doing God's
will; that this is 'their' highest perfection, and
that God is pleased with them, inasmuch as they
are doing His will. God takes into consideration
the situation in which we are placed, and will adjust His judgments to our environment. God is

larger than man, and if He is more just He is
more loving, and will be faithful to us. God
chooses the state of life we are in. Our judgment
will be shaped by the manner of our life in that
state. Assuming that man has embraced the
state he felt God called him to, one is accountable
to God not for his state, but for his life in that
state. Let us then serve God faithfully wherever
we may be. This is our duty. Let us repeat
that mothers cannot be wiser than to train their
little ones up to a burning confidence in Mary,
from the beginning. The sweetness, love, goodness and strength of Our Lady impresses a man's
heart, and when this devotion is distinctly associ-
ated with childhood and home, the morning and
evening prayers at the mother's knee, the hymns,
processions and feasts in her honor, all these have
a claim and special grace to touch the hearts of
men, hardened though they be by this world's
selfishness and reverses; these serve to bring
back the warmth of the old fireside, and to revive
the sweet fragrance of innocence and early piety.
The thought of a mother is so knitted to love,
tenderness, unselfishness, that the very idea
merits for her a world of power to attract men's
souls to God. It may seem too human, but it is
a fact, that devotion toward our Heavenly Mother,
awakens in us a knightly feeling, a grand, pure
chivalry. The gentleness of this superb creature,
the motherliness and life-long conviction of her
love for us, and pure, unselfish interest in our

welfare, must prove a human excitant of honor and gratitude that easily develops into full-bloom conversion of a man's heart to God. All this is implied in the primitive fact that God has given Mary to us, and for that reason she should be a great weapon in the great war of salvation. Then again it seems to be human in us not to offend a woman so easily as a man, and whilst in itself it is infinitely more grievous and reprehensible to offend Our Lord than Mary, yet a merciful God has taken advantage of our disposition to bring us to love Him and refrain from offending Him, through the thought of the Great Woman Mary: "Son, behold thy Mother." The following story exemplifies this: St. Brigitte, distressed over her son's death, came by a vision that showed her the scene of judgment, which revealed the Sovereign Judge with Our Lady by His side. The devil appeared before the Judge and made this plea before Our Lord: "Thy Mother hath wronged me in two ways. On the eve of the young man's death she made her appearance in the death-chamber, and during his agony held me at bay, so that I could not tempt him. Again, when as an officer of Justice, I should have the young man's soul before Thy tribunal with charges I had to prefer against him, behold, Thy Mother catches him up in her arms and brings the soul to judgment. These two great wrongs have I suffered at her hands; and it is only right that Thou shouldst give me redress,

o

and command the soul to re-inhabit the flesh and resume its life again."

When the evil spirit had finished his plea, the Mother of God arose and said: "Though the demon is the father of untruth I must allow he has just spoken the truth in this case. But Charles served me all his life and had the disposition, if need had been, to lay down his life for me; so I, in turn, have brought special help to his death-bed and judgment." After Our Lady had said this, Our Lord spoke up: "My Mother," said He, " rules here as queen and sovereign in My kingdom; and, she may, according to her good will and pleasure, issue dispensation in the matter of My laws. Under the circumstances she was perfectly right in what she did inasmuch as she acted wholly within her powers." With a stern command the Judge imposed silence upon the evil spirit and he vanished from the scene. The vision ended with this, leaving in its wake the sweet consolation to the saint of knowing that her son was saved, whilst it created the obligation on her part of praise and thanks to the powerful advocate and patroness of mankind in heaven and on earth, and of adoration of the tender mercies of God, Who desireth not the death of the sinner but that he should live and have life.

RESOLVE:

I SHALL pray to Our Lady, spouse of St. Joseph, to obtain for me a happy death, that is, one in the grace of Her Son.

PRAYER:

GRANT us, O God, a becoming mind and heart toward Thy incomparable Mother to the end that, loving and serving her sweetly in life, we may participate and ultimately enjoy in death the power of her arm against the spirits of evil that rally round the death-bed to make a last final assault, and that we may die in peace, through Jesus Christ, Our Lord.

CHAPTER XXIV.

MARY AND THE SINNER.

SURELY this is a delicious theme, and, we may say, one that finds in itself the most important application of all that Mary is to us. As a matter of fact, Our Lord came down from heaven for our salvation. This is His first and only purpose. We may say, then, as a matter of fact, that the world would not have had Our Lady had it not been for sin. Happy fault! cries out the Church when the glories of the resurrection remind her of the splendors of Divine Mercy. Yet, Our Lord came to abolish sin, not to encourage it. Our Lady is ours to enable us to avoid sin and to help us to forgiveness upon condition that we shall draw away from our wickedness and turn our hearts from evil to good. "Because for this end thou hast put thy fear in our hearts, to the intent that we shall call upon thy name, and praise thee in our captivity; for we are converted from the iniquity of our fathers who sinned before thee." (Baruch iii. 7).

The sacrament of Penance which brings the Blood of Christ directly to bear upon sore, bleeding and sinful humanity is not an aid or incentive to wickedness; on the contrary, it augments one's sinfulness were one to sin the more easily because

he may be so easily forgiven. Our Lord is first
and above all things Saviour; and, Our Lady is
first and above all things the Refuge of Sinners.
In an apostrophe which he addressed to Our
Lady, St. Augustine says : "O Mary, I am exceed-
ingly pleased and dare much. I repeat, I dare
much and my boldness runs high because a
wondrous solidarity unites us. For, after all, it is
for our sakes that thou art what God has made
thee, and as for ourselves, it is through thee we
have become what we are. If, indeed, there had
been no transgression of the law of God on our
part we would have had to do without redemption. And if the redemption had not been
necessary there had not been a necessity that
would bring a Redeemer into the world. To
what end then shouldst thou have become the
Mother of the Saviour, if there were no need of
Salvation?" (Super. Joan Ap. Moralis, lib. iii
Tract. 10).

In the light then of christian philosophy, so
clearly and simply set forth by St. Augustine,
Our Lord and Lady have come into the world for
precisely such as have drawn them thither by
their needs—for sinners. This one observation
offers a devout mind great stores of matter for
his meditation. It will cure the uncharitable and
the spiritually proud of their pharisaism and
obnoxious conceit. Sovereign mystery of heaven,
it is to the dead soul of the sinner that the Great
God of heaven comes, to resurrect it, to vivify it,

sanctify it and save it! Can despair live in the
atmosphere of this glorious thought? The Saviour, the Redeemer, as these hallowed titles imply,
are for such as are to be saved, such as are to be
redeemed,—for sinners. And who is not a sinner? If there be one such, then Jesus Christ has not
come for him. The sinner is the magnet of the
Redeemer. For this reason we find the saints
wooing the Redeemer by the confessions and
avowals of their unworthiness and sinfulness;
for this they uncover their bleeding hearts, their
faults and infirmities. These confessions were
not meant to drive Our Lord, Who is Whiteness
Itself, from their souls; they were not utterances
of despair, but on the contrary a magnet to draw
the Saviour's attention upon themselves, by the
vision of their needs. The more one realizes himself, what he is, and what he is capable of being,
if abandoned to the empire of his own corrupt
heart, the more will he realize that he needs Our
Lord, and that this is a lasting need. The longer
we are good it is none the less a fact that we are
still ourselves and still need Our Lord. This
consciousness of their own needs is a per-
manent law of saints; the foundation of their
sanctity and the merit of their great achievements is that through all progress and growth
they still feel that they need as much, and even
more than ever, the Lord's help upon their needs.
Jesus and Mary are from the first for sinners.
The thought is as deep as God Himself. It offers

fuel for gratitude, that will keep our souls burning
with that sentiment for ever and ever. Our Lady
is destined to do her noble work amongst sinners,
and to be in their midst, like the blue-purple iris
queen-flower in the marshes, scattering its various
beauties upon the fetid and stagnant waters.
Again, who is not a sinner? who does not need
Mary? Are they who thrive to-day upon the
eagle-heights of contemplation made of different
clay and with different natural propensities from
the wretches, who people and haunt the slums?
No. By withdrawing His hand in the one case
and increasing His grace in the other, the situation would be reversed, and the contemplative of
to-day would be the derelict of tomorrow, and
vice-versa. We all remain sinners as long as we
live. We all need Mary, and we need her always.
St. Anselm vivifies the sentiment. "I am convinced," said the saint, "that it is for sinners rather
than for the just that Mary has become the Mother
of God. Her own Son, out of His goodness, has
said that He came not for the just, but for sinners,
and the Apostle says in turn, that Christ came
into the world to save sinners, amongst whom He
looked upon Himself as the chief. So it is indeed
for sinners, that is to say, for myself and my
likes that Mary has become, the Mother of God.
How in the world then does the enormity of my
sins appear as a reason for my not hoping for
pardon, whereas it is precisely to mend my sins
that the wonderful benefit of pardon has been

given me *through Mary*." (Lib. de Excellent. Virginis. C. I.). That there is spiritual pride in the world is to be expected from the native tendency of the soul after the fall and the whisperings of the devil; but, it is to be observed, in the writings of the saints and fathers, that they show, invariably, the real interior conviction of what they themselves are — sinners; and, in this they prove themselves real saints.

"For a just man shall fall seven times." (Prov. xxiv., 16). The day when one fancies he is not as capable as any other man of doing any wrong, were it not for God's gratuitous gifts to him, is a day of triumph for Satan over that man's soul. It is a matter of Catholic theology that when one wishes to bring upon himself those rich graces of Jesus Christ's passion that are peculiar to the Sacrament of Penance, and wishes to have let in upon himself the great volumes of cleansing and sin-preventing graces, he must confess some sin, or the sacrament of penance cannot operate. True, sin remitted once is still sin committed and offers sufficient matter for interminable absolutions, at the same time, it is sin, though it is sin absolved. It is logical for a sinner to have recourse to Our Lady. She came into existence for his sake. She awaits his return to her for help, and she is even anxious, if we may so express it, for the sinner to come back to her. And oh, how much Mary can do for us sinners! Abimelech purloined the spouse of Abraham, and

God said to the King: "Now, therefore, restore
the man his wife, for he is a prophet; and he
shall pray for thee and thou shalt live." (Gen.
xx., 7). Those who offended Job were com-
mended to seek the prayers of the prophet before
God would forgive them—"And My servant Job
shall pray for you: his face I will accept that
folly be not imputed to you." The Lord, also,
was turned at the penance of Job when he
prayed for his friends. (Job xlii., 8-10). The
Israelites, when closely pursued by the Philistines,
asked Samuel to pray for them: "And they said
to Samuel: Cease not to pray to the Lord Our
God, for us, that He may save us out of the hand
of the Philistines,—and Samuel cried to the Lord
for Israel, and the Lord heard him." (I Kings,
vii., 8, 9). It does not shut them out from power
to intercede for us when the saints are gone out
from life. They are strong in death: Jacob
stretched his hands over the heads of Ephraim
and Manasses and said: "Let my name be called
upon them, and the names of my fathers, Abraham
and Isaac." (Gen. xlviii., 16). Let it be understood that Abraham and Isaac were then dead.
Moses sought their power to intercede for his
people: "Remember, Abraham, Isaac and Israel,
thy servants." (Exodus xxxii, 12). Our brethren
who are gone can help us. "O Lord Almighty,"
says the prophet, "the God of Israel, hear now
the prayer of the dead of Israel." (Baruch, ch.
iii., 4). If the living and the dead have the power

of helping us with God, we are naturally led to
inquire into the basis of this power. They are
the 'friends' and 'servants' of God. Is it not,
then, correct to allow Our Lady at least as much
as God's other friends and servants? And is it,
indeed, as so many sectaries insinuate, superstition to accord more power to the 'Mother' than
to the 'friend,' 'minister,' or 'servant?' We are
all sinners. Mary is for us, and no one has such
power to help us as she. This is the will of God,
and whilst the character and works of intercessors,
and even of our Mother, are motives to prompt
heaven to grant grace and forgiveness, the Lord
Himself is the original and primary source of all,
and it is always understood that it is His mercy
that yields to the prayer: "Hear, O Lord, and
have mercy, for Thou art a merciful God, and
have pity on us; for we have sinned before Thee."
(Baruch, iii., 2).

THOUGHT:

I AM a sinner, therefore I need Mary. I am a
greater sinner, and therefore have a greater need
of Our Lady: I am the chief of sinners like
Saul, who became Paul, therefore I, above all,
have need of Mary.

ILLUSTRATION:

THE Rev. Father Clement, a priest distinguished
for his great eloquence, and at the same time his
indefatigable zeal and piety, was, by the providence
of God, called to the bed-side of a young man who

was stricken with apoplexy. This fatal disease smites with the quickness of a thunderbolt and leaves its victim's mind a blank. This was so in the present instance. The good priest had run upon the call with fleetness, but of course he found the stricken man unconscious. The call had come in the early morning and the good priest, who loved each one of his flock as his only child, and lavished his whole soul upon each one, lost no time but hurried back to the church in order to celebrate a Votive Mass in honor of the Blessed Virgin for the benefit of the sick man. Father Clement was one of those lofty, ardent, self-sacrificing priests who love with their whole might, a priest such as the faithful love, whom the poor and sick call in truth their father, who lives poor, and dies poor, an Alter-Christus. When a priest like Father Clement, a man of God, after his own heart, mounts the altar, stands before the throne of grace with Jesus Christ in his hands, there is no favor the Father of Mercies will not grant him. Father Clement had not quite finished the Mass when a message was conveyed to him that consciousness had returned to the sick man. The zealous priest, appreciating the value of an immortal soul, again lost no time in getting back to the sick room. He found the young man in possession of his senses and he rejoiced at this, but far more did his own priestly soul rejoice within him when he saw the young man manifesting the greatest sorrow for his sins, showing deep compunction and shedding tears of repentance. What was wrought in the invalid was indeed extraordinary, for, he generously tendered his life to God in expiation of his past. He proceeded at once with his confession and received the Lord's Body and Blood together with the last anointing in the most edifying dispositions. The young man's life had been disorderly, and the world around had known of his way of living. He was looked upon in general as a man who, whilst he professed Catholicity, was in his practical life more like the pagans. These circumstances made good Father Clement piously curious to know the singular meaning displayed in the young man's regaining his senses, which enabled him to make his peace with God, when the very jaws of eternal death were about to close upon him. " How does it come to pass, my child," said the good Father, "that God has wrought this wonder in your behalf?" With quick, rapid pulse, panting chest, with a voice broken with sobs, the young man replied—"Alas, my dear Father, I can only lay the grace at the door of God's mercy, softened, no doubt, as it has been, by your own excellent prayers together with the ardent prayers of my good and dear mother, who is dead. When my dear mother was in her dying moments she called me to her bedside and communicated to me the alarms she felt over the dangers that were before me in life: She said moreover—'My child, all my comfort is that I leave you in the care and protection of the Blessed Virgin, the Immaculate Mother of God. Promise me, my child, one thing I have to ask of you : promise it as a proof of your love for me. It is not much and it will not cost you much, dearest. Find time, some way, each day to say your beads.' Father, I made that promise to my mother and, believe me, I kept it. During these eighteen years I have not failed to say my Rosary every day, and in this consisted all my religious practices and devotions. As for any other religious thing, I have simply done nothing."

When he had told his story he grew suddenly weak and speechless. The noble hearted priest, overwhelmed with emotion, knelt by the bedside. He prayed in thanksgiving to the mercies of God and the glories of the great Queen Mother. With tears of love, he watched and prayed during the agony of the dying young man. He saw that soul snatched by Mary's hand from the gates of hell, cleansed and made innocent again. He sees it now leave the body to go to his Father in heaven and to the Immaculate Mother, the lustre of whose glory he was to intensify by adding a new saint to heaven. When the soul had left the body of the young man, Father Clement withdrew from the chamber of death, bewildered, yet happy, and glorifying in his heart the marvels of God's mercy and the power Jesus has imparted to His august Mother. From that day, the good

priest's voice was never silent on the greatness
and power of the Mother of God.   Wherever and
whenever he had the opportunity Fr. Clement
extolled the Rosary; and he registered a promise,
besides, to promulgate it as long as he had a
heart to love and a tongue to speak.

RESOLVE :

I SHALL love the Rosary: I shall be generous
and find time each day to recite the beads.   I
know I waste enough time each day which would
be sufficient for the accomplishment of this act of
piety, and which I could and shall profitably
employ hereafter in saying the whole or a decade
or two of the Rosary.

PRAYER :

GRANT, O Lord, that we poor miserable sinners
may have the wisdom and grace to carry the
Rosary about with us, as a sword of salvation
hung by our side, unsheathed, or in the scabbard
of our pocket, and to recite it daily, walking,
standing or otherwise, as we may, so as it shall
be to us not as the rusty weapon, but a bright,
sharp blade made so by use; whose flash of steel
shall hurl terrors at our triple foe,—the world,
the flesh and the devil, and cleave through them
a path of salvation for our souls.   Through
Jesus Christ, Our Lord.

CHAPTER XXV.

MARY'S SECRET.

THE devout are of the conviction that Our Lady was never refused aught, and furthermore, that she never would be. The Church calls Mary the Seat of Wisdom, and we, therefore, have no alternative but to look upon Our Lady as being wise. Accordingly, we are to presume that she knew the nature and extent of her own powers; and, with this fact clearly before us, it is not in reason for us to suppose that anything which God could not allow with consistency would ever become the burden of her suppliant lips. Saints, in the latitude of their powers, are more or less restricted to what is designated the 'ordinary' power of God: but it is no exaggeration to say that Mary can do all things she wishes, without restriction, as we see from the fact that God went so far as to modify the order of His providence at Cana, upon her request; because, she will only wish what is obtainable, being, as the Church justly styles her, 'Virgin Most Prudent.' "Mary's credit is so great with God," says St. Anselm, "that there is no wish of hers but shall be executed." (Orat, xlvi, ad Vir. Mar.). "If we could suppose," says Suarez, "the case where the Blessed Virgin were to make a request, and that the whole court of heaven were lined up in opposition to her, just as we find the case, in Daniel, of one angel resisting another, Mary's prayer would prevail over theirs: Hers would contain a value and efficacy out-valuing the united prayers of all the saints." (Suarez iii, p. 3, disp. 23, sec. 2). Other bases of Mary's tremendous power are indicated, such, for example, as her virtues and merits; her unique daughtership; that she is the oldest daughter of God—going before all mankind in predestination and election at the instance of her superior perfection, though others were born before her; or again, that she is the Spouse of the Holy Ghost. The following specimen conveys the impression of some, anent the chief source of Mary's power to intercede for us: "When God suffers violence to be done Him, and does the will of man, after the manner of Joshua in arresting the course of the sun, 'the Lord obeying the voice of man.'" (Joshua x, 14). He does not forfeit any of His power when He yields to the breadth of His goodness: 'He will do always the will of such as fear Him,' is the excellent assurance we have of the Psalmist. And after all, it is as much the property of goodness, when it is found linked to power, to give way before timid weakness and humility, as it is to make a firm stand against pride, and to squelch rebellion. This law is both instinctive and universal. It supplies power to every kind of weakness. It balances the world; and, we find that it reaches even as far as the very brute. This law is the mark of God put upon all things, and in religion God should furnish our eyes with a most perfect model of this law. In point of fact, He has done this very thing when He displayed the strength of His power by the weakness and nothingness of the means He employed, as we find it in the triumph of His cross, by the reign of the 'Lamb,' Ruler of the world, and as we find it in the word of St. Paul, who gives us all christianity in a nut-shell: "When I am weak, then I am powerful." (II. Cor xii, 10). To be in harmony with this law, the highest power and the sovereign empire in the sight of God are to be found in the hands of the weakest and humblest beings. "One is my dove, terrible as an army set in battle array." (Cant. vi, 3, 8, 9). "Since now Mary is the most delicate, the humblest of creatures, the Creator ought to be, in a way, under Her command. She herself has admirably intoned the song: He hath put down the mighty from their seat and hath exalted the humble. He hath regarded the humility of His handmaid: Behold, from henceforth all generations shall call me blessed. For He that is mighty hath done great things to me." (La Vierge Marie dans le Plan Divin, Liv. iii, ch. 5).

As the beloved of the Father and His only daughter, God cannot resist Our Lady. If indeed, when all others had pleaded for this in

P

vain, the wise woman of Thecua exercised that
great power over the bosom of David and
brought with her womanly pleading the angry
king to forgive and recall his fugitive son Absolom,
we may well believe that Our Lady's face of
sorrow, and her sweet, slender, grief-worn body,
after long mourning, will not plead in vain. Not
for a husband, nor a son slain by a son, mourned
she, the world's Mother, but a Divine Son struck
down in innocenee by His own Father, and taken
by bloody violence from His Mother's arms. If
David heard the widow of Thecua, surely the
Lord will hear her who stood at the foot of the
cross. When He is, as it were, deaf to all others,
the mourning Mother of the slain Jesus will move
the heart of God in behalf of us poor, exiled
children of earth: "Why hath the king spoken
this word, to sin, and not bring home again
his own exile." (II Kings Ch. xxiv. 13).
And how the Salve Regina accords with this
prayer of the widow of Thecua! 'To thee do we
cry, poor exiled children of Eve.' "Mary has
but to ask and her Son will grant what she asks,"
says St. Bernard. "The prayer of Deipara has in
it the power of command," says St. Antoninus.
Yet far deeper than all other reasons for this
power of Mary is a christian philosophy which
Nicolas has developed for us and which moves so
smoothly along with the current of St. Paul's
thought, with that of David, the prophet, and,
most of all, with Our Lady's own confession

touching the secret of her greatness and power before God. It is the law of God to resist the proud. So has it been written. That pride goes before a fall has entered into the very tissue of the world's moral standards of judgment. No matter what one may have to offer, the human family is so constructed that it most loathes to have anything at the hands of the high-minded and stiff-necked. If this is the law, it follows that it is, on the other hand, in human nature to help the lowly and weak, to smooth their path, or to receive, at their hands, without natural resistance, the knowledge, advice, help or whatever else they may have to offer us; and, we may be sure, from what has been revealed to us in Holy Scripture, that lowliness of spirit must go before the blessings of God, and that the blessings of God will surely follow by the laws of heaven. If the world then has no advocate so powerful before the throne of God as Mary, the reason is that there is no creature that ever was so thoroughly lowly, so self-unconscious, so exquisitely timid, so profoundly humble as she. At the same time, however, as we place the great secret of Mary's power in this point, we do not mean to exclude other sources of her strength. Among such is her spouse-ship with the Holy Spirit.

This of course supplies her with great power. We all know that a queen-wife has a certain authority over her consort. An example of this is witnessed in the mighty influence which Queen

Esther exerted over the heart of Assuerus. The title of spouse has in it something more than sentiment. Whether king or not, a husband cannot be indifferent to his wife's wishes, and where they are just, or, at least, are not unjust, he feels himself more or less under obligation as a husband to acquiesce in his wife's will and pleasure. I say where a spouse wills what is just and not, as it is in many cases, when a wife's animosities enkindle feuds and troubles for her husband which serve no just or wise end, but only gratify a woman's spite—which history proves she is very capable of entertaining. Our Lady is and must be an ideal spouse, worthy as creatures may be of her most wonderful relation to the Third Person of the Blessed Trinity. The Holy Spirit will not be anything but a divine, and as such an ideal consort. "The spirit of the Most-high shall overshadow thee." Therefore we must expect the Third Person of the Blessed Trinity to be disposed more or less on account of His relations with Mary to heed the requests of His Immaculate Spouse. When, however, all other titles, virtues, merits, and prerogatives ripen into the incomprehensible dignity of the Divine Motherhood, we may well say that Mary's prayers, in power and efficacy, are promoted into the realm of command.

THOUGHT:

INSTINCT in man and brute teaches, with faith, that the high shall be brought low and the lowly raised. Viewed from this standpoint of Christian philosophy, as well as from all others, Mary has the most power before God of any creature, so, let us pray through Mary.

ILLUSTRATION:

To find honor with God, to be the recipients of His graces, and, all the while, preserve ourselves in a true spirit of lowliness and in a sense of our own nothingness is a wonderful behavior. It is, we may say, easier to know God, that is to say in so far as man may know Him, than to know one's self; because, it is pleasant to know God and mightily disagreeable to know one's self. It is for this reason that we find such difficulty in knowing ourselves. Our pride balks at it; our self-love is hurt by it. St. Francis of Assisi used frequently to say: "My God, my God! Who art Thou, and who am I?" In order that they would not get beside themselves over the graces and favors He has given the saints, God invariably suffers them to remain the victims of some imperfections, or indeed pride would prove too much for them. If nothing God does to us, or we ourselves do, can ever seduce us from our true, inward knowledge and consciousness of what we are, we have, indeed, made great strides heavenward. When God honors us with graces and virtues we find in this a true test if we are honest and true to God, or whether treason and dishonesty do not still lurk within us. From this we learn if we are saints or demons.

The great charm of saints is that with their
poverty, chastity, mortification, charity, and all
the rest, they are still honest and true to God,
that is, lowly in spirit.   This is the dividing line
of saints and devils.   This noble virtue is the ring
that denotes the true metal.   We choose an example of this true spirit in Frances de Bermond,
who, known in religious life as Mother Jesus-
Mary, was selected by God to be the instrument
of His hand in the establishment of the Ursulines
in France.   She was truly a holy woman, for God
favored her abundantly with extraordinary manifestations; and yet nothing whatever appeared
outwardly upon her, either in word or look, or in
any manner that could betray in the least her interior wealth of grace, or her secret manifestations
from God; nor could anything about her create a
suspicion that she looked upon herself as, in herself, anything different from what she always was,
or the rest of the world around her.   When it
came to pass that the nuns found the holy woman
in ecstacy, she used to say upon coming out of
her holy swoon: "O my dear Sisters, you are all
too patient; you should not have to wait here
whilst I am 'sleeping;' you should retire or
awaken me."   Such tact and modesty was indeed
a charming thing, and a sign of true lowliness of
spirit.   Upon an occasion, when she felt obliged
to refuse the daughter of a wicked woman a
place among her pupils at the convent, the mother
of the girl took a turn at abusing the saintly nun

most shockingly. The virago raised her voice to a high pitch, spoke and gesticulated violently, and seasoned her coarse display with ribald and blasphemous observations and epithets. Humility, charity, and their usual attendant, peace, did not forsake the saintly woman. "Thank God," said she to her nuns, "if we are so treated it will make us all the better servants of the Lord." This love of humiliation, as the very name signifies, is what the world cannot understand. The saints know the value of being humbled, that is of being made humble. If we were wise and humbled ourselves, the task of getting the strongest virtue in christianity would not be so painful. It is like the cross, as we are authoritatively assured : If we throw it away we shall have to take up one more heavy. The author of the spiritual combat urges all who desire to be virtuous, to court humiliation, to love and court those people who are disagreeable and obnoxious to us. Wherever we are, or in whatever sphere of life we may be cast, if we are to be true to God, we must be prepared to accept humiliation. When Mother Jesus-Mary went to Lyons for the purpose of establishing a foundation of her Order in that city, she and her religious were made the butt of .mockery and frequent gibes. "You do well," · said a woman, one day, to the Mother Jesus-Mary, "to leave Avignon and come to Lyons. Here you can get back on to the right road again, for of course everybody must know of the kind of life you were leading in Avignon where your husband was hanged." "Ah," replied the good nun, with all the sweetness and equanimity imaginable, "it is true, my Spouse was hanged upon a cross." It is needless to say that such wonderful calmness and charity can only spring from a lowly heart, and that the life ornamented by such precious gifts can produce only the most edifying results. When this holy woman had occasion to communicate by letter with a woman of quality, one of her nuns, who happened to be expert in pen-craft, asked if she might not be allowed to write the letter in the good mother's name. The holy woman declined with the observation that this course would draw down upon her praise that was not due to her, and that, moreover, the lady in the case should be made aware of the little capability there was in her of doing anything well. With her religious she was an equal rather than the superior. She was severe only when strict duty demanded it. As she was in earnest in practising the virtue of lowliness of spirit, she tolerated nothing different in the case of her spiritual children. Her ideas on command were both true and humble.

Power did not prove a stumbling block to her profound spirit. The power of command does not come from enmity to those whom we command; the end of government is not to hurt those under us and to make their life harder. So, charity attended the government of Mother Jesus-Mary.

A command is a command when it is delivered
with sweetness just as well as when it is dispensed
in a tone of severity or grumpiness. Authority
must have force and must demand obedience, at any
cost, but force and kindness are sociable elements
in government. Mother Jesus-Mary knew that
her power of command was not given for her own
self-love, an outlet to her own passion and feeling, but for the good of her subjects, hence
lowliness of spirit characterized her reign. Hers
was a true government, and none the less so
because she governed as a mother. As we learn
from St. Teresa, God does not want tyranny.
Our Lord appeared to her and she says: "He
told me to say to them this was tyranny." (Life,
c. xxix. 7. Coleridge, i. Vol. p 93). St. John
Chyrsostom says "it is the rule that they who
abuse authority deserve to be deprived of it."
(Hom. xii. in epist. ad Rom.). When a nun who
had been tendered a charge, alleged her incapacity
for command over others, Mother Jesus-Mary
answered with great force: "Neither do I understand how you should command them; you shall
ask them and they shall be obedient according as
your requests shall take the place of command."
Mother Jesus-Mary only brought out in her life
the virtues of those whose hallowed names she
bore united. She obeyed and ruled like them—
for love and by love. To rulers and subjects
alike the virtues of the Sacred Heart appeal. To be
ever meek and lowly of spirit is the message of

the Sacred Hearts of the Lord and His Mother to
the whole world.

RESOLVE:

I SHALL rule humbly if God lays power upon
me; I shall rule from faith and reason, and not
passion; I shall rule for the ends God has predestinated when. He invested me with power of
authority.   I shall obey and rule for the glory of
God.

PRAYER:

O, GOD, Who knoweth the pride of our bosom
and how self-love adroitly turns Thy gifts into
instruments of ruin, grant us grace always to command with temperance, mildness, and lowliness of
spirit, whilst conserving authority and force; and,
on the other hand, to obey those whom God has
placed over us with alacrity, sweetness and submission, even as Thy Mother both commanded
and obeyed Thyself, finding in the same source,
Thyself, the gift to command and obey. Through
Jesus Christ, Our Lord.

CHAPTER XXVI.

HUMILITY OF MARY.

HUMILITY is the touch-stone of true christian holiness. Upon this ground St. Paul has placed the reason of Our Lord's being raised up. In his epistle to the Phillipians, II Chapter, the apostle says that Jesus Christ 'debased Himself,' that is to say, made Himself of no account. 'Wherefore,' (for this reason) God also hath exalted Him and hath given Him a name which is above all names. The humility of Jesus led to the obedience unto death and the cross. (v. 8). No less is it the humility of the Master that forces every knee in heaven, on earth, and in hell to bend. It is the Lord's humility that compels every tongue to confess that the Lord Jesus is in the glory of the Father. (v. 2). Is it not true that we seek but too often our own glory? God's gifts we boast of at least in thought, and our manner not infrequently conveys the impression that the talents we have, or the virtues we are endowed with, are not so much the fruits of heavenly kindness as the real fact of the matter so distinctly teaches. Pride is robbery, and St. Teresa has most accurately and profoundly defined humility as 'the truth.' The things we do, the good we accomplish, the very virtues, I say, we practise, are

to ourselves as a cause primary and sufficient.
With a certain amount of theoretic sincerity we
commiserate the lack of gifts in others, and acquit
such of so much fault in the matter of talents or
spiritual gifts; we thank God and impute in the
same fashion what we have as coming from God,
but there is a sentiment in the background that
throws a shadow upon the theory. Far and away
within us we are not so true. We take, if not all,
at least a good part of the glory of what we do
and of what we are. 'The glory of God through
me'—we write the 'glory of God' in small letters,
and the 'through me' in capitals; we subordinate
the end to the means. In this we commit robbery. "It was no robbery for Christ to think
Himself the equal of God." (v. 6). We take
the credit of what we are and of what we do,
whereas St. Paul says distinctly: "It is God Who
worketh in you both to 'will' and to 'accomplish' according to His good will." (v. 13). We
do not thank God for our good purposes, our
pious and worthy desires, nor for the means we
have access to, or the success that attends the
execution of our enterprises. "For all seek,"
says St. Paul, "the things that are their own, not
the things that are Jesus Christ's." (v. 21). "We
are ambitious and seek what is not our own."
(St. Paul i, Cor. xiii, 5). What a reproach it is
to be robbers of God! Better far never to have
done than to have done and taken the glory of
our action to ourselves. Our Lord's teaching

surely had a fear back of it, for the Saviour warned, as well as instructed, that "Whosoever shall exalt himself shall be humbled, and he that humbleth himself shall be exalted." (Matt. xxiii, 12). Our Lady could not by any possibility be so humble as Our Lord, because Jesus came down from infinite heights. Never having possibly been so high as God, she could not have come down so great a distance as God. But Our Lady was next to Jesus in humility. When the announcement was made to her by Gabriel did she for an instant get beside herself? Did she forget her creatureship? Did she glorify herself? Did she lose sight of her position before God? The simple, modest words of the wonderful Virgin will tell the whole world the story of the humility of her who was predestinated to be the Mother of God: "Behold the handmaid of the Lord."

Did she attribute the divine vocation to herself? Never for one instant. Mary was calm and exhibited no flurry, no false and pretended humility, no aped surprise. She in no way considered herself. Self was dead. 'I no longer live' was supremely true of her. Did Mary look for the 'accomplishment' which St. Paul has just told us is done in God, to her own purse, so to speak. To look for the means to God is the logical consequence of one's being thoroughly convinced that the affair is originally the will of God and His own work. When we are persuaded that it

is God's work entirely, we very naturally look to
God for help, and we have a very natural and
calm confidence in Him.   Many failures in life
emanate from the fact that people do not see the
will of God in their life, and consequently vacil-
late in half certainties and luke-warm confidence
in their having the means to carry out what they
have in hand.   When a christian knows he is
doing what God has asked him to do, and we
come to consider the infinite resources of God,
the endless treasures of His power, goodness and
mercy, it is difficult to fancy failure a possibility.
Our Lady looked to God for the accomplishment
of the work she humbly saw was God's: "How
shall this be done unto me?"   Surely the temptation to pride offered in Mary's case, is the
greatest that had ever been or could ever be possible in the world.   She was being called to the
highest dignity possible to a creature.   Did Our
Lady persevere in her humility?   When she grew
in the realization of the wonder vouchsafed her,
when the thrill of the conception came upon her
in the peculiar presence and action of the Holy
Ghost, did she forget for one instant Whose work
was being done, or Who was achieving it all?   No.
St. Elizabeth occasioned the reply to this question: "Whence is this to me," said she, "that the
Mother of my Lord should come to me?" (Luke
i, 43).

   St. Elizabeth must have known by inspiration
that Mary was the Mother of the Lord to be

born. She informed her illustrious cousin Mary
of the effects of her presence upon her own
unborn child. "As soon as thy salutation
sounded in my ears, the infant in my womb
leaped for joy" (v. 44). With the same calm
peace the glorious Virgin confesses the wonder:
"My soul doth magnify the Lord."—Yes, what
you say is true, dear cousin! And Our Lady
proceeds to tell how it all came to pass; she tells
how she was selected by God for the work.
Here we find but one thing: We see no record
put forward of glories and perfections, of sacrifices and deeds to which she imputed her
selection. She lays all to one thing: "Because
He hath regarded the humility of His handmaid."
She tells why the whole world will call her
blessed and gives all the credit of it to God:
"For He that is mighty hath done great things
to me." Does she search for her own glory?
She turns attention off from herself and points
to the Author of all so as to direct thither the
streams of praise and glory from the world: "And
Holy is His name." Did she lose herself for
one instant? did she grow arrogant, presumptuous or familiar toward God so as to lose her
humble fear? "His mercy is from generation to
generation to them that fear Him" (v. 50). She
informs us of the basis of election and sounds
the key to the plan and spirit of the mission of
Jesus Christ: "He hath showed might in His
arm; He hath scattered the proud in the conceit

of their heart" (v. 51). Mary responds and
insists on the purpose of God to put down the
mighty from their seat and exalt the humble
(v. 52). Here we contemplate Our Blessed
Lady unveiling before the world the secret of
her exaltation and assuring us in her own words
of the reason why God preferred her above all
other women for the dignity of being His
Mother. Here Our Lady instructs us on the
fundamental spirit which we too ought to cultivate in our life. Mary's one sermon to the world
is upon the necessity of being humble, of
accounting ourselves as nothing and of giving to
God the things that are God's. First and above
all, and at all hazards, let us have lowliness of
spirit whoso, or whereso we may be. St. Bernard
has pitched upon the basis of the great things
wrought in Mary and points it out to us when he
says: "Her purity hath given much delight to
God, but it is by her humility she has deserved
to conceive the Lord."

THOUGHT:

THE one message of Our Lord and of Our Lady
is couched in the Master's own words: "Learn
of Me, because I am meek and humble of heart."
(Matt. xi. 29).

ILLUSTRATION:

THERE is no denying or questioning the saints
understood the meaning of the word: "God re-
sisteth the proud, but giveth grace to the hum-

ble." The stamp of these words is upon all
lives of such as the Church calls saints, though
not upon the lives of all such as the world calls
saints. God can neither deceive nor be deceived ;
but this cannot be said of man. The importance,
moreover, of this sublime truth is fully and above
all other things made to stand out with boldness
in all the teachings of saints. St. Jerome tells
us of St. Paula, a widow, who could point to an
ancestry among the noblest and wealthiest of the
Roman families, as one who had brought, in spite
of her education and lineage, the practise of the
first christian virtue to so high a degree of perfection that she might, for all that appeared in her,
be easily taken for the lowliest of her domestics.
The noble Father assures us that as she stood
with a galaxy of virgins grouped about her, her
dress, her words, her deportment, and everything
about her, was of such a character as would naturally convey the impression that she was lowest in
rank of all present. St. Jerome tells us that she
surpassed all others by virtue of her great humility. So from the very beginning the importance
of this virtue in the real christianity is evident.
Like a golden thread it goes through all the lives
of saints. In the great variety of spirits, designs
and vocations in saints, all have shown perfection
and solidity on this point. Whilst St. Thomas
of Aquin was following his course in theology,
his fellow-students all looked upon his taciturnity
as stupidity. They labelled him the 'dumb ox,'

Q

and the 'great Sicilian ox.' The world since
that time has been made familiar with the beautiful genius of this Giant Doctor. All have since
admired his keen penetration and marvelled at
the great depth of his knowledge and the uniform
soundness of his judgment; and, as we look back
upon the school days of this wonderful Doctor,
we fancy with delight and admiration this prodigy
of wisdom suffering his brethren to do all the
talking, and with exquisite modesty accepting at
their hands the service of rendering the explanation of abstruse things and having it believed by
all about him that he was really obtuse. It
turned out, one day, that a fellow-student, with a
feeling of compassion for the stupid Thomas, un-
dertook to explain the lesson to him. Thomas
listened with the greatest humility and silence.
Duty at last forced him to break the seal of his
lips, and to make the promise of that glory which
he would one day shed upon the kingdom of God
by his glorious writings and his incomparable
learning. Albert the Great, his teacher, ques-
tioned him on some very abstract point and drew
from Thomas a display of intellectual brilliancy
and huge power that fairly flashed like meteors,
electrified his fellows, and inspired his illustrious
preceptor to cry aloud: "We call Thomas the
dumb ox, but he will awaken the universe with
the bellowings of his doctrine."

St. Francis of Assisi cared for this virtue as a
delicate flower, and protected it in his life by every

caution. He appropriated nothing to himself of the things which he did; there was no reserve made for his part in the great things that emblazoned his life. All this is revealed in his answer to a certain religious who was at a loss to know how it came to pass that so many people sought him out and made so much of his counsels as to invariably yield to him. " He Who knows the hidden recesses of the heart," said St. Francis, "needs no assurance that this is not on my account but His own, Whose eye discerns what is good and what is wicked. What man doeth is God's, not his own. Hence all praise should find its way to God." In this conduct St. Francis has bequeathed to his children the legacy that all founders have left with their children — that all should learn of them what they themselves had learned of the Master; namely, to be meek and humble of heart. St. Francis de Sales drew in words a picture for a friend in which he fancied himself upon a scaffold, or again burned at the stake under an unjust verdict and sentence, and finding in the ordeal the keenest delight at parting with both honor and life so as to be made agreeable to God if 'God would only allow it. This saint has left these words on record: "The humble are blest for they shall get securely into port. This beatitude above all others is dear to me and it would be my wish that if on the last day any justice shall be found in me that this shall be kept from the world and known only to

God." So all along the line of saints we find the lesson of Our Lady's Magnificat well acquired and admirably digested in the lives of the chosen of God. David, her kingly and devout ancestor, had founded a house whose chief strength and holiness, from the king himself down to Mary, is set forth all in one word, which shows at once the danger of taking glory unto ourselves, the necessity of its quick and effectual resistance, the pledge of the Lord's assistance and what is, after all, the truth of this whole matter. "Not to us, O Lord, not to us, but to Thy name be glory given."

RESOLVE.

I SHALL welcome, or at least be resigned to the miseries of life, and shall bear with the events, the trials, and even the sinfulness of my life with the view of reaching through them a larger lowliness of spirit.

PRAYER:

O GOD, Who hast said that Thou shalt save an humble people (Psalm 27-28) and with Thine own lips hast announced the blessedness of the poor in spirit (Mat. 3) impart to us in Thy mercy, the grace of humility so that we may will to be with Blessed de la Colombiere whatever will promote this virtue in us and to renounce all graces that would deprive us of the charm and glory of this, the virtue of Thy Sacred Heart, O Thou Who livest and reignest, One God, forever and ever. Amen.

CHAPTER XXVII.

OUR LADY, MODEL OF THE LOWLY AND REFUGE OF THE PROUD.

TRULY is Our Lady a benison to all mankind, not alone by the force of what one might call her official capacity as an instrument in the incarnation, or the formal fellowship in the redeeming operation, but by her own personality, the sweet, delicate low-liness, the power and inspiration of her precious and noble example. The world knows, especially the christian world, the dangers of high-minded-ness. Upon this point there seems to be no dis-pute. The only question is centred in the point of establishing in any one case the fact. Upon this, as all other points of life, men are more or less and to a greater or lesser degree deluded. If we are convinced that a certain other man is really proud we sigh, shrug our shoulders, shake our heads, and prophesy, or at least entertain strong suspicions on his perseverance. Any catastrophe that overtakes him brings no sur-prise to such as have known his inordinate self-sufficiency. We do not see it in ourselves, though it is possible that we ourselves are co-equally delinquent on the point, only we fail to see our-selves as others see us. Our building seems fireproof, waterproof and storm-proof, and before

we know, a crash comes and then we investigate
and find the truth. The *Spiritual Combat*, that
noble book that St. Francis de Sales always carried about with him, speaks to this purpose in the
following words: " Self-knowledge is clearly
needful to all who desire to be united to the
Supreme Light and uncreated Truth ; and the
Divine Clemency often makes use of the fall of
proud and presumptuous men to lead to it;
justly suffering them to fall into some faults which
they trusted to avoid by their own strength that
they may learn to know and absolutely distrust
themselves. Our Lord is not, however, wont to
use so severe a method until those more gracious
means of which we have spoken have failed to
work the cure designed by His divine mercies.
He permits a man to fall more or less deeply in
proportion to his pride and self-esteem ; so that
if there were no presumption (as in the case of
the Blessed Virgin Mary) there would be no fall.
Therefore, whensoever thou shalt fall, take refuge
at once in humble self-knowledge, and beseech
the Lord with urgent entreaties to give thee light
truly to know thyself, and entire self-distrust lest
thou shouldst fall again perhaps into deeper perdition." (Spiritual Combat, Co. ii). It is not too
sweeping to affirm that the root of all disorders,
of confirmed habitudinarians, of drunkards and
licentious men, is arrogant self-sufficiency. The
independence of counsel, and contumacious self-
opinionatedness of victims of these brutal vices

is proverbial.   Why should so many bright men become notorious for excesses which, if not continuous, are at least periodic?   The probability, and we may say the certainty, is that they are guilty of pride, and are visited by the fatherly vengeance of God, Who seeks to check this internal disorder and lead such men to better know themselves.   Men who, to our seeming, were very pillars of granite, have been seen to fall, and by the shock have been made aware for the first time of that truth which God spoke in the very beginning: " Remember, 'man, for dust thou art." Pausing amid the ruins of his former greatness, amid the thousand splinters and broken timber, the twisted rods of his dignity and once admirable character ; gazing upon the relics of his once honored name, the levite, the statesman, the professor, the inventor says to himself with a dejected look, a despairing, willowy fall of the head and a sad, tearful voice :   " Aye — ' Dust thou art.' "

In Church and State minds have there been which could not brook the tameness of an humble life ; they have let out their reins upon ambitions, till these, like furious steeds, have defied control, drawn their riders on, and dashed them finally to pieces over deep and fatal precipices.   They could not see others preferred before them ; they could not bend to Providence that rules all.   They did not stop to meditate on the character, life and teachings of Jesus Christ.   Were they as bright as Our Lord ? — They hadn't thought.   Had they such worthiness and virtues as the Master? Had they so noble lineage? If they only had known how to suffer others who were, let it be granted, inferior to themselves in talent or otherwise, to be esteemed above them, they would have been honored by God for that noble simplicity of their character, admired by posterity for the granite strength of their virtues, and lived in the history of christian art by the recollection of their holiness. In one word they would have been saints. "Be ye holy" — God gives and God takes away. God gives talents to us for employment, and then again tries us by asking us to bear up with their disuse — which is not abuse, but in this case, the best possible use — from illness or disability, through dearth of opportunity or appreciation, which, in the mysterious course of Providence, always loving and wise, is shown to be of life's sad truths, stranger than fiction — "Open Thou my eyes, and I will consider the wondrous things of Thy law." (Ps. cxviii. ii.). Proud men complain. They are not treated as they deserve. Others get on by some secret influence or 'fate,' as worldlings call it, who have not half the brains. Others are better known, and are brought out and made much of, with only a third of the ability; others are summoned to positions who have not half the power of adjustment; others have gotten on by cavil, by over-shrewdness, and by resorting to measures if not foul, at least such as a well-bred, dignified gentleman would not stoop to employ,

as we find the case often in political life. These
are the soliloquies of the proud man. He forgets
that we are more than Ethnicians; that we are
christians, and must be prepared to suffer even
injustices. Granting all that he alleges, and it
cannot always be denied but what he says is often
so, still we must bend in all things to God, adore
His wisdom, and if, indeed, others are in high
positions, and we get no credit for all that we are
or have done: "Blessed are those who suffer for
justice sake." Eternity is to come. No man can
stop us from becoming saints, and if we are, then
what matters it if we lose the clap of hands that
will wrinkle, wither and crumble, or the praise of
those who cannot reward us? The holier has the
better in life's struggle, and the possibilities of
holiness are not restricted to person, position or
place. To be holy is the highest any one can
reach, and God is the only true Riches, Honor
and Glory. The highest in the esteem of God, is
he who does best God's will in all things that oc-
cur in life, by accepting God's providence, by
bearing with its pains, not grumbling over its dis-
appointments—which would be an incongruity
inasmuch as there is neither reason nor rhyme in
anything that God does not wish: "I have de-
lighted in the way of Thy testimonials as in all
riches." (Ps. cxviii. 14). The very things we
complain of are the same that fashion us for eternal life. All men must be tried; God sifts,
humbles, purifies and instructs. Great qualities

and high endowments are for God's sake. The high-minded may forget this. They may look upon all things from their own point of view as for themselves. Their own self-will, which is the essence of pride, constitutes their law: "The Lord hath made all things for Himself. The proud man is an abomination to the Lord." (Prov. xvi. 4, 5). "Thou hast rebuked the proud; they are cursed who decline from Thy commandments." (Ps. cxviii. 21).

Unless we submit to those ' wondrous things of God's law,' become resigned to thwarted ambitions, the dissatisfactoriness of our part in life, to the seemingly wasted opportunities, and so on down the line of human possibilities, our pride is not overcome. The providence of God is, from end to end, disposing all things sweetly if we do not impede its action. God permits strange and sometimes awful things, but His eye is fixed upon you. He has not forgotten you. He knows everything. "Why sayest thou, O Jacob, and speakest, O Israel: My way is hid from the Lord; and my judgment is passed over from my God." (Is. xl, 27). The proud must not lose courage: Neither ought the world to crush them, but rather help them to overcome themselves. Let us go to Mary to help us; to aid us in this matter before Our Lord: "O Most Blessed Humility of Mary!" cries out St. Augustine, "it has placed mankind in the possession of Our Lord. It is this that brought to life those who lay dead, this that has renewed the skies, purified the world, opened up paradise, and delivered souls out of the darkness of hell." (Serm. 35 de sanct.). The victims of pride should seek Mary. St. Bernard calls our attention to this great source of strength: "If," says the saint, "you should be tossed about by the waves of pride or ambition, or detraction or envy, look to yonder star in the heavens, cry to Mary." (Brev. Holy Name B. V. M.). We must not lose heart if we find ourselves harassed by this passion. The very discovery of it is a blessing, and if by the grace of God, we vanquish it, all the greater will be our reward in the next world. Let us then repress the pride within us that lifts itself like the mountain; by self-violence lower it to the plain, and by pushing on our victory drive it back till it becomes concave like the valley, so that we shall be not merely not proud, but positively lowly in spirit. This a true sign of our christianity; here is where we are distinguished from all others. The prophet has foretold this true influence of Christ's coming: "Every valley shall be exalted; and every mountain and hill shall be made low. . . . And the glory of the Lord shall be revealed." (Is. xl, 4, 5). Where there is this meekness of spirit there is God's glory and not our own petty and wicked pleasures in grand or petty larcenies from the glory of God. God's lesson to us is to seek heaven and God's glory; that outside this all motives are sheer folly, intol-

erable in His sight, and all revenues therefrom
vapid and punishable; 'all flesh is grass and all
the glory thereof as the flower of the field.'
"Shall we rule ourselves, or shall God?" "Behold," says Isaias, "the Lord God shall come with
strength, and His own shall rule." (Is. xl, 10).
To accomplish the work of becoming lowly in
our judgments and affections, and satisfactorily
resigned to those rough ways of life, we must
turn our eyes to heaven for strength in the most
dreadful struggle of the human soul: "It is He
that giveth strength to the weary and increaseth
force and might to them that are not." (Is. xl,
29). Up from the tempest of the Spirit, up
from the turbulent waves, our cry shall ring out:
"Ave Maris Stella!"

THOUGHT:

In all the happenings of life, the bitter and the
sweet, we must confess a providence of God and
say: "Thy will be done."

ILLUSTRATION:

When the prophet foretold that every valley
shall be filled, he proclaimed the rule of Christ's
kingdom and set forth the criterion for judging
true holiness: Not, indeed, that we shall judge
any other, but that we shall ever keep in mind
how God, Who knows all, and has the right, will
pass judgment upon ourselves. The deeper
declines the valley, the more humble and lowly

we become in spirit, the more God will bless us
and fill us with Himself. The process of getting
rid of self is not agreeable. The metal is in
fusion, and the recrement must be gotten rid of;
the scoria, the dross, that which is not God —
Ego—'I no longer live.' The Ego sizzles and
suffers in the process of purification, but look
forward to the splendid glory, when God shall
exalt you. Our Lady was the humblest of God's
creatures, and behold, therefore, how the Mighty
God filled her, accordingly, with Himself: ' Hail,
full of grace,' humble, unselfish, God-loving, God-
seeking soul, 'the Lord is with thee.' "Come,
Holy Spirit, fill the hearts of the faithful." The
fires of self and selfish loves are gone out — our
hearts are ready for Thee to 'kindle in them the
fires of Divine Love.' God will exalt the lowly:
Their glory is reserved for a future day: ' Behold,
from henceforth all generations shall call Me
blessed.' Has not God kept His promise and
exalted His humblest of creatures? Behold the
nations, peoples, and tribes, kings and vassals
have always paid tribute of honor, glory and love
to the august Mother of the Redeemer. In
the fourth century, when Nestor invaded her
title of Mother of God, the Fathers of the Council
gathered from the four quarters like a storm of
indignation, and in their united powers broke
upon the impudent heretic with a fury of defence
that swept away every vestige of hope from the
bosom of the calumniator. Again, what a glorious

scene it was when, in the ninth century, Charle-
magne brought together more than 300 mitred
dignitaries, cardinals, graces and lords of the
Church, with the blazing pageantry of full court
to assist at the consecration of a church dedicated
to Mary, and in the present instance, under act
of consecration by Pope Leo III.   Did not
the prophecy ring out—"All generations shall
call Me blessed," when pontiff and emperor, the
high and the low, were brought to solid unity in
doing honor to the spouse of an artisan, the
descendant of a defunt dynasty, the most hidden
and lowly creature in all the world?

In 1528, when the Lutherans decapitated a
statue of God's Mother, Francis the First raised
with his own hand a statue of silver to Mary in
the presence of the highest in Church and State,
of eminences, princes and ambassadors.   Emperor Ferdinand III. had an image of God's
Mother raised on the public square of Vienna, and
the whole city was set off with the most brilliant
illuminations imaginable in honor of the Queen of
Heaven.   On December the 8th, 1854, the millions of Mary's children throughout the world
thrilled with joy and the air was filled in every
part of the world with song of praise and hymn
of thanks, when Pius IX. told the world, without danger of either deceiving or being deceived,
that Mary was Immaculate in her Conception.
If we, too, shall bear the seething cauldron for
the few brief moments of mortal existence, like

Our Lady, in the measure of our lights and graces, God will place palms in our hands and exalt us: No, it is not to be in this world but after our death, and in that happy country where honors are true, safe and everlasting.

RESOLVE :

AT every turn in my life, and in whatever passes with me, from within or without, I shall be resigned and say: "Thy will, O Lord, be done."

PRAYER :

GRANT us, O God, the grace to watch out, during life, for our pride, and to bring our minds and hearts into submission to Thy judgments and commandments; and, in the multifarious daily permissions that surprise our knowledge, grace to be of one disposition with the prophet who said: "The Lord ruleth over me; I shall want for nothing." In one word give us, O Lord, through Thy Mother, the supernal eye to catch the beauty of the winding path, the jewelled loveliness of tears and the sublime picturesqueness of a disrobed, cudgelled and conquered pride. Through Jesus Christ, Our Lord.

CHAPTER XXVIII.

FAULTS, A DISEASE AND CURE.

IF any one were bold enough to say that a person who has been once justified can escape all sins, even venial sins, during the whole course of his life, without having to attain success in so doing by virtue of a special privilege from God, as the Church maintains the case to be with the Blessed Virgin, let him be Anathema. (Trent. Sess. 6. Con. 23). What is God's purpose in allowing us to groan in these shackles of vice, if not the stronger ones of steel, at least lesser ones of tough cord? "All we like sheep have gone astray, every one hath turned aside into his own way." (Isaias liii. 6). Some overcome the larger sins and heroically control the passions of the more fierce and fiery mould, and yet we find that these err in some minor detail, or encounter defeat in some infinitesimal thing. They subdue the lion, but seem to be outdone by the mouse — that petty conqueror of female courage! What, I repeat, is the lesson? What the great meaning of this temptation that swaggers down the path of just and noble souls, and exerts its tyranny in holy quarters out in the world and spares not the hidden places of monastery or hermitage? St. Gregory furnishes us with the reply to this great

and important question, which we should all
know so thoroughly as to profit by the instruction
which God's singular providence is intended to
convey. Our saint says: "Just as when the
promised land was divided up between the various tribes of Israel, the Chanaanites, who were a
Gentile people, were not destroyed, but, on the
contrary, suffered to abide in the midst of the
tribe of Ephraim, as a tributary, according to the
Scriptural report; because, the Chanaanite people means vice, and we often possess great virtues
upon our entrance into the promised land, inasmuch as we are strengthened, within, by the hope
of eternity; but since, however, we keep on with
our petty vices, notwithstanding our sublime virtues, it may be said we suffer the Chanaanites to
dwell within our borders." So far St. Gregory
tells us clearly with St. John that all men have
sins or imperfections. Now the saint resumes:
"But these people pay us tribute because we
make these very defects which we cannot wholly
bring into subjection, minister to our spiritual
progress by their humbling us, with the view,
namely, that our soul, with all its high state of
virtue, shall have an opinion of itself so much the
more meek and lowly as it shall witness its incapacity, when left to itself, to surmount and do
battle with the most feeble defects. It is upon
this point precisely that Holy Scripture says:
" See how the Lord suffers these people to dwell
among the Israelites for their instruction." (Moral,

R

lib. iv., ch. 22). According to the Fathers of the
Church, the lesson which David received from his
fall, the same which St. Peter, who denied his
Master, learned from his apostasy, was to become
humble, self-diffident, and God-reliant. To ward
off the danger of the contrary spirit God put
that sharp goad in St. Paul's side which left him
no peace, presumably, night or day. The fear of
their ever growing self-reliant characterizes all
the saints, and permeates all their lives, teachings
and works. "And after all," says St. Gregory,
"when lighter vices remain with us the message
embodied in the fact is that we shall place ourselves under obligation to cultivate great circum-
spection, wariness, and precaution in our victories,
lest our enemies, who never die, should some day
get the upper hand." (St. Gregory). "That day
shall be when we shall have fancied that we have
conquered wholly or in part by our own strength."
O, ye saints, remember David and Peter! The
very universe shook in the fall of these great dignitaries, and the vibrations are felt to-day in the
holy places where devout people ponder the fall
of the prophet and the apostle, the King and the
Pontiff. "In this way," continues St. Gregory,
"the Israelites are instructed by these nations,
still reserved within their country, that when we
show the white feather in the matter of small
faults, we shall learn our weakness from the resistance which these smaller vices offer us, and become instructed, I repeat, upon the fact that it is

not upon our own resources that we have succeeded in overcoming the more difficult vices."
(Moral, lib. ix., chap. 22).

Underneath all our daily faults, beneath the
surface of the insurmountable little vices of the
advanced and really virtuous souls, we find the
hand of God, and, luckily, the hand of our
Father. The hand of our Father? The same;
for, happy are we, indeed, when God can teach
us in so mild a way the lesson of repressing our
pride, without having recourse to more terrible
calamities, more horrible falls. Blessed and wise
are we if we read aright the message of each fault,
if we follow its index pointing to our hidden
pride and that greater or lesser presumption
concealed within us. If, then, these gnats buzz
around us, and providence, together with human
infirmity, prevents our having a gnat-net, life may
not be so sweet to us but it will be truer for
being humbler. The secret of great vices
suffered by God to affect the lives of some is, as
we have already observed, their indomitable
high-mindedness. Celebrated drunkards, wine-
saturated sots who disfigure every stage of
society; libertines who are such fine beasts and
such lamentable specimens of men, learn the
lesson of your vices; listen in silence, prayer
and meditation to the gurgling sound of that rill
of secret pride that gives rise in that corner of
your heart to the stream of corruption that flows
out upon your lives. Kill the germ. Let such

as find themselves down, in treating this disease, apply the remedy to the true cause of their misfortunes, and purity and sobriety will supplant these hideous and monstrous passions, as grapes grow on vines and figs on fig trees. Let the just, the devout in the world, in monastery, in desert-hut attack the root and source of their imperfections and daily faults, for where there is no pride or inordinate weakness of self-love there is no sin. Whilst the germ lives there will always be disease. If the Christian world would only set about practising the fundamental virtue of Our Lord's Heart and Our Lady's Magnificat, what often occurs under our own eyes would be averted; for whilst some take to themselves from small faults the correction and warning of God, others are so self-sufficient that God has recourse to drastic measures and permits them to be the victims of beastly passions that prey upon their conscience and happiness, make their life a misery, a torture, and, we may say, a hell, because these men will not know themselves; they go their own way, will have no advice from anyone. They are haughty and independent, made so, mayhap, by their talents or their past success in business, or some kindred reason, and to crown the disaster they are so blind as not to decipher the dreadful, large print of their shameful vices and, in all cases, refuse to accept the humiliation of seeing themselves as they are; but, till they do, they will remain the ignominious

slaves of tyrant-passion.   God makes no truce
with the stiff-necked.   God's providence works
wonderfully well in this matter.   If one cannot
overcome little faults how in the world can he
overcome large ones?   This is the mystery of
God's mercy in teaching us by the little faults
'Without Me you can do nothing.'   When the
smaller misdemeanors fail to reach the goal, God
allows us to make a fatal tumble.   A day of
battle will dawn and the sun will set that evening
upon our shame and humiliation.   Humility is
a fundamental virtue as Our Lady teaches us.
God did not have to teach His Mother humility
by any such means as faults.   Her humility was
perfect " Because He hath regarded the humility
of His handmaid."   She was spared their daily
commotions in this life because she never erred
in humility.   Wise are we then to make up to
Our Lady in our daily faults.   We commit an
impatience, a word that lacks due kindness, a
discoloration of the truth, or we add a tint to
evade a slight confusion, we nurse a secret
vanity, or we woo a word of praise.   To these
thousand and one ways of sinning daily, all
emanating from the common source of self-love,
we shall have to employ hereafter in our life that
admirable resource of the wisdom and mercy of
God which teaches us to make these very faults
turn and serve us for the extinction of our pride—
which will bring us into imitation of our Mother
in heaven in a fundamental point.   The most

clement Mother of God, having been the humblest of God's creatures, is the best able to teach us the lesson of Her Child's Heart, and the one after the Great Master Himself Who can furnish us with the strength to overcome this, our greatest adversary, and drive him from his hiding place within our own breast.

THOUGHT :

IF I am vanquished in small matters, how do I come off so well in the larger contests? The answer is: I have been presumptuous and am in danger of it, and God is teaching me to depend upon and give glory only to Himself in all my victories of the soul.

ILLUSTRATION :

ST. AUGUSTINE furnishes us with a delightful scrap of the inner knowledge of his dear and sainted mother which commands our interest, from the character of the knowledge imparted, and contracts added interest from the close relationship between the historian and his subject — two saints, mother and son. St. Augustine, with admirable uniformity, shows us in everything the saint's touch; he never strikes a false note. Predestinated by God to be the exponent of the nature and power of Divine grace, he was to be in his own life the most striking example of it. No one in the light of such a destiny should have more humility than he among the saints, and it is no chance observation to allege that none have had. He shows his own moral nakedness and leprosy before the advent of grace in his heart, in no sketchy way. He has not skimmed it over with vague platitudes, but has gone down in his confessions before the world to the facts and figures, so that the world would know the son of Monica as he was. This wonderful truthfulness of the saints, or, what is the same, this lowliness of spirit of his, did not seek to set off his saintly mother as all heavenly in her nature, as a saint to the manor born. He showed in himself, and in his mother, that they were both clayey, human, subject to danger from passions — of themselves, nothing.

Saints, when their portrait is offered to us by biographers, must be true to art. The suppression of the truth, which obtains when the little bits of nature, the side-lights, are withheld from us, is a deprivation of a background; and the effect of this bad art in biographers, or word-painters, is that when the lives of saints should soothe the eye of the soul and uplift us and spur us with hope of emulation by the reflection that saints, too, were human like ourselves, and had earned perfection by toil and struggle, the fact is, the figure produced before us dazzles the eye, pains it, and we turn away with pure awe and bewilderment, and not with what we should have reaped from the vision; namely, courage and determination, crowned with hope and confidence to follow in their footsteps. Saints are drawn for us, who were born so, as it were; whereas, in point of fact, they became saints. A biographer of a saint must draw with a free hand. In many cases this is not so. The intention has always been beyond reproach, but the work has been bungled, and poor execution defeats the best end. A skilled marksman, whilst he may not aim too high, must not misjudge by aiming too low; he must poise his barrel, gauging the direction and force of the wind-currents, so as to hit the bull's-eye. Then again, a figure too large is a disfigurement as well as a dwarfish one. Biographers may love their theme ever so much, but they must not be too narrow, nor biased by their affections at the expense of truth. In all things, truth has its own charm. We know that saints had imperfections, but these are kept from us by biographers. Why, bless you, we want to realize that they were like ourselves, and we want to do our best to be like them. This is accomplished when the lights and shades of their life are given.

How true and lovable St. Teresa is in telling us of her earlier infirmities of spirit. By this she becomes a reality to us. St. Bernard unveiled his short-comings to his religious. In the present instance, too, St. Augustine shows us that a saint is not born. We all take courage therefrom to know that if, indeed, we find inclination at work in us, we, too, can overcome ourselves. St. Augustine, with consummate simplicity and exquisite truthfulness, gives the affair of St. Monica:

"In spite of the precautions that were thrown about her," said he, "she suffered herself to get wound little by little, into the meshes of a passion for wine, as she told me in motherly confidence. As a matter of fact, her parents, with all the confidence in the world in her sobriety, had no hesitation to dispatch her, according to the usage of the times, to draw wine from the 'cave;' but she could not help putting the wine vessel to her lips and swallowing a few drops, before tilting it into the bottle. But she never took more than a few drops because a delicate taste revolted at it. She had not, so far, contracted a marked passion for the liquor; she was acting, up to the present, under obedience to one of those impetuous movements which children cannot master, and which show themselves in foolish pranks. But as he who is careless in little things, falls little by little into greater ones, it came to pass that, by increasing the draught each day, she finally came to the point where she could polish off a full cup with evident relish. — She had contracted the wine habit. A domestic, who usually accompanied her to the wine-cave, had a quarrel with her of a day, and·taunted her with her vice; she called Monica a tippler, a drinker of wine. This stung her to the quick. She opened her eyes with horror upon the shameful habit she had gotten enveloped in, and set to work at once with a resolution to get rid of it." (Conf. i. ix. C. 8). What do we find in this narrative, but the old story? Monica did

not suspect her natural propensities. She trusted
her own strength. She failed to realize the dangers of life, and to take cognizance of her own
natural infirmities. When, however, the accusa-
tion of her fault was thrown at her face by a
domestic, she felt humiliated, but she accepted
and bore all with humble resignation. Somehow
we love her more for this little episode in Monica's
life. It makes us realize that she was human like
ourselves, that she, if left to herself, or if she had
not humbled herself when her fault had been
brought home to her, might have become an inebriate. Let us ask again why those persistent
drunkards we see about us, do not rise up and
vanquish their loathsome passion. "Ah," say such
men, "it is human to err." True, but St. Bernard
rebuts: "It is human to err, but devilish to go on
in error." (Serm. xi. In Ps. Qui. Habitat.). Pride
blinds these men to the miserableness of their
character, and the lowness of their condition.
When, again, the sadness of their state is brought
home to their minds and convictions, by some
true relative or friend, it is likely these slaves of
vice will turn upon their real benefactor, and reward his good Samaritanism with a ton of
insolence, for his benefaction and kind advice.
If this is not the result, and we find they are
simply and doggedly indifferent, this is the silence
of contempt for advice. They go on in their
wild career; they make little account of God or
His sanctity—which, as we know, is nothing short

of a Satanic pride. But if the vice-chained do fortunately listen to friendly counsel, and make an effort to rise up, is it not too often the case that they try to do so, and aspire after reformation, and essay to conquer their passions by their own natural will-force? Whereas, the purity, sobriety, patience, charity, and the rest of christian virtues that owe their strength to human force, are empty and unreliable. The Master's word is clear, 'Without Me you can do nothing.' Besides, we are not merely men, we are fallen men, and have, besides, to live as christians. Granting, that, as men, we appear to accomplish reforms, these will not stand the test of the tempest of temptation unless God is in the boat with us, and His hand is stretched forth to calm the stormy passion. This, to my mind, is the solution of the question of all virtues, of temperance, chastity, patience and the rest. Let us then go to Mary, and by this flower-decked and pleasant path come to Jesus: under her most glorious leading, we shall be brought to the sacraments and prayer, and our vices will scatter like wool before the gale.

RESOLVE:

My principle shall always be: "Without Thee, O Lord, I can do nothing." I shall have Our Lady teach me this truth.

PRAYER:

O God, Who didst suffer the Chanaanite to dwell in the land of Israel, and Who sufferest,

even in saints, faults and imperfections to harass
their souls, open our eyes to the message of these,
our daily errors, imperfections and sins, that we
may read therein the principle of human frailty,
and the necessity of humbly depending for all our
strength upon Thine own power and mercy.   O
Thou Who livest forever and ever, One God,
world without end.   Amen.

CHAPTER XXIX.

MARY, MODEL OF CHARITY.

WHERE there is true charity there is no room for envy or jealousy which is an altogether selfish, unjust and rude proceeding and, for all its hideous character, a wide-spread disorder. Cain slew his own brother under the accursed domination of this passion. Now charity, to be worthy of the name, must see but one object and one motive in life — God. His gifts to others, consisting of graces and talents, we are all under more or less obligation, from a spirit of justice and charity to admire. There is a beautiful and rich thought expounded by St. Augustine to the effect that the second fruit of an action or gift remains for such as sympathize with him who is the doer of the act or possessor of the gift. If we turn the matter over well this is found to be perfectly in line with christian unity, sympathy and charity. Our heart opens to another's virtues and actions, and this starts a circulation. We are not tied up, or isolated, or better still, insulated. His current does not pass off. It passes through us, thrills, helps, augments the grace in us which moves him who generates the current. To my mind, if I may venture to express a critical observation, this selfishness defeats the action of the Holy Ghost to a greater extent than is readily fancied. In the great variety of functions and vocations in the christian life, there must be sympathy in all for all; for, the one great and primitive fact that overtops and outranks all other titles and gifts which any one of us may claim is that we are Catholics, children of God. If God has given others talents and graces, we must see God's will in the matter. Alas, we are sometimes confronted by a spiritual avarice in the individual in this matter which brings systems to be misunderstood because of the unbrotherliness and aristocratic exclusiveness of some member of the body. Cain wanted all for himself. His brother's virtues and gifts made him angry; yet, "charity seeketh not her own." It seeketh God through us but not through you or myself more than through others.

Is it not known, however, to be a fact that sometimes men seem as though they would rather have a work left undone because it had not pleased heaven to accomplish it through themselves? Then again some of us are secretly pleased that we have gifts, graces and opportunities that others have not received; and the source of our pleasure seems to lie not so much in our possessing these things as in the fact that we are made to differ from others, by reason of them. Our Lady's spiritual charity was perfect. She reached out to others, extended the blessings she received out to the world. She wanted the world to become like her Son and herself. The reason

is simple—Mary sought not her own, but God's:
"O Virgin, blessed and honored," says St.
Anselm, "not on thine own account, but for our
sakes, also, how great and wonderful is all that I
see happening through thee. In looking upon it
I find myself tuned up with joy, and yet, for all
my happiness, I dare not express it. If, O our
Queen, thou art the Mother of God, are not
thine other children the brothers of God?" It
would be well for those of us whom the graces
and blessings of God have occasioned to be so
exclusive and selfish, would we in our prayers repeat these words: "Are not these other children
the brothers of God?" When Our Lady beheld
herself raised to the lofty dignity of the Divine
Motherhood she rejoiced to see others elevated.
Would to God, we, her children, were like our
Heavenly Mother, we should not then entertain
the pride-born hope of attaining greatness by
making others smaller, of making ourselves giants
by standing near a dwarf, or proving we possess
them by denying the gifts and goodness of others
or by the thousand ways in which it is possible to
harm and belittle another, positively or negatively,
through jealousy. The charity of Our Lady showed
itself in an absence of anything rancorous or
bitter, haughty or ironical. Envy that has in it
the rancidity of a diseased and cancerous piety
perished in her presence. There was no impatience or anger in Mary. "A mild answer break-
eth wrath but a harsh word stirreth up fury," says

Proverbs (xi. 1). Charity breeds unity, sympathy, joy; it is no accepter of persons; it extends itself to all the sons of God, to the world.
Our Lady is a blessing upon the world then; and
the explanation is simple,—Mary loved all mankind, her charity was noble, pure, unselfish. The
unworthiness, the wickedness, and ingratitude of
others did not induce her nor influence her to
uproot or diminish her love. "Carefully examine
the evangel," says St. Bernard, "and if you find
in Mary anything that savors of menace, of harsh-
ness, or a mark of the faintest indignation, I am
satisfied that you shall not trust in her and that
you shall fear to approach her. But, if, on the
contrary, you find her all tenderness, all sweetness, and all mercy which we claim as her heritage, then thank the One Whose compassion, so
full of benignity, has given you a mediatrix in
whom there is nothing to inspire you with the
least doubt." (Serm. in verb. Apoc.). "O thou,"
cries out St. Anselm, "before whose purity that
of the angels pales, who art above the saints in
charity, my spirit looks out from the shadow of
death to implore with ardor the look of thine immense compassion, whilst at the same moment it
covers itself over with shame at the sight of thy
brilliant purity." The practical charity of Our
Lady has been dwelt upon,—the glowing love for
the world proven in works, and this in turn shown
by Our Lady's consent to the Divine Motherhood
with its dreadful responsibilities. The whole

world was upon its knees begging her to consent to the Motherhood of the Lord ; the cry awakened her love which then burst forth in the 'be it done to me according to Thy word.'

It will edify us to review this consent and the charity it implies in the words of St. Augustine : "Give thy answer, O Blessed Virgin," says this great saint, "the angel awaits thy consent. Why does the messenger have to await thee ? Hast heard him ? The Holy Ghost shall come upon thee, and the virtue of the Most High shall spread His shadow over thee, so as thou shalt become Mother without losing thy virginity. The gate of heaven, formerly shut up by Adam, is opened ; and through this gate the messenger has come forth. God is upon the threshold ; He is waiting for the angel whom thou keepest waiting. O Mary, the world, all captive, begs thee to give thy consent; the world makes thee the pledge of its faith before God ; it begs thee to wash out the injuries of thy parents. Entrance into heaven is permitted unto us if thou givest thy consent, and thou shalt be of service to thyself and to us, for thou wilt make our pains cease." St. Augustine then addresses the angel : "O thou angel, messenger of so great a King, bearer of a Divine secret, take part in favor of the world, thou who knowest the secrets of heaven. Thy companions will rejoice if thou aidest the world. As for ourselves, the sword of impiety has separated us from thy society ; see that through thee we may

be united again. Cast thine eyes upon the barren
misery of our prison and hasten to say to Mary:
How long, O Virgin, shalt thou keep thy messenger waiting, who is in such a hurry? Dost
see, God is expecting me in the vestibule of
heaven. Say the word and receive His Son.
Give thy word and feel the effects of the virtue
of God. Open thy womb of rose, perpetual
Virgin. Thy word at this moment opens heaven
or closes it." "Behold," she says, "the handmaid of the Lord." Let the King enter into His
chamber, "be it done unto me according to Thy
word." There is no delay: the messenger re-
turns and Christ enters into His virginal dwelling.
He receives the garment of flesh in the womb of
the Virgin. "A trifle of flesh was transported into
a treasure of Majesty; man espouses the divinity;
the flesh receives its recompense." (Serm. xvii,
in Nat. Dom.).

Have we the charity of Our Heavenly Mother?
Do we do our duty in charity to God's Church
by moral and material help? Do we open the
gates of heaven by spreading the Church — by
prayer and good example, bringing on conversions to the truth? Our Lady's charity was
not confined to the spiritual, but overflowed
in liberality to the poor as Her Son proves
in His conduct. Those who hoard their gains and
lock up their mercy in iron vaults from the poor;
those who love and worship money, and do not
heed the needy nor support the orphan; the rich

who do little for the temple and kingdom of God,
and who have bowels of stone toward the orphan,
the waif and the foundling, will fare ill at God's
hands on the day of judgment. St. Peter speaks
of such as have their hearts exercised with
covetousness, as children of malediction. (ii Peter ii
14). Cursed are the avaricious. Now, Our Lady
is a blessing for such if they will look to her to
strike, with the rod of Jesse, their hearts of stone,
and open up in their souls the wells of Divine
charity, that will water their lives and give them the
beauty, the richness, and the fruits of cultivated
fields in place of the cold, barren sterility of the
heart paved with metal. The Mother of God,
the Mother of the poor, of the orphan and
the outcast, the Mother of the savage and be-
nighted peoples, looks down upon the rich, and
appeals to their sympathy and their purse. There
she stands in the heavens, with the moon beneath
her feet "because," says a holy writer, "she has
set beneath her feet all earthly things." (Homan).
There she stands, clad in silvery light, who gave
her life to God's kingdom, who wedded poverty
with her adorable Son. The fortune her beauty and
nobility might have brought her she gave to the
cause of salvation. And not only did she give
whatever was hers to God, but more and above all,
she gave herself. She gave not only the fruit, but
the tree itself. Now you, her children, who have
this world's treasures, aid by voice and by purse
Holy Church, enrich her temples, equip and sup-

port her schools, support and multiply the institutions and undertakings of charity. This practical
charity in the work of the redemption will be a
blessing to you to-day and tomorrow. What!
You refuse! Keep then your fortunes, see the waif
and orphan lost to the faith of Jesus Christ and
His Mother, because protestant institutions can
accommodate, when we, for dearth of resources,
must deny them subsistence. See the savage lost to
us because our missionaries are not supported —
yes, lost to the Master and Mary. What then? In
In the autumn of your life the gold and russet
grandeurs of the day will know the shadow of
God's displeasure. St. Peter says the curse of God
is for you, and your hoarded gains will occasion
God's just eternal wrath, when this earthly scene
is closed upon you. In time look to Mary, you
envious, you jealous, you indolent of soul, you
breakers of peace among men, and you avaricious
and miserly Christians; you all, who have not
charity, in anyone of its branches — look to yonder Virgin, robed in azure and silver, who gave
her only begotten Son to the work of mankind's
salvation; study, compare, and ask yourself if in
charity you comport yourself as children of
Mary; then draw near and warm your cold hearts
near the red flame of the burning and Immaculate Heart.

THOUGHT:

I MUST love all men and repress envy, especially
must I love all christians, and this love must find

proof and expression in a sympathy with their graces and talents, in helping them in their spiritual and temporal needs, in the one case by a word of counsel, or a prayer, in the other by a shilling or two from my purse.

ILLUSTRATION:

ENVY is chiefly at the root of such sins as we commit against our neighbors. The hate it begets has set no bounds for itself. The terrible picture of a brother standing over a murdered brother with dripping knife, is the best sermon on the fierceness of this passion of envy. The bloody Cain is a lesson to the world on the lengths to which this awful passion will carry those who cultivate it. The princes of the priests, under the dreadful tyranny of this vice, were drawn on to murder, and that, as we know, of no mere man, but of a God. The brothers of Joseph, through jealousy, held counsel upon his destruction, and only compromised their treachery in the end by bartering him to the Ishmaelites, who would bear him off to Egypt as a slave. History tells us how Saul grew jealous of David upon the latter's victory over the giant and allowed the passion to develop in his bosom till the next thing we come upon is his attempt to assassinate the young victor. If, indeed, in our case, murder does not follow in the trail of this passion, it remains to be seen, in another world, how, through its influence upon us, we have choked the good

that others could have done and forfeited the
riches of grace and merit that might have arisen
from sympathy with them. Through jealousy
we should not be like the dog in the manger.
Yet, how often have we ourselves stood in the
path of others? We have shut our eyes to the
merits of others. We have not acknowledged
their talents, virtues and the good they have done,
or could have done, if we but showed ourselves
humble, generous and unselfish toward them. To
my mind, more evil has emanated from lack of
encouragement than from abuse of it, when given.
Envy leads us to minimize the good points of
others so far as to deny them outright—which
is an error against the truth. Pride is the root
of envy. St. Teresa, I repeat, has said that
humility is the truth. This is so, whether it concerns others, persons or things. In all we must
love the truth. The holiest amongst us may be
assured that it is time well spent if they examine
their hearts on this score. Will some of us not
find still a twinge in our feelings, when the
achievements or good points of others provoke a
favorable observation? Envy is a serious matter
and calls for closer attention than, it is safe to
say, it receives: It merits deeper research, and
could be advisedly mentioned more specifically
in confession.

In the year 1643 an affair occurred which must
inspire us all with decided impressions on the
point we are considering, though the recital is

made at so late a day. The affair is reputed to have occurred in a village situated in the western part of the continent of Europe. A marriage had taken place during the day, and the wedding feast or reception was under way. The guests were seated about the festive board, and looked upon the newly wedded twain with admiration that broke out in no end of fine words passed upon the beauty of the pair, in confessions of present pleasure felt by all, and in hopes expressed to the effect that the future of the two would be long and prosperous. Glasses tinkled, peals of laughter rang out, strains from the violin and mandolin fascinated the flower-scented air, whilst the brilliancy of the scene charmed the eye. The bride had been the famous beauty of the village, and many beaux and gallants who had presumably all the desirable qualities of birth and fortune sued for her hand. She finally, however, made her choice of him who is now sitting by her side. The chosen one was young and handsome, and had about him that certain air which can leave no doubt of pedigree with such as ever behold it in any one. The rejected suitors had in the meantime conceived a dreadful jealousy toward their rival, and met together in a public inn to fetch upon a plan of satisfying their wounded pride and assuaging their burning envy, which had by this time developed in them all a hatred that was maddening. Their jealousy grew with each moment, as is characteristic of vice,

and rose to an awful pitch, with this result: The
wedding guests were interrupted in the midst of
their revelry by the entry into the banquet hall of
a group of masked persons. The first thought
of the wedding guests was that the newcomers
were friends of the married couple who had an
agreeable surprise in store for the feast as their
joint contribution to the event. Accordingly all
made way for the masked group, so as to afford
them the opportunity to carry out without hindrance their agreeable plan of entertainment. Several of the masked persons beckoned the groom
into an ante-chamber, and he readily obeyed so
as to lend himself to the plan of his disguised
friends.

It was not long before these same masked men
came back into the banquet hall bearing with them
a bier, ornamented magnificently and covered over
with a black drapery. This they deposited in the
middle of the banquet hall, and the masked group
proceeded to dance fantastically around it, and
without inspiring the slightest suspicion glided out
of the room with measured and graceful pirouettes
and gracious farewells. The guests stood in anxious expectation over the issue of this bizarre
proceeding. Time wore on and the masked band
did not appear again. They waited and waited.
Finally impatience overtook the guests and they
made after the strange actors of this scene. No
sign of them was visible in or about the house.
Even as yet, the guests did not anticipate anything

but a pleasant issue and all the more flattering surprise for their suspense. They waited on till patience was exhausted entirely and there was no hope of seeing anything further of the masked parties. They made, however, one more search, but all in vain. At last, one of the wedding guests hit upon the idea that it was a part of the real plan that the guests themselves should uncover the bier and, perhaps, or, in all likelihood, it would reveal a huge wedding cake, the givers of which had chosen to be left unknown. The idea was hailed as a capital one, agreed to by all present. The bride and the wedding guests drew near and gathered around the bier, all curious and hopeful. The bride drew the cloth from the bier. There lay the dead husband of the bride. The masked men had murdered him. Their jealousy had grown to frenzy.

RESOLVE:

WHEN I do perceive annoyance in me at another's good things, or any signs of secret gladness over things going ill with my neighbors, I shall trample on this spark of envy which, if left to go unchecked, might not stop short of a total conflagration of the soul.

PRAYER:

O GOD, Who Thyself permitest the honor of Thy saints amongst men, and praisedst with Thine own ruby lips the Baptist; Whose August Mother rejoiced always in seeing her fellows and children increase in beauty, strength and glory before Thee, uproot in Thy mercy all envy from our hearts that the charity of Thine own Heart and that of Thy Mother's may glow in our bosoms, unchilled by any jealousy toward our brethren. Through Jesus Christ, Our Lord.

CHAPTER XXX.

MARY, MODEL OF TEMPERANCE AND CHASTITY.

THE proto-sin was, in its outward aspect, glut-
tony. Lack of temperance occasioned the collapse
of the human family in the beginning. Of course,
if there had been no inward disorder, no selfishness, there would have been no outward expression.
The apple was the cheese in the trap, which drew
out the inordinate cupidity, which should never
exist within us so as to overwhelm our reason and
faith. The apple was the test, the proof. By it,
God discovered whether, in the depths of our
heart, we loved ourselves or any creature more
than we loved Our God. But the "curse of Eve
is turned into blessing in the case of Mary," says
St. Augustine. Our Lady has not inherited our
first mother's palate; the lawless appetite of Eve
has not come down to her extraordinary daughter,
Mary. She, the great Virgin, is, then, a benediction to the world of gourmands and dainty feeders,
as well as a reproach to fastidious and swinish im-
bibers. Man's constitutional and hereditary
appetite for over-indulgence in carnal things, and
his propensity to drink and the like, have everything to do with salvation. The stronger our
attachment is for such things, the greater will be our
danger of offending God, because when we sin,

this comes about through the cause assigned by the Apostle: "But every man is tempted by his own concupisence, being drawn away and allured." (I. James ch. i, 14). I say if we school our appetites there will be no chance of our sinning. "Then, when concupisence hath conceived it bringeth forth sin; but sin, when it is completed begetteth death." (v. 15). Proclivity to drink is commonly observed in anyone; and the excesses of such a sinner are decidedly noted down; but, on the point of esculents in general, their possibility toward evil is not taken at its proper value. Food supplying power to the human body, like fuel to the furnace, must be under rule, or it will occasion harm in us. Physical labor, in the measure of our powers and our appetites, is a safety valve. Eat heartily and lounge and you cannot avoid being beastly in your tendencies. Other causes may occasion an explosion in us, but it is sure that over-feeding must give us an over-heated concupisence, that tends toward destruction and death. Let us be christians at table. It is a curious thing, that in the face of the penitential spirit of the Gospel of the Church and saints, that so few of our moderns — especially men—fancy that eating, to the worst extent, is a specific sin in itself, or that it has relationship with other specific sins. Their regrets begin and end in the discomfiture of a pain or unpleasant congestion of the stomach. Over-feeding, however, is in itself a nauseous sin, and is, besides, an avenue to other sins which call the body into action. With the resources of Providence, the intemperate need Our Lady. Being so humble and temperate, Our Lady has spread abroad the blessings of sobriety and purity. Purity follows humility and sobriety. The unwedded, the widowed and the wedded, all look to Our Lady for a blessing. "We admired," says St. Augustine, "what Susan has to show us in the way of observing conjugal chastity; but we prefer Anne in the goodness of her widow-hood; and we have still a greater admiration for the virginity of Mary." "Lust," says this Father, "is a vice of the soul perversely loving corporeal pleasures, neglecting temperance, which joins us to things spiritually more beautiful and incorruptibly more sweet." (Lib. xii. C. 8, De Civ. Dei). "Blessed art thou amongst women." God wills that we shall seek in Mary, the blessings of sobriety and chastity. "Mary is blessed," says St. Augustine, "for her humility, for her charity, for her sweetness, for her zeal, her generosity, her sobriety and her chastity." All this is very just, because we find Mary has excelled in her humility, and has had abundant charity; that she was uniformly sweet, zealous in her activity, prodigal in her generosity, austere in her sobriety, pure and without blemish in her virginity. (Spec. B. M. Lect. xv.).

It is worthy of observation that in the Catholic Church, both in the religious and the scholastic life, the sexes are separated. Distrust of human nature is for vigilance and avoidance of any danger to the purity of one's soul. A blanket may stifle a flame, but no number of woollen folds will quench the fires of the human heart. In coat of gold or in rags a woman is a woman and a man is a man. The holiest may awaken dangerous thoughts. The human family is weak, and we must avoid all dangers. Above all others, parents should be convinced of this. Mothers ought to forbid promiscuous playmating; they ought to see that their daughters will not accept employment where intercourse is with, for example, one person of the other sex. St. Bernadine of Sienna says: "The impression which the Virgin produced on persons inclined to concupisence was of such character that she never appeared in their eyes to be capable of stirring up passion." (Serm. secund. post. dom. Palmarum). But one could not say this of any other creature. What a wonder of all that is chaste was she whose power and beauty of soul so redounded to her body, as to steep it in its own chaste influence, and cause it to lift men up and purify them even with its graceful symmetry, olive eyes, and its lily whiteness. What now must be the effect of that soul whose marvellous chastity is projected directly upon us. Did ever fabled stone boast of such power to awaken purity? Did the face of Moses ever evince such power with its dazzling rays, as Mary's calm and sweet face? What, then, I ask, must be the influence of Our Lady's soul, of her merits and intercession, to make us pure in mind, in heart and body; chaste in our thoughts and loves, in our deportment, dress, words and looks; honest, not subtle in our speech and carriage, simple, straightforward; tender, not soft; true, not mad; simple, not foolish? Our Lady resembles myrrh. 'I yielded a sweet odor like the best myrrh.' (Eccl. xxiv, 20). Myrrh and stacte and caisia perfume thy garments. (Ps. xliv, 9). So might the Blessed Virgin say with Proverbs vii, 17: 'I have perfumed my bed with myrrh,' because the odor of myrrh was death to worms; in the same way did the holiness of Our Lady throw its rays upon others and straightway kill the worm of carnal concupisence and quiet down all wicked excitement of lust. (Morales In Cap. I Matth. lib. ll, tr. 10). St. Gregory goes on to recite the properties of myrrh as witnessed by Dioscorides, the Greek physician, and by Pliny, and urges their applicableness to Mary, Our Lady, as follows: "Our Lady eliminates wicked desires from us; she cleanses our hearts; she preserves us from the putrefaction of sin, she rids us of the stench of bad example, she cures us of the evil of the lips, she strengthens our understanding, she is death to the worm of carnality. She deals peremptorily with our needless cares, she roots us in our good resolves and brings around our perseverance." (Loco cit.). We cannot say more for the chastity of Our Lady and the blessing it is to the world, than to observe that her body was of such holiness as to furnish the flesh and blood of Virtue Itself, the Lord Jesus Christ, the Redeemer of mankind; that her mind and heart were so pure as to make her the chosen guide, preceptress, and, with all it implies of familiarity in touching, nursing and ministering, the Mother of Jesus! Let us ornament our household with images and paintings of Our Lady, in order to look upon her often, and to, each time, turn away purer, to see her often, in order to pray to her often, so that we who experience the misery of carnal trials and the painful consequences of human perverseness, may obtain the grace to esteem holy chastity, the strength from on high to be courageous in temptations of this painful nature in order that the world may become purer because we have been true children of Mary. The Sacraments of the Church, prayer, devotion to Our Lady and prudence in avoiding the occasions of sin, will keep us chaste.

THOUGHT:

I MUST be temperate in eating and drinking, with a view to keeping the body under discipline, and through all temptations preserving it pure with a rigid and stout hand.

ILLUSTRATION:

HOLY purity is a precious jewel. We carry it in frail pots, or caskets of thin glass. "The flesh is weak." Oh, so weak! We might slip, fall, and crack or blur the jewel; or, it may be lost or stolen from us. Yes, thieves covet it. We must 'pick our steps' (Prov. 14, 15) proceed with care, and even charter a convoy to protect our treasure. Like good works, the bodily perfections that would excite the cupidity of thieves must not be paraded and worn, as it were, outside. Sometimes lack of modesty in dress is the evident source of the perils and thefts suffered by people in their purity. Then, again, people who have valuables about them are not wont to take paths which it is known that robbers infest. To live up to the standard of a clean life, a standard set up by christianity, every means must be brought into requisition: occupation, distraction, and all natural means, but, above all, supernatural means—the Blessed Sacrament, called the 'wine of virgins,' prayer, fasting, and, under advice of our director, a lash of the discipline may prove the peculiar grace to subdue this demon. We must do all that lies with ourselves and trust to God for the rest. The *Spiritual Combat* lays down rules of warfare, and insists that in the temptations that contravene the Sixth Commandment no arguing, or debating, or consideration must be made on the nature of the sin, its hideousness or the like, but that to be pure one must turn on his heels at a thought and run. If you stop to wrestle with the devil on this point he will overcome you.

T

St. Jerome writes of himself and of his terrible assaults by lust: "Often," says the saint, "I threw myself at Our Lady's feet and wept abundantly. Often through the day and night I cried out for mercy and beat my breast with my hands until it pleased the Lord to calm the tempest and grant me repose. Often have I blushed before the face of my cell as if it could know my hideous passions. I buried myself in the heart of forests where I sought refuge in the midst of wild rocks in order to mortify my miserable body and there find rest. Then peace came back to my heart when it seemed as though my own was mingled with the songs of praise chanted by the choirs of angels. I redoubled my fasts and macerations and devoted my mind to labor with an unquenchable ardor." Is not my soul as much to me as Jerome's was to him? Ask yourself this question. Why then such small pains to be clean in your life? 'The idle brain is the devil's workshop.' Once a young hermit who passed considerable time in idleness was beset with unchaste impulses and in his tribulation appealed to his abbot. This holy man discerned at once the source of all the trouble and set the young hermit to fill in his life with a great amount of labor. Some time after, the good abbot in fatherly solicitude inquired how things went with him — was he still troubled with his horrid temptations. The young hermit replied: "Oh, indeed how could I be for I have scarcely time to breathe."

St. Joseph Cupertino used to say: "Do you care to resist the attacks of impurity, approach the Holy Table often; because, there where God is found so much the devil cannot stay very long. God will bring victory around in time, for, God can do more with His grace than Satan with his strategies and assaults." St. Fulgentius has well said that virginity is humility of the flesh and that humility is virginity of the heart. St. Anthony confirms the need we all are under of cultivating. humility if we would be pure. "Through its perils only the humble can pass in safety." St. Ambrose also has said: "Do you wish to be chaste, be humble; do you wish to be more chaste, be still more humble." We know from the Holy Scriptures that purity is a gift of God. "We cannot be otherwise continent unless God giveth us to be." (Wisdom 8, 21). Yet in the struggle of the poor feeble human family with the lust of the flesh, Mary, the Mother of God, has always played an important role. The lives of the saints, of Jerome, of Augustine and the rest, show the hand of the Mighty Empress of Heaven in the direction and protection of the thoughts and affections of her devoted children. No saint ever passed over Our Lady in the important work of salvation in seeking victory over their passions. Neither can we afford to do so. "Absolutely" speaking in the light of speculation man can—'absolutely' speaking I say — be saved without her. We cannot allow that Christ lacks sufficiency, but

witnessing the conduct of Our Lord toward His
Mother, the lives and practices of saints, we wisely
appreciate the fact that if we wish to show like
results, we ought to employ the means they employed, and not try to invent new ways of salvation or to retrench the old.   Practically Mary is
necessary to our salvation.   Practically we cannot
be saved without her help.   Facts are facts.   If
we 'can' be saved, in absolute, speculative possibility, without Mary, shall we be saved without
her?   My answer is "No."   No saint has done
so in the past and it would be neither wise nor
pious in anyone to attempt it now, and if tried by
design would be a bad omen.   Let us repeat once
again that in chastity, as in all other virtues, we
ought to have recourse to Mary as to a trusty
weapon.   "Whoso then feels within himself the
war," says Innocent III, "with the world, the
flesh and the devil, let him fix his eyes upon the
army set in battle array, let him cry out to Mary
and she through her Son will dispatch help from
on high and will guard him from sin." (Serm.
de Assump. B. V. M.).   .

RESOLVE:

I SHALL confess my sins and receive Our Lord's
Body as often as I ought.   Three Aves to honor
her Immense Purity I shall utter each day.   When
the sky begins to darken, I shall prevent the
storm; should it burst above my head in fury I
shall still breathe in peace and say in the con-

fidence to out-live it: "Holy Mary, conceived without sin, pray for us who have recourse to thee."

PRAYER:

O GOD Who didst give to Thy Mother's soul and body a beauty and a charm to breathe forth clean thoughts and chaste loves upon all who came into her presence, deign, in Thy mercy, to have us be wise in employing every means to promote purity in our lives, and especially to be prudent in shielding ourselves in all our contests of the flesh behind Thy Mother's sure protection. O Thou Who livest and reignest with the Father and the Spirit, one God forever and ever. Amen.

CHAPTER XXXI.

MARY AT THE DEATH-SCENE.

THE Church teaches us that it is pious and useful to employ the intercession of saints, and whilst we may not be able to point to a formal and direct precept to call upon the saints, the Church and the practice of the faithful invite us to do so. The opinion, indeed, prevails among theologians that failure to conform to this practice is a sin, particularly where it is a question of Our Lady. "Although it would not seem to exceed, in itself, the bounds of a venial sin if one were not to implore the help of Our Lady, still this may furnish an index to a disposition of mind mortally sinful; in other words, such reluctance would excite the suspicion of an heretical spirit; and, furthermore, any one who should go so far as to neglect so great a help toward salvation would be showing great carelessness in this one important matter and incurring a greater or lesser danger of falling." (Lehmkuhl, Vol. I, p. 216). We ought, then, to pray to Our Lady each day. To act otherwise by design would be a grave thing, whilst to do so by indolence would mean a severe prejudice to one's soul—"pray for us, sinners, 'now.'" In our Preface it was announced that the present volume was intended for such as feel the thrill of

life within the Church, and we have reached that
point when we are to look back and to glean the
purpose of the observation — why the demonstration of devotion to Mary had a particular message
to the faithful.   The ground of distinction is, that
for those who have not the faith but tend toward
it, it may be that in the beginning they do not,
acccording to their present lights, take Our Lady
fully; and we might observe that with such we
could tolerate the speculative view of Mary, and
trust in their sincerity and in the growth of grace
in them to lead them forward to the spirit of faith
on this point, and the practical view, namely, that
we shall not be saved without Mary.   If we need
Our Lady during life, we surely need her in a
special way upon the solemn occasion of death.
The Church confesses and urges this necessity
in the prayer she has attached to the Ave : "Holy
Mary, Mother of God, pray for us, sinners, now
and at the hour of our death."   If we are being
lost, whilst breath tarries we have yet an opportunity to snatch the crown with our pale fingers
and be saved; and if we are, on the other hand,
so far saved, the demon still hopes to destroy us,
and the crown may slip away from our grasp.

In either case, defensive or offensive, the devil
throws all his diabolical resources into the one last
effort to damn us.   Alas! for its enemy as well
as for the soul, the adage works — "Where there
is life, there is hope:" "Woe to the earth and to
the sea because the devil has come down unto you,

having great wrath, knowing that he hath but
a short time." (Apoc. xii. 12). The hour of
Death is a solemn one, terrible and important
beyond calculation. A last struggle with the
hopes in a most desperate effort to sustain the
demon ; win or lose — all ! The spirit of evil and
darkness will bring to the event a force perhaps
never as yet known to or fancied by the soul in its
most lugubrious straits. Surely he will do all that
God permits him to do though, indeed, he cannot
tempt us beyond what God permits, or indeed we
should have no chance against him. The dying
moments of the saints bear strong witness to the
fact. Fancy the very bones of an Alphonsus
Ligouri, or a Rodriguez, as they crackled and
their emaciated, shrunken and arid flesh sizzled
in the fires of torture, in the death struggle when
Lucifer hoped at last in a final mad effort to conquer and sully the purity of these saints. David
mentions this hour: "The sorrows of death
surrounded me." (Ps. xvii. 5). Fever, aches,
and weakness rack and torment the frame. An
aged father, a devoted mother, a husband, a child,
will stand or kneel by our bedside — we must
part. "The torrents of iniquity troubled me."
Ps. xvii 13). In the words of Innocent " the
conscience is disturbed and driven, as it were, to
hate itself." 'O God' I shall do better tomorrow,
let me live,' and yet again as heart faints and lips
purple ' let me live, Lord, I shall do better, I shall
mend the wrongs I have done. I shall never

neglect Mass again; I shall go to confession regularly; I shall always give good example. To-morrow, tomorrow, Lord!' The physician feels the moribund's pulse and whispers to the relatives or friends: He is dying; he has but a few hours, a few minutes. 'If it please Thee, Father in Heaven! tomorrow!' prays the moribund. 'This night!' is the low moan, the cold, freezing answer, the terrifying whisper of Death. The hope of living to do penance dies in the invalid's bosom. Terror seizes him,—'At last, at last, my hour is come! Merciful God, have I truly re-pented?'—"Unless ye do penance ye shall all perish." The frame quivers, drops of sweat sparkle on his cooling temples. Then a spas-modic glow sweeps over his being, as hope of living flits across his fancy and vanishes. 'I must face God and give a strict account of my steward-ship!"

Earth darkens and eternity opens up before his fancy — heaven or hell! As if tracked by a hound the soul is cornered by Death. It cannot escape any longer or put off the answer — heaven or hell? Only fools chide all fears, for it is written that ' no man knows!' The best of us do not know the issue. "The sorrows of hell en-compassed me, and the snares of death prevented me." The devil summons his minions.— "They surrounded me like bees." (Ps. cxvii. 12), "and they have stretched out cords for a snare. (Ps. cxxix. 6). The demon charges his

satellites: "Mark, this battle decides it! eY
know his weakness, lay well your traps; sound his
pampered lust; haunt his vision with fair forms;
ye know his love for liquors, parch him with
thirst, and suggest that his health demands it. Ye
know his dislikes and how hard it is for him to
forgive; administer plenty of reasons why he
must not be expected to forgive; whisper that
it is only, after all, a just indignation." No man
can contend single handed with the powers of
darkness in life, much less can he do so against
the fury, the terrors, the craft and the snares of
Death. The Holy Ghost assures us that we are no
match for the demon and his. "He delivered me,"
says David, "from my strongest enemies, and
from them that hated me, for they were too strong
for me." (Ps. xvii. 18). St. Bernard estimates
the struggle to be as terrible as the 'demon's wish
to retain us is horrible.' St. Anthony saw in one
of his visions a figure monstrous and horrible,
looking upwards with huge hideous arms outstretched in a mad, frenzied effort to intercept
the flight of souls to heaven, some of whom the
hideous creature succeeded in dragging back,
more of whom it strove in vain to detain in their
heavenward flight to glory. The Church has
been preparing us by a life-long prayer for victory
in this last and grim battle. Mother Church takes
no hazard with our capacity to pray, at that awful, critical, crucial moment, the parting of the
road. At her request, day after day, we secure our-

selves against the possibility of our incapacity to pray at that moment, being wearied and exhausted by fever and pain. Day after day we have been sending troops ahead of us to the scene of conflict. The Church and the saints teach us all through our life that Mary must have a hand in that final, decisive contest of the immortal soul with the full roster of evil spirits. From this prayer of the Church, making special mention of Our Lady, and of the 'hour of our death,' makes it agreed that the final rally of demons is terrible. Yes, but Mary, besides being fair as the moon, and bright as the sun, is terrible as an army set in battle array. She has her artillery of graces and the prestige of her august saintship. She has her troops of winged warriors, her Michael, her Gabriel, her Raphael, and countless hosts of cherubs, seraphs, principalities, powers, and the rest. It was foretold by God, and His word is truth. This is the hour when his word will be fulfilled in our regard — "And she shall crush thy head."

Fancy this glorious Virgin in her warlike splendor, drawn by angels upon the concave moon, fancy the war-blasts of golden trumpets, the numbers, the brilliancy, and the might of the celestial army. Only the eyes of faith, 'tis true, can make the power of such a scene possible. We feel it is too much importance to attach to a mortal, a puny creature; but, then a soul is the image of God. Here is the secret of all. "Beau-

tiful is mercy in the time of tribulation," says
(Ecclesiasticus xxxv, 26). The greater our
suffering and misery and lack of all trust in human
aid, the sweeter for this does the pity of God
taste, and, above all, at death, is this true. In
that supreme moment of human helplessness, the
mercy of God will shine most radiantly, for then
the die is cast for eternal happiness or unterminat-
ing woe. "At that hour, then, God is present
with His children to help them; and He beats off
the demons and temptations, particularly when
the Virgin Mother of God is invoked, whom,
therefore, the Church teaches us to salute and
pray to as follows: Holy Mary, Mother of God,
pray for us sinners, now, and at the hour of our
death." (Corn. A Lapide, Comment in Sac.
Script). The zealous father of his family, the
priest of God, visits often his dying children; he
refreshes them with frequent communion; as often
as they express the wish, he is summoned to pac-
ify their conscience and to help them to overcome
the devil, because the priest knows the deceits of
the devil, and brings light and strength in the
name of God to the living, the dying and the dead.
Much is needed in death, accordingly, we must
pray much. Never to have fallen, is not an infal-
lible assurance that we shall not fall under the
reinforcements in the enemies' lines at the last
storming. Neither must we despair if we have
unfortunately lived a life of slavery in sin. At
the last moment, Mary can and will, if we call

upon her, save us out of the very jaws of damnation, and the claws of Lucifer. When our friends are breathing their last, let us all gather around and join in the prayers the Church has composed for this solemn emergency, and with faith and charity, softly whisper the *Ave*, the *Memorare*, or some other familiar prayer of Our Lady, into the ears of our expiring brother. In this we are helping to beat off the devil, and to send, at last, the soul of our brother before the judgment seat with the sign of redemption, faith in Our Lord, and the passport to its glories, signed by the Holy Name of Mary; and let the choirs of heaven mingle with the army of the Church militant, and both sing aloud, "Adored be God, and praised be Mary, His August Mother."

THOUGHT:

I KNOW not what the devil has concealed. He is deceitful. Perhaps he covers over his strength presently to make me over-reliant in myself, or too little reliant upon God. Perhaps he is planning to wait for the final struggle, the desperate assault. One thing, I shall make sure to have Our Lord and Lady with me. Daily, I shall rehearse the death-scene, and to the end I shall make my life one preparation for the battle: "Holy Mary, Mother of God, pray for us sinners, now and at the hour of our death. Amen."

ILLUSTRATION:

A YOUNG Parisian of good family, not unlike a good many others, whom we ourselves have known, had succeeded in drowning his faith in an endless round of pleasure and excesses. He had broken the hearts of his parents, so that they could have no more to do with him. His allowance at home being cut off, he found himself for the first time in his life under the necessity of providing his own subsistence.

After a time he ran across an engagemement as professor in a college, but before very long he was dismissed from his chair owing to his lewd and scandalous manners. From this out, he went from bad to worse, on to no end of debauchery. His wickedness brought him so low in mind, body, and circumstances of poverty and wretchedness that disgust, sadness, and in the end despair, which always follows upon the heels of presumption, took possession of him so far that he resolved upon doing away with himself in the river. He proceeded at once to carry out his design. The next thing we find him upon the bank of the river making his preparation for the fatal plunge and surveying his watery grave, when a voice came up to him from the waters below, saying, "Beware! Beware!" The voice had come from a boat hard by where some fishermen, who had escaped the suicide's notice in his perturbed state of mind, were arranging their nets. He gathered up his effects and proceeded further down the bank of the river in search of a lonely spot that would be more favorable to his dark purpose. On the way, the thought struck him: In a quarter of an hour they will pull my carcass out of the river and expose it in the morgue, but my soul! my soul! where shall my soul be? He stopped short at this terrible thought, and his blood almost froze in his veins at the answer which he had to give to this question. He bethought himself a few moments, turned and went back. He took the first street that led up from the river and walked along to its very end, not knowing whither he was going. The end of the street brought him to a sharp halt, and for the first time he raised his eyes from the ground, where contemplation, full of terror, had kept them fastened. As he did so, the first object that met his eyes was the famous church of Our Lady of Victories. By some instinct he entered the church, dragged himself as far as the pulpit with a weary body, and a mind and heart replete with painful, sickening emotions. Night had fallen and the lamps were burning brightly before the miraculous statue of Our Lady, which arrested the attention of the poor outcast. In the midst of the lights he caught sight of Our Lady, and all at once some strange feeling, as he afterwards said, came upon him, an emotion deep and powerful. He rose up instantly and flew to the door of the church as though an enemy were in pursuit of him.

That whole night the young man was the prey of strange terrors,.which he could not express and the origin and motives of which he could in no way explain to himself. He resolved to return by the morning to Our Lady of Victories. At day-break he made his way to the holy shrine drawn thither by some secret force. Immediately he got inside the church he looked toward Our Lady's image and saw the good Father Desgenette in prayer before it. The young man approached and called out to him: "Father." "Well, my friend," replied the good priest. "To tell the truth, Father, I don't know why I called to you, but be assured that in any case it is not for the purpose of confessing that I did so." The man of God headed him off with great sweetness,—"That is not the question," said he, "but you look very sad, tell me what ails you." "Ah, indeed I am sad, yes, very, very sad, oh, so unhappy," said the poor fellow. "Yesterday I was passing your church and slipped in. I desired to come again this morning and now that I have met you I must tell you of the strange emotions and impressions that are upon me."

The good priest listened with that sweet patience, that charity that seeketh not her own, that Christ-like yearning and unquenchable thirst after the repentant sinner. All is over now; grace has triumphed. Our Lady reckons another victory. She has rescued another soul, torn, tortured by despair, from sin, and has snatched another soul from the very gates of perdition. The man of God heard the recital of the young man's wicked life, heard of the circumstances of his contemplated suicide, together with his providential coming to Our Lady's Church, and had also the priestly pleasure of seeing the young man bathed in tears of contrition and then falling upon his knees begging to be confessed. From that moment a complete change came over the poor young man. A new heart was created in the once degraded creature who through all his disgrace, whether saved or lost, should bear with him to heaven or hell the character imparted in baptism. The new Saul becomes a vessel of election. This is hard to imagine and a difficult proceeding to the spiritually proud, who shorten the arm of God and make iron rules for Him Who can raise up children from the very stones, and make, in the twinkling of an eye, the greatest saint out of the lowest of sinners. Yes, it is true. God called this young man — this sinner, this suicide-to-be, this debauchee — to the holy priesthood, and to that further sublime privilege of the apostolate. Upon his ordination to the sacred priesthood, he went out as a missionary to the savage islands of the far East. He abandoned home and country, father and fields, to labor among the savages. His heart yearned and burned to spread the knowledge of that grace which had acted so wonderfully in himself. He sighed and panted to extend the knowledge and

U

power of God's Mother, and prayed incessantly to lay down his life for God, and to pick up and wear the martyr's crown, so as to witness the sooner and surer in their brightest effulgence, in their vasted might and their most glorious beauty, the world's Redeemer and the world's Mother and Empress, Mary, the glorious Mother of God, cast in a scene of rapturous and imperishable splendors before which Tabor's effulgence and earth's best glories grow pale, sink, and vanish.

RESOLVE:

COME what may through every report, through misery, sin, blood, carnage, I know there is one who, by the mercy of God, will never forsake me nor fail me if I but turn to her — the Mother of Jesus. I shall never, never lose confidence in Mary, the Mother of God.

PRAYER:

O GOD, Whose mercy is above all Thy works, Who desirest not the death of the sinner, but that he may be converted and live, grant us the grace to love the sacraments of Thy Church, to pray always as we need, and to seal our hopes of mercy, pardon, and peace, by a love, a hope, and undying confidence in her who is at once a Tower of Ivory, a Help of the Weak, the Refuge of Sinners, and the Mother of us all. Through Jesus Christ, Our Lord, Who liveth and reigneth with the Father and the Spirit one God, forever and ever. Amen.

www.ingramcontent.com/pod-product-compliance
Lightning Source LLC
Chambersburg PA
CBHW020942030726
47496CB00005B/1313